Running With
The Wind

What Reviewers Say About Bold Strokes Authors

KIM BALDWIN

"'A riveting novel of suspense' seems to be a very overworked phrase. However, it is extremely apt when discussing Kim Baldwin's [*Hunter's Pursuit*]. An exciting page turner [features] Katarzyna Demetrious, a bounty hunter...with a million dollar price on her head. Look for this excellent novel of suspense..." – **R. Lynne Watson**, *MegaScene*

"*Force of Nature* is an exciting and substantial reading experience which will long remain with the reader. Likeable characters with plausible problems and concerns, imaginative settings, engrossing events, and a well-tailored writing style all contribute to an exceptional novel. Baldwin's characterization is acutely and meticulously circumscribed and expansive." – **Arlene Germain**, reviewer for the *Lambda Book Report* and the *Midwest Book Review*

RONICA BLACK

"Black juggles the assorted elements of her first book, [*In Too Deep*], with assured pacing and estimable panache...[including]...the relative depth—for genre fiction—of the central characters: Erin, the married-but-separated detective who comes to her lesbian senses; loner Patricia, the policewoman-mentor who finds herself falling for Erin; and sultry club owner Elizabeth, the sexually predatory suspect who discards women like Kleenex...until she meets Erin." – **Richard Labonte**, *Book Marks, Q Syndicate, 2005*

"Black's characterization is skillful, and the sexual chemistry surrounding the three major characters is palpable and definitely hot-hot-hot. If you're looking for a more traditional murder mystery, *In Too Deep* might not be entirely your cup of Earl. On the other hand, if you're looking for a solid read with ample amounts of eroticism and a red herring or two, you're sure to find *In Too Deep* a satisfying read." – **Lynne Jamneck**, *L-Word.com Literature*

ROSE BEECHAM

"...her characters seem fully capable of walking away from the particulars of whodunit and engaging the reader in other aspects of their lives." – *Lambda Book Report*

ROSE BEECHAM (CONT)

"When Jennifer Fulton writes mysteries, she writes them as Rose Beecham. And since Jennifer Fulton is a very fine writer, you might expect that Rose Beecham is a fine writer too. You're right… On the way to a remarkable, and thoroughly convincing climax, Beecham creates believable characters in compelling situations, with enough humor to provide effective counterpoint to the work of detecting."
– *Bay Area Reporter*

GUN BROOKE

"*Course of Action* is a romance…populated with a host of captivating and amiable characters. The glimpses into the lifestyles of the rich and beautiful people are rather like guilty pleasures… a most satisfying and entertaining reading experience." – **Arlene Germain**, reviewer for the *Lambda Book Report* and the *Midwest Book Review*

"*Protector of the Realm* has it all; sabotage, corruption, erotic love and exhilarating space fights. Gun Brooke's second novel is forceful with a winning combination of solid characters and a brilliant plot."
– **Kathi Isserman**, *JustAboutWrite*

JANE FLETCHER

"*The Walls of Westernfort* is not only a highly engaging and fast-paced adventure novel, it provides the reader with an interesting framework for examining the same questions of loyalty, faith, family and love that [the characters] must face." – **M. J. Lowe**, *Midwest Book Review*

LEE LYNCH

"There's a heady sense of '60s back-to-the-land communal idealism and '70s woman-power feminism (with hints of lesbian separatism) to this spirited novel—even though it's set in contemporary rural Oregon. Partners Donny (she's black and blue-collar) and Chick (she's plus-sized and motherly) are both in their 50s, owners of the dyke-centric Natural Woman Foods store, a homey nexus for *Sweet Creek*'s expansive cast of characters….Lynch, with a dozen novels to her credit dating back to the early days of Naiad Press, has earned her stripes as a writerly elder. She was contributing stories to the lesbian magazine *The Ladder* four decades ago. But this latest is sublimely in tune with the times." – **Richard Labonte**, *Book Marks, Q Syndicate, 2005*

Visit us at www.boldstrokesbooks.com

Running With The Wind

by

Nell Stark

2007

RUNNING WITH THE WIND

ISBN 1-933110-70-8
ISBN 978-1-933110-70-7

THIS TRADE PAPERBACK IS PUBLISHED BY
BOLD STROKES BOOKS, INC.,
NEW YORK, USA

FIRST EDITION, MARCH 2007

CREDITS
EDITORS: JENNIFER KNIGHT, CINDY CRESAP, AND J. BARRE GREYSTONE
PRODUCTION DESIGN: J. BARRE GREYSTONE
COVER DESIGN: SHERI (graphicartist2020@hotmail.com)

Acknowledgments

My name may be on the spine, but this book belongs to many people. Lisa: thank you for being my love, my inspiration, my fellow brain-stormer. This novel would never have been conceived without you. You are the wind at my back. Radclyffe: oh Captain, my Captain, thank you for this amazing opportunity. Your encouragement, support, and professional example are priceless. Team BSB: I couldn't ask to be a part of a braver and more talented group of authors and support staff. Thank you for your stories and your hard work. Jennifer Knight: you were instrumental in improving the quality of this book—thank you for helping me make it stronger. Cindy Cresap: I can't tell you how much I enjoyed cracking up at your editorial comments as you took me to task. "Fingers!" Julie Greystone: thanks for your careful fine-tuning of my story. Your eagle eye is much appreciated. Ruta: thank you for believing in the merit of this tale from the very beginning, and for being so proud of me. And to the rest of my family of choice: Your unconditional love is an anchor in my life.

DEDICATION

For Lisa—my reason.

BY THE LEE

Corrie looked at the front door of the Newport Yacht Club, then back toward her car. It would be so easy to just drive home, so easy to make up a story: traffic, a flat tire, food poisoning. Heaven knew her stomach felt sick enough—looped up and twisted like a mess of fouled lines.

She turned her attention back to the door, to the shiny brass knob set into the freshly painted wood. Walking away now meant contending with the disappointment of her parents, but even more importantly, Will would know that she couldn't handle it. He'd get that infuriating big-brother grin on his face, the one he always flashed at her whenever she was acting like a spoilsport. *It's not whether you win or lose...*

No, she had to be gracious—gracious and congratulatory and polite, to both her brother and Denise, despite the fact that the woman who had been her lover was going to be her sister-in-law in less than a year. Who was she kidding? Will had the right to gloat. He'd won and Corrie had lost, and if she had to shell out a single penny for alcohol tonight, she was just going to damn the torpedoes and go home.

She turned the handle and stepped swiftly inside before she could change her mind. There was the familiar mahogany wood paneling; there was the curving staircase and the podium set to one side. Nothing had changed and nothing ever would. Not here, not with the good ole boys in charge. A member of the club staff whose name she couldn't recall looked up from the podium and gestured toward the door to her right.

"Good evening, Ms. Marsten. The party is just through there."

"Thanks," Corrie said. She walked to the door and pushed it open. Almost immediately, her mother's voice floated across the room.

"Corrie, darling, over here!"

Corrie jammed her hands into the pockets of her slacks and made her way between the tables, nodding at so many familiar faces. At least no one else knew the sordid story. Denise's reluctance to come out to her parents had spared Corrie public humiliation. She stopped beside her mother's chair, nodded at the cousins arranged around the table, and leaned down for a swift kiss on the cheek.

"Hello, Mom." She frowned slightly. "Where's Dad?"

Cecilia Marsten sighed. "On the dance floor, acting like a fool." Gold hoop earrings jangled as she shook her head. "If he re-injures his back, it's his own fault!"

Despite her dark mood, Corrie smiled. She squeezed her mother's shoulder and looked out toward the small space that had been cleared for dancing. Sure enough, there was her father, trying to do the Swim to Britney Spears. It really wasn't working. At once mesmerized and mildly horrified, Corrie failed to notice that someone had come up behind her until a strong arm encircled her shoulders and a set of knuckles roughly mussed her hair.

"Argh!" she yelped, twisting away and spinning to face her assailant.

"William," her mother said in an exasperated voice, "please do not turn your sister's hair into a bird's nest before the photos."

The sight of Will grinning mischievously, his offending hand now resting on Denise's slender waist, was enough to make Corrie want to slug him. She grabbed for the back of the nearest chair instead. *You're smarter than him*, Corrie reminded herself. *Smarter, and you fuck better*. She'd managed to wheedle that much out of Denise the last time they saw each other. What a blowout that had been. Denise hadn't admitted it in so many words, of course, but Corrie could read between the lines. Which made her marrying him even more egregious.

"Hey, li'l sis, glad you could make it," Will drawled, pulling Denise closer and caressing her possessively from her hip up along the side of her ribcage and back again.

Corrie's gaze followed his fingers before she finally looked Denise in the face. Those perfectly plucked eyebrows had drawn close together into a frown, and suddenly, Corrie remembered how smooth and soft they had felt as she had traced them with one forefinger in the aftermath of their lovemaking. She remembered the awe, the joy, the love bursting beneath her skin overflowing the borders of her eyes, and how Denise had clutched at her, looking up at her as if she were some kind of goddess.

Now, her dark brown eyes were guarded. Wary. That hurt.

Never again, Corrie thought for the thousandth time. *I will never be that gullible again.* Denise playing turnabout had been bad enough. But engagement? Marriage? *Un-fucking-believable.*

"Will," she said flatly. "Denise. Congratulations. Please excuse me. I'm going to get a drink."

"William," she heard, as she walked toward the open bar, "why do you always have to antagonize her like that? You're not teenagers anymore. Look, now you've made her upset."

She didn't need to hear Will's answer to know what it would be. *I was just fooling around, Mom. Just having some fun. Just teasing.* And his excuses had always worked, too—ever since she was old enough for him to push around.

"You don't know the half of it, Mom," she said under her breath.

The bartender noticed. "Talking to yourself already?" he asked in a far too chipper voice. "That can't be a good sign."

Corrie pretended she hadn't heard and settled onto one of the shiny black stools, resting her elbows on the lacquered wood. "Shot of Ketel One and a light beer to chase, please." She stared down at her hands as the bartender moved away. There were still faint red lines across her palms from where they had bitten into the metal of the chair. *So fucking angry. And for what? What will it get me?*

"Corrie?" A soft, hesitant voice at her elbow made her blink and spin on the stool. The young woman standing nearby was looking at her with a hopeful expression as she ran one hand through her short, dark hair.

"Storm? Sarah Storm?"

Storm's answering smile rivaled the glittering disco ball hanging from the rafters. "You remembered. Wow!" She shuffled her feet slightly. "I really thought you wouldn't."

"Aw, now, why's that?" Corrie leaned back against the bar. Suddenly, she felt better. Much better.

Storm shrugged self-consciously. "I dunno. It's been awhile."

"Only a few months," Corrie said. "Besides, I wouldn't forget you. You were the superstar of your session."

Storm blushed a deep red. Her skin had lost its summer tan, but freckles still liberally sprinkled the bridge of her nose. And she was wearing a tight, silvery top that did nothing to hide the contours of her arms. *Sailors always have the best biceps.*

The bartender, at that moment, set the drinks down on the bar.

"Just a sec," Corrie said, before expertly throwing back the shot. Cool and clear and easy down her throat, followed by the smooth bitterness of the beer...she looked up into Storm's admiring eyes and felt the knot between her shoulders ease. "Anyway, this is a nice surprise. What're you doing here?"

"Oh," said Storm, as her fingers idly twisted the hem of her shirt. "Your parents sponsored mine to join the club. They've become friends, I guess."

Corrie nodded and took another pull off her bottle. "And sailing? How's that going? Several schools were recruiting you, if I remember correctly."

"I, uh, picked Yale."

Corrie's eyebrows arched involuntarily. "Top school for women's sailing in the country this year. You should be really proud."

"Yeah," Storm said and fidgeted some more. Corrie hid a smile behind her beer. "So," Storm said, after an awkward pause, "how are you?"

"Fine, just fine." Which was a lot closer to the truth than had been the case five minutes ago. "I'm doing the grad school thing over in Wakefield, and I'll be head of sailing instruction there this summer."

"Awesome! So awesome. Really great!"

Corrie just nodded and sipped. Essence of cool. The kid kept asking her questions, and she kept answering—deflecting them back once in a while, but mostly just enjoying the attention. The crush. Because that's what it was, even if Storm couldn't recognize it, and Corrie had a strong feeling that she couldn't. Or wouldn't.

She sure did have a nice body. Lean—almost wiry, but not quite. Full breasts, and that tight shirt showed off a hint of six-pack abs, and—*Why the hell am I checking her out? She was my student this summer.*

The crackle of a microphone interrupted her self-recrimination. "All right, ladies and gentlemen," the DJ began, "please take your seats. It's time for some bride and groom trivia!"

Corrie frowned. "Trivia? What the fuck?"

Storm shrugged and looked guilty for not knowing what was going on, as though it were somehow her responsibility to have the answer to Corrie's rhetorical question.

"Hustle, hustle, hustle!" the DJ said. "I have a prize sitting right here for the person who first calls out the correct response."

Corrie rolled her eyes. "Looks like we'd better get back to our seats."

Storm nodded and smoothed the folds of her short black skirt. It showed off her legs—strong and shapely. "It was really cool. To see you again, I mean."

Corrie reached out to touch her arm. Storm's skin was hot, even as it puckered into goose bumps. When she arched one eyebrow, the kid blushed.

"Likewise," Corrie said, pitching her voice low. "Good luck with school and sailing." She squeezed lightly before moving off toward her family's table. She didn't look back, but even so, Storm's gaze was a palpable warmth on her neck.

The glow wore off almost immediately as she sat down next to her mother and across from Will, who had his arm around the back of Denise's chair. As they watched the DJ's goofy antics, his fingers stroked lightly across her shoulders. Corrie's jaw tightened, and she tried to ignore the sight by leaning over to her mother to chat about—something. Anything.

"So, Mom—"

"Let the fun and games begin!" the DJ boomed out.

"Oh, not now, dear," Cecilia murmured as she surveyed the crowd of friends and family. "I want to pay attention to the trivia."

Corrie sat back with a sigh and folded her arms beneath her breasts. *Hell*, she thought. *This is my own personal hell.*

"Let's start with a few easy ones. Who can tell me—what's the groom's favorite baseball team?"

"The Yankees!" shouted one of Will's best friends. A chorus of groans, boos, and hisses reverberated throughout the room.

"That's slander!" Will yelled back.

Corrie could tell he was struggling not to give his buddy the finger. She grinned faintly. The right answer was the Red Sox, of course, and the lucky winner received a small flask of liquor in the shape of a boat. The damn thing even had a sail, on which was proudly emblazoned: *Marsten and Lewis.*

Cecilia lightly patted Corrie on the knee. "Aren't those cute? I picked them out from the bridal store downtown."

"Very cute," Corrie managed, barely resisting the urge to massage her temples. Definite headache coming on.

"Next question!" said the DJ. "What is the bride's favorite color?"

The color of my eyes, Corrie thought. Denise had told her that once while on a picnic at Brenton Point. She risked a quick glance across the table. Denise was whispering something into Will's ear. He nodded, and she gave him a kiss on the cheek. Corrie's stomach rolled.

"Yes, green. Exactly right," said the DJ, handing off another flask to one of Denise's cousins. "Now here's a tricky one—how did the bride and groom first meet?"

Corrie's chair scraped against the floor as she surged to her feet. "Bathroom," she said tersely when her mother looked up, startled by the sudden movement. "Back soon."

She hurried out the doors and down the hall, past the host and down another corridor. That question, that goddamn question. She could remember, down to the taste of sea salt in the air and the sound of her own voice, how she had proudly introduced her family to Denise Lewis, her crew for the Olympic Development Regatta.

"Corrie!"

A mere two steps away from the sanctuary of the women's restroom, Corrie stopped, sighed, and turned around, only to see Storm jogging awkwardly toward her, her dress shoes clicking loudly against the polished wood floor. She struggled to wipe the frown off her face. The poor kid didn't know what the hell was going on, after all.

"Hey again," she said as Storm came to a halt. "What's up?"

"Well..." Storm hesitated, then finally dared to look directly at Corrie. "I know it's none of my business, but...you look upset."

Storm's earnestness, the sincerity in her voice, loosened the pit in Corrie's belly. "I'm not having the best day ever."

Storm nodded. "I just—well, can I help, in any way?"

The question was sweet and wistful, charged with Storm's clear and simple longing to comfort. To make it better. And she would do anything; Corrie could tell. Desire flared—bright and sharp—burning away the self-pity, the shame. The weakness. A hot knife cauterizing the wound, closing it off. *Fuck you, Denise. Fuck you and your bullshit. I'm done wallowing.*

And in that single, perfect moment, she saw herself—a sleek ship running free before the wind, leaving behind the tangled mess of sails and line that had very nearly pulled her into a broach. As the pressure in her chest eased, she took a slow, deep breath and looked down into Storm's clear, almost colorless eyes. The decision was so easy.

"How old are you?"

Storm blinked at the unexpected question. "Nineteen. Why?"

"Then you can help." Corrie firmly took Storm's hand and led her into the bathroom, then locked the door behind them.

"Wh—what are you doing?" Storm asked as Corrie gently pushed her back against the door.

But Corrie didn't speak. Bracing herself on the wood, she leaned down and kissed Storm, swallowing her little gasp of surprise, teasing her innocent lips apart with light strokes of her tongue. It didn't take long before Storm was kissing her back, clumsily but enthusiastically. Corrie felt tentative hands skate along her sides to clutch at her waist. Finally, she pulled away just far enough to focus on Storm's dazed eyes.

"You okay with this?" she asked softly. When the kid nodded, Corrie brushed one thumb across Storm's swollen bottom lip. "I really want to touch you. How's that sound?"

Storm's swallow was audible and her entire body trembled. "Good."

"Yeah?"

Another nod.

The triumph was so sweet. "You think I'm your hero now?" Corrie murmured as her hands drifted beneath Storm's top. "Just you wait."

And then she was easing the bra up to cup Storm's breasts, and Storm banged her head lightly against the door as Corrie squeezed and pinched and twisted. Every tiny movement forced another small sound of need and pleasure from Storm's throat. This, this was a buzz, a rush far more potent than alcohol. Creating this need, holding it in the palm of her hand—trapped, desperate for release, totally dependent on her will.

She kissed Storm again as she let her touch wander down beneath the waistband of Storm's skirt and stroked the muscular abs with her knuckles. "You have an amazing body," she whispered into Storm's ear before curling her tongue around the sensitive lobe. Storm's hips bucked involuntarily. "I want to fuck you."

Storm froze. Corrie pulled back a little, but kept her fingers where they were, still lightly stroking.

"I—" Storm struggled to speak, wetting dry lips with her tongue. She cleared her throat. "I've never...I mean..."

"I won't if you don't want me to," Corrie said steadily. She kept her gaze focused intently on Storm's swirling, dilated eyes, like the restless summer sky before the first thunderclap. *Give in to me,* she urged silently. *Let me feel you.*

"I want you to." Storm trembled again.

Corrie kissed the side of her neck, laving the spot with a gentle tongue. "I'm glad," she said against Storm's hot skin. Her kisses trailed down to Storm's collarbone as she gradually hiked up the skirt with her right hand until she was touching the narrow strip of cloth resting in the hollow between Storm's hip and thigh. Corrie nudged Storm's legs further apart with one knee and slowly followed the hem in toward the centerline of her body, in and down.

She bit down lightly just as her fingers brushed Storm's swollen clitoris through the fabric.

"Oh—" Storm called out, releasing her grip on Corrie's waist to press her hands back against the door.

Corrie returned her lips to Storm's ear. "Feels good, doesn't it? Shall I do that again?"

"P—please," Storm stuttered, her hips shifting vainly.

Corrie's blood thrilled to the sound of that word—the needy, helpless plea. *Right now, she needs me more than she needs to breathe.* So what if Denise didn't want her, didn't need her? There were so many who did. Who would. This kid was just the tip of the iceberg.

Corrie stroked her with one light fingertip until Storm was whimpering with every breath, her head twisting against the door, eyes squeezed tightly shut against the unbearable pleasure. And then Corrie slipped beneath the scrap of cloth to dip into Storm's wet folds with her middle finger, her wrist tendons straining as she simultaneously pressed her thumb against Storm's clit.

Storm cried out wordlessly and Corrie could feel her body tighten, gathering itself for the leap into ecstasy. Ignoring the slight cramp in her palm, she circled harder with her thumb and slid just the tip of her finger inside, and then Storm groaned her name as sensation took over, as she shivered helplessly and flooded Corrie's hand.

Corrie kept still until Storm's breathing began to settle. She eased her underwear back in place and lightly kissed Storm's trembling lips, then moved away to rinse off her fingers. Oddly enough, she felt no desire to be touched in return. Her own pleasure had somehow flowed and ebbed with Storm's.

Someone knocked at the door. Storm's face drained of color, but strangely, Corrie felt no panic, not even a whisper of butterfly wings unfurling in her gut. The debilitating anger of just a few minutes ago had passed. She was calm. Empty.

"I'll handle this," she said, stroking Storm's arm lightly before opening the door.

Denise.

Corrie glanced back at Storm. "I need to talk to Denise for a minute," she said. "See you back in the hall."

Storm nodded, slipped over the threshold, and was gone.

Denise stepped inside, straightened to her full height—which still meant that the crown of her head only came up to Corrie's chin—and put her hands on her hips. Corrie leaned nonchalantly against the doorframe.

"What the hell are you doing, Cor? She's just a kid!"

Corrie shrugged. "She's legal, and I didn't hear her complaining."

"What if her mother had been on the other side of this door—instead of me?"

Corrie rolled her eyes. "Look, D, I don't need your approval, and I sure as hell don't need you telling me what to do. You forfeited your right to be involved in how I live my life when you fucked me over for my brother."

"You're being juvenile about this."

"Maybe so, but at least I'm not a slut!"

Denise pulled away, surprise and anger warring on her face. "What the hell is that supposed to mean?"

Corrie laughed sharply. "That's what they call people who sleep with two different family members in the same month."

Denise flushed down to her neck. "I do love him, you know," she protested. "I love him in a way I never loved you. You and I...I mean, I'm not—"

"I've told you before and I'll say it again," Corrie snarled. "I don't want to hear your 'explanation.' The two of you deserve each other."

"And you deserve casual fucks in the bathroom?" Denise's heart-shaped face grew softer then, and she reached one hand out as though to touch Corrie's cheek. "Come on, Corrie. Can't we move on, here? Move past this?"

Corrie evaded her touch and pushed off the wall. "Believe me when I say I'm not punishing myself over you. You don't want me—fine. There are dozens—hell, hundreds—of people who do. Just keep out of my way."

Denise sighed and lowered her hand. "I still care about you," she said softly. "You know that, right?"

"Oh, yeah." Corrie's lips twisted. "You've got a great way of showing it." She pushed open the door, walked out, and didn't look back.

❖

Quinn sighed as her ball headed straight for the gutter yet again, and she turned her back on the pins. "I think I'm hopeless without the bumpers," she said, trying hard to keep her tone light. *It's just a dumb game. Not a big deal.*

Drew patted her on the shoulder when she sat down in the bucket seat next to his. "No worries, Quinn, no worries. Next time for sure."

She reached for her soda in an attempt to hide her frustration. This entire night was going exactly as she had known it would—badly. Or, she reconsidered after a few sips, maybe not badly so much as just not fun.

Krista stepped up to the lane, which prompted Drew to elbow Quinn in the ribs. *Ow!* Quinn nearly lost her cool and scowled. Instead, she shifted away from him and half-heartedly took his hint.

"All right, Krista. Here we go. Time for a strike!"

Krista smiled in reply but turned and grinned affectionately at Megs. There really was a huge difference between a smile and a grin, Quinn reflected, especially if you'd been halfway hoping that you'd be getting one and were instead seeing the other. Not that she'd ever really expected anything to come of this, but, *hope springs eternal.* And she had to give Drew credit for finding someone she was actually interested in this time. His last attempt had been an unequivocal disaster: Allergic Allie, who had started sneezing the second Quinn had walked in the room. She'd turned out to have histamines to pretty much every animal on the planet. Not exactly the kind of person a vet student could date comfortably—or at all.

Krista, on the other hand, had a cat. She was working on her Master's degree in Drew's department—electrical engineering—and in her spare time, she liked to read historical fiction. Quinn knew all of this about her because they'd chatted over lunch the week before, and for the first time in perhaps ever, she had actually felt comfortable talking with someone she didn't know very well. As an added plus, Krista was attractive without being stunning. Beautiful women made Quinn nervous.

So yes, okay, she'd had some hopes for tonight. Maybe not high hopes, but she could definitely see herself becoming friends with Krista, and she'd even thought once or twice or five times about what it would be like to kiss her, and—

Seven pins clattered to the floor. Impressed, Quinn clapped. Drew shouted something goofy like "Yeehaw," and Megs wolf-whistled. Krista blushed slightly, looked over her shoulder, and winked.

I really should try to get rid of those extra ten pounds, Quinn thought for the millionth time. Megan's physique was nothing if not enviable. Her gray shirt stretched tightly across strong shoulders that tapered to a narrow waist. A swimmer's body. Or perhaps more accurately, a windsurfer's body—that was her sport of choice according to Drew, who worked with her at the boathouse during the summertime.

Another clatter of pins and a cute little whoop of pleasure announced that Krista had bowled a spare. Megs jumped up to give her a high five. Their hips bumped lightly as Krista returned to her seat.

"Nice one," Quinn said with feigned enthusiasm, studiously ignoring the lurching of her stomach. She sipped at her soda again and tried to just enjoy the night—the banter of Drew's group of friends, the cheesy eighties music blaring from the bowling alley's speakers, and the occasional exultant holler of someone who'd just managed a strike. But the trouble was, she didn't really know Drew's friends very well, and she wasn't good at small talk anyway. And to be honest, she'd been a little kid in the eighties and couldn't tell Pat Benatar from Cyndi Lauper. Not to mention the fact that every time someone got a strike, she felt like an idiot for not being able to roll a bowling ball in a straight line.

As the night plodded on, Quinn watched how Megs touched Krista often in light, almost teasing ways—a few fingers resting briefly on her arm, the slight brush of their shoulders, the gentle press of their thighs as they sat side by side. How very animated Megs was—how she nodded and gesticulated as she told funny stories, and how captivated Krista was by her display.

I'm just not exciting, she realized. *The only stories I have are about school and animals, and even if they were interesting, I'd be too introverted to tell them. It was like that in high school and college. Why should now be any different?*

It was sad to see Krista slipping away, but on the other hand, it was a relief. Krista wouldn't be able to say, "You never want to go out," like Quinn's short-lived high school boyfriend, Brian, had claimed. And she'd never be able to accuse her—as Sue had in college—of caring more about her studies than about their relationship. Life was simpler this way. Easier.

"Hey, guys," said Drew after their second game finally ended. "Anyone up for going to the diner?" He waggled his eyebrows. "Milkshakes, spicy fries, quadruple bacon cheeseburgers..."

Quinn looked around. Almost everyone was nodding. She stood up quickly. The idea of spending more time with other human beings was about as appealing as...well, as that quadruple bacon cheeseburger. Fortunately, she had just the excuse.

"I need to head out," she said as the others collected their jackets, wallets, and purses.

"What? C'mon, Quinn."

She cut off his wheedling plea with a swift shake of her head. "I need to run over to the humane society and check on a few kittens." Which was a lie, but it sure did sound good. No sane person wanted kittens to be neglected.

Drew huffed a loud sigh. "Fine." He grasped her shoulders gently and smiled down at her. "I'm really glad that you hung out with us tonight. You should tag along more often."

"I had a good time," Quinn lied again, glad that it was so easy. And then she walked to the door and pushed it open, zipping up her coat against the chill October air. She didn't look back.

COLLISION COURSE

Seven months later

Corrie woke a few minutes after dawn, to the sensation of warm sunlight across the bridge of her nose. She lay still, eyes closed, mentally taking stock. Monday. First real day of work for the season. Someone—Brad—in bed next to her. She'd ended up choosing him over Megs last night. Curtains rustling in a light breeze. She flexed her toes and took a deep breath, testing out her mood—like pushing a sore tooth with her tongue. But there were no twinges today, only a lingering satisfaction with her conquest and a pleasant rush of anticipation for the day ahead.

She opened her eyes to the sight of Brad's well-muscled back, already tan from hours on the water. He had a mole between his shoulder blades. She'd kissed it playfully last night before falling asleep. Corrie turned over and slid out from under the crisp cotton sheets, snagging a pair of black swim trunks and a dark gray sports bra from the back of her desk chair as she moved toward the door.

She pushed it open gently, knowing that Frog was lying just on the other side. His collar jingled as he got to his feet, barked, and cocked his big gray head at her. She scratched the silky spot behind his right ear.

"Sorry, bud," she whispered, shutting the door behind her. "I know you hate sleeping out here." She straightened up, adjusting the frayed collar of the T-shirt that had slipped over one shoulder. "Let's go grab some breakfast, huh?"

Fifteen minutes later, she was standing at the kitchen sink sipping at a tall mug of steaming black coffee and munching on a slice of last night's pizza while her laptop booted up. Across the room, Frog was noisily devouring his kibble. Corrie stared out the curtained windows toward the gentle slope that led down from her bungalow to the shoreline. A partially completed pier jutted into Point Judith Pond, just past the skeletal frame of what would someday be a large shed—almost a barn. Polishing off the pizza, she wiped her hands on the dishtowel and quickly brought up her Internet browser. It opened to NOAA's forecast page for Wakefield, Rhode Island.

"Eight to ten knots right now," she muttered, scanning the page, "and up to fifteen by late this afternoon." She looked out toward the water again and nodded, content. *Not bad.*

She walked quickly back to the bedroom to collect her wallet and keys and tucked them into the waterproof pocket in her trunks. Brad was snoring and had shifted to take up almost the entire bed, his arms and legs splayed out haphazardly across the sheets. Corrie grinned smugly. She leaned down to kiss his shoulder, and he stirred just a little.

"There's coffee in the kitchen. See you 'round."

"Mmm, yeah," he said, and promptly fell back to sleep. She laughed and walked down the hall, pausing briefly in the bathroom to brush her long, blond hair back into a ponytail, before threading it through the ragged Hoyas cap that rested beside the sink.

"Let's get out of here, Frogger," she called, moving purposefully through the small den and toward the front door.

Once outside, she took off at a brisk jog, turning right out of the narrow gravel driveway and heading northeast along the edge of the inlet. It was a two-mile run to the Sailing Center—the perfect morning warm up. She took a deep breath of cool, late spring air and quickened her pace a little. The easterly wind smelled pungently of sea salt, and it made her eager to be out on the water.

Upon arriving at the boathouse, she immediately unlocked the equipment shed's double doors as Frog ran up and down the pier, half-heartedly chasing seagulls. Several rows of windsurfing boards and sails extended off to her left, a forest of lifejackets to her right. She eyed the windsurfing equipment for a few seconds, then shook her head and continued further into the building, past the unmanned rental counter.

"Better wind for a Laser," she said under her breath. Halting in front of a long wall honeycombed with narrow compartments, she finally selected a sail before moving across the hall to pick out a complementary mast and boom. Tucking the sail and its lines under her right arm, Corrie cautiously walked the long, thin mast and its companion boom out of the shed and down the pier before setting everything down in front of a row of Lasers, all up on blocks.

At first glance, the boats registered as nondescript. Only fourteen feet long and just over four feet wide, they certainly didn't have the inherent majesty of the large keelboats moored out in the harbor. Even the beginner tech dinghies had permanent masts and lines. *But that's what makes you special, isn't it?* Corrie thought as she unfurled the sail and began sliding its sleeve down the length of the mast. *You're a little puzzle. And if I put these pieces together right, you'll out-maneuver just about anything.*

There was something exhilarating about assembling a boat like this—about raising the mast and running the lines yourself. The accountability was both frightening and appealing. Do everything properly, and you'd have a boat that you knew, inside-out and backward. Do anything wrong, and it would fall apart on the water.

Once she had double-checked her knots, Corrie slid the assembled Laser onto a cart, then rolled it down the ramp next to the pier and into the water. Seaweed brushed against her legs as she tied the boat to a pylon with an expert bowline knot. She glanced back to check on Frog, who was happily rolling in the sand along the beach, before hoisting herself into the shallow cockpit and dropping both her rudder and centerboard into the water. She leaned over the bow long enough to pull herself toward the pier and undo her knot, then pushed away and let out the mainsheet so that her sail could fill. It caught the wind immediately, and as the boom swung out to the leeward side of the boat, the shift in weight distribution was enough to tilt the windward side up at a precarious angle.

Corrie threw her weight out to port, tucking her feet under the narrow piece of fabric, the "hiking strap", that ran the length of the cockpit. She made minor adjustments to the mainsail and tiller as her weight balanced out the force of the wind on the sail and brought the boat back down to a flat position. Her stomach muscles quivered as she held her torso perfectly flat over the water, steering with only the tips of her right fingers. Lasers were so damn sensitive—to touch, to weight, to wind shifts—and besides the accountability involved, she loved the precision they demanded.

Just a few years ago, sailing this particular boat would have been a luxury. She'd been completely focused on training in the 470, a two-man Olympic racing craft. Back then, sailing had felt more like work than pleasure. The regattas every weekend, the time trials, the relentless jockeying with other sailors for position. *That's over now*, she reminded herself, leaning out even further as the hull reacted to a gust of wind. For several months after her failure to win a spot in the Olympics, Corrie hadn't been able to make herself go anywhere near a boat. She had worried that she would always associate sailing with Denise's betrayal and Will's gloating. Even just looking out at the water had hurt. But all of that was in the past. Sailing was in her blood and the tide had called her back. This was her slice of ocean, her club, her boat. Not his. She smiled broadly at the morning sun. *Now, finally, I can just enjoy it.*

Content to hold her course for the present, Corrie sailed east toward the narrow inlet that connected the pond to the ocean. In less than two hours, the Sailing Center would be swarming with new students of all ages—some frightened, some arrogant, some comically eager. But for this one small part of the day, all she had to answer to was the wind and the water. She tossed her head back, enjoying the taste of the salt spray on her lips, and she let instinct take over.

❖

An hour later, Corrie boosted herself from the cockpit to the wooden slats of the pier. She looked up at the willowy redhead who had secured her boat and now stood shading her eyes against the bright glare of the morning sun.

"Hey, Jen."

"Hey, you. How was it out there?" Jen's Brooklyn accent was more pronounced than usual—a testimony to the fact that it was still morning and she wasn't ready to be awake. After last night's party, Corrie wasn't surprised.

She got to her feet, undoing the Velcro straps of her sailing gloves in the process. "It's nice. Decent wind and steady for now. Only a few little gusts. Should be a good day for the rookies."

Jen laughed. "They'll still be scared to death."

"You know me, I live for the girly shrieking." Corrie squinted at the boathouse. "Looks like some of them are already here."

"Yes, and they're all asking for the head of instruction," said Jen as they began to walk back. She looked pointedly at Corrie, who groaned.

"You can run, but you can't hide. I gave them a very precise physical description."

"Thanks," Corrie grumbled. "Thanks a lot." She took a deep breath. "You ready for this?"

Jen shook her head. "I am going right back inside, where I belong. You're the social butterfly." She veered off toward the equipment shed with a little wave as Corrie sighed and reluctantly picked up her pace. She loved sailing and enjoyed teaching, but fielding a barrage of half-anxious, half-demanding requests was not her idea of a good first day.

After a solid half hour of reassuring concerned or confused students—and in one case, the overprotective mother of a twenty-year-old guy whose face had been flaming in embarrassment—Corrie found herself alone and with a few minutes to spare before she would be required to officially open the instructional season with a welcome speech. A knot of instructors had gathered just outside the boathouse doors, chatting idly about their plans for the night.

"Hi, Cor," Brad said, reaching out to squeeze her left shoulder.

"Hey," she said, but was careful not to return his touch. It wouldn't do to have him getting the wrong idea, after all. A night of fucking was exactly that—no more, no less. She looked away and immediately noticed Jen's raised eyebrows from across the circle.

When Corrie shrugged and put on her innocent face, Jen couldn't help but roll her eyes. *There she goes again*, she had to laugh to herself. *I must be almost the only friend she hasn't seduced at one point or another, and that's only because I'm as straight as they come.* It had been that way for a while now, but somehow Corrie managed to keep them all friends. Take Brad, for instance—by the half-smile on his face, a little wistful but resigned, he apparently knew the drill.

"We'd better head inside, guys," Corrie called, effortlessly taking control of the group. "Almost time to get this show on the road." But just as she was about to lead the way through the double doors, she caught sight of Frog racing full tilt toward two people nearby.

❖

"Remind me again why I'm doing this?" Quinn asked her companion as they turned the corner and saw the mass of people gathered outside the University of Rhode Island's Sailing Center. *Big crowd. That's just great.*

"Because you can't study all the time," said Drew. It was the same answer he'd given her twice already this morning. "And because it'll be good for you to get outside. You're way too pale."

"Pale is healthy." Quinn wondered why she kept letting Drew persuade her into situations like this. She pinched his tan forearm lightly. "What part about the risk of skin cancer don't you understand?"

Drew sighed and shook his head. "This is exactly what I'm talking about, Q. You need to get out. Loosen up. Go with the wind for a while." He caught sight of several of his fellow instructors gathered in a loose cluster in front of the boathouse and pointed them out to Quinn. "Look, there's the gang. I'll introduce you to everyone before we get started."

As they approached the group, a large gray dog came bounding out of the surf directly toward them, wagging its skinny tail. It stopped just short of Drew and Quinn, shook itself vigorously, and shoved its nose against Drew's hip.

"Ugh," said Drew, looking down at his water-splattered T-shirt. "Thanks, Frog. You're a pal." He reached down to pet the dog's head anyway, but Quinn had beaten him to it. She knelt on the ground, one hand rubbing behind Frog's ears and the other patting his sleek, barrel chest. He whined deep in his throat at the attention and happily licked her face. Quinn laughed.

"Hey, buddy," she crooned. "You're one fine looking Weimaraner. Who do you belong to, hmm?"

"That would be me," Corrie said as she came up alongside them. "Sorry for the impromptu bath, guys."

Drew shrugged. "Not like I wasn't expecting to get wet today anyway." He looked down at Quinn, who didn't seem to realize Corrie had joined them. He tapped her on the shoulder. "Earth to Quinn. I've got someone you need to meet here."

Quinn got to her feet reluctantly, giving Frog one last pat on the head and turned toward his owner. At a few inches taller than Quinn, Corrie looked the part of an all-American athlete. Her slim, muscular legs, toned arms, and tightly rippled stomach were already darkly tan. Freckles liberally sprinkled the bridge of her nose, above which two green eyes studied Quinn intently.

"This is Corrie Marsten," said Drew. "Head of sailing instruction this season and a legendary sailor 'round these parts. She's my crew when we race the two-man boats, though I bet we'd do a lot better if she skippered."

Corrie rolled her eyes and scratched behind Frog's left ear. "Whatever, Harris." What Drew didn't know, of course, was that skippering one of those boats made her think of Denise. And besides, she would have never admitted this to him, but sometimes it felt really good to just relax into the rhythm of the boat and let someone else make the tough calls.

Unperturbed, Drew carried on. "Corrie, Quinn Davies. She's an old buddy from college who's in vet school here. And my roommate for the summer so she can escape her crappy landlord."

"Hi," Quinn said as she shook Corrie's hand. Rough calluses slid across her soft palm. "Great dog you've got there."

"Yeah, thanks," said Corrie, reaching down to stroke Frog's head. "He's my best buddy."

"Why 'Frog?'" Quinn asked.

"He looked like one," Corrie said. "Back when he was a tiny puppy—just like a little gray frog." When Quinn laughed, she shrugged. "Fortunately, he grew out of that. So hey, did you sail with Drew up at Dartmouth?"

"Oh no," Quinn answered quickly, shaking her head for emphasis. "I've never sailed a day in my life. We lived across the hall from each other freshman year. That's how I know him." She nudged Drew with an elbow for emphasis, and he poked her back playfully.

"Ah. Cool." Corrie smiled—an easy, open expression that Quinn felt herself return—and adjusted the rim of her baseball cap. "Welcome aboard, then." She looked up at Drew and nodded toward the boathouse. "See you in there."

Quinn watched her jog off, feeling her involuntary grin slowly fade. For some reason, she felt warm, as though she'd been on stage in a spotlight that had just been turned off.

"...that's Corrie," Drew was saying as he opened the boathouse doors for her. "What do you think?"

"She's very charismatic, isn't she?" Quinn said, still struggling to sort out her own impressions. Corrie's easy confidence was intriguing, but her effortless and completely natural beauty had also triggered more than a few of Quinn's familiar insecurities about her own body. *I could look better if I worked at it*, she thought for the millionth time. *But there's nothing I can do with my hair, and my face is always going to be too round.* Quinn's slightly wavy, nearly shoulder-length brown hair always felt unruly, and on particularly humid days, unkempt. And each time she looked in the mirror, it was easy to see that she'd inherited the roundness of her father's features without his defining cheekbones. Dropping a few spare pounds wouldn't fix that.

Realizing the pointless trajectory of her thoughts, she forced herself to look around as she took a seat next to Drew in the chart room—a large, open space that took up most of the first and second floors of the boathouse. A full bar extended along half of the right wall, while a huge fireplace was centered in the left. A small stage shared the far wall with a long sliding door leading out to what looked like a deck.

"Nice space, huh?" Drew asked proudly. "We have socials in here every Friday after the weekly races, sometimes with a DJ and sometimes a live band."

Quinn nodded absently, then stiffened as the shrill whine of a microphone echoed through the room. When it cut off just as abruptly, the chatter in the hall stopped. As Corrie stepped gracefully onto the stage, the young guy sitting to Quinn's right leaned over to his buddy and murmured something emphatically. Quinn caught the word "hot" and shook her head. If looking like that meant being drooled over, maybe she was better off.

"Welcome to the summer program, everyone," Corrie said, her gaze sweeping across the room. "I'm Corrie Marsten, head of instruction. You can call me Corrie, or Cor, or Mars...but anything that sounds like 'Ms.' or 'Miss' Marsten is off limits." She waited for the small current of laughter to subside before moving on. "This year is especially exciting since we're hosting a regatta this year in early August—the Rhode Island 470 Invitational. We're expecting it to be a big race, and we'll need a lot of you to participate in some way."

As she continued to discuss the specifics of the regatta, Quinn found herself wondering yet again whether it had really been a good idea to give in to Drew's insistence that she take sailing lessons. She needed to study hard this summer if she was going to pass the qualifying exam on her first try, and she blatantly refused to cut down on her volunteer hours at the humane society. Drew was just trying to help, as always—

to get her to meet people and have fun—but these lessons could easily turn into a significant time sink. *Well,* she considered resolutely, *if they do, then I'll just quit. No harm in that. Drew won't give me a hard time if I try it and don't like it.*

She tuned back in to the proceedings just as the instructors finished introducing themselves. Emboldened by her recent decision, Quinn turned to face Drew.

"All right, Drew," she said firmly. "Teach me how to sail a boat."

❖

By the end of the day, Quinn was exhausted. Her arms and legs ached, her palms hurt from gripping the mainsheet, and she had a mottled blue-black bruise on her left knee where she'd whacked it against the thwart during one of her first tacks. But as she sat in safety position just inside the mooring field, she only felt exhilarated.

Drew had spent the morning teaching his small group the basics of sail theory, as well as the safety rules of the club and the procedure for checking out equipment once they received their ratings on the tech dinghies. Then, they'd spent the hour before lunch practicing in the "simulator"—an old, beat up tech on wheels that could be turned in a full circle so as to allow beginner sailors to experience tacks and jibes before going on the water. After lunch, they rigged up several boats and took them out, and the afternoon was filled with "follow the leader" maneuvers, capsize drills, and finally, landing practice.

The best part of the day had been when Drew had pushed Quinn's boat away from the pier—when she'd finally been on her own against the waves and the wind, alone and free. Sure, she'd messed up a few times at the very beginning, and she'd very nearly capsized after letting go of the rudder during her first jibe. But she'd gotten better after that. More comfortable. *I love that I'm the one doing it all*, she thought. *No one to answer to, no one else to rely on. Just me.*

She watched intently as Cindy, a middle-aged English professor, approached the pier for her last landing of the day. Drew supervised from the edge, offering the occasional tip but mostly allowing his students to make their own judgment calls. As Cindy successfully turned up alongside the dock, Quinn took a deep breath and grabbed the tiller extension tightly, ready to maneuver out of her head-to-wind position.

"All right, Quinn!" Drew hollered. "Bring it on!"

After a few fumbling moments, Quinn got her boat moving and sailed as close to the wind as she could, toward the leeward side of the pier. She watched the distance close, chewing nervously on her lower lip as a small gust caused her speed to increase. Almost immediately, she stopped trimming the sail and allowed it to flap in the breeze. *When in doubt, let it out.* The boat slowed and she exhaled in a relieved sigh.

"Nice," said Drew. "Way to counteract that puff."

Realizing that she still had several boat lengths to go, Quinn pulled on the line just a bit until her sail stopped flapping and the wind propelled her forward once more. She repeated the process several times, before the bow settled gently against the side of the dock.

"Great job!" Drew said as she secured her boat to the pier. "You rocked that one, Q. If we could give ratings the first day, you better believe you'd have one."

Quinn let out a shaky sigh and forced her tired fingers to undo the cleat hitch that tied off the main halyard. "No way am I ready to go out on my own yet." She somehow managed to let the boom down gently into the bottom of the boat, then turned back to Drew. "But thanks. That was really fun."

"Do you mean it?" he asked as they carried their sails back to the equipment shed. "You had a good time out there?"

"Definitely," Quinn said, amused by his earnest tone. "I love how it's both academic and athletic. How you have to be thinking about wind physics the whole time, even while you're shifting your weight and holding on to the lines." She smiled at him over her shoulder as they pushed through the door. "I like your sport, Drew."

"Glad to hear that," Corrie's voice rang out from behind the counter in front of them, where she was helping Jen manage the influx of sails and lifejackets. As they put their stuff down, Corrie reached out and plucked a strand of seaweed from behind Quinn's left ear. She held it up between them. "You'll start a fashion trend."

Quinn laughed self-consciously. *Trust me to come in looking like some kind of sea monster. Great.*

"First social's this Friday, right?" Drew asked as he signed their equipment back in.

"Oh yeah," Corrie said. "Should be a blast."

Drew poked Jen in the shoulder, hard. "You gonna be there, Jenny?"

Jen tried to smack him with a nearby towel, but he leapt back out of range, smirking. "How many times, Harris?" she asked menacingly. "How many times have I told you not to call me that?"

Corrie rolled her eyes at their familiar antics and turned back to Quinn. "How about you, Quinn? You coming?"

Quinn shrugged, surprised at the question. *Why would she care?* "Oh...I don't know. I have a lot of studying to do."

"Just come once," said Drew, still keeping a cautious eye on Jen and her towel.

Corrie smirked. "Cheap drinks, good music, and warm bodies. Everything a sailor needs."

If Quinn could have stopped herself from blushing, she would have. *Yeah*, she thought, embarrassed. *That sounds right up my alley.* "We'll see," she said. "Thanks." And then she hurried out the door before any of them could say anything else.

❖

Corrie stretched and massaged the back of her neck, wincing when she encountered a sunburned patch of skin. The infernal paperwork was finally done. Every student who had joined today was entered into the system, and it was past time to go home. She looked out her window at the dark sky and sighed.

Frog's tail suddenly thumped against the floor just as someone knocked at the door. Corrie looked up, blinked, and frowned deeply. *What the fuck?*

"Will," she said, trying to keep her voice flat. No need for him to realize just how much he rattled her. "What the hell are you doing here?"

"Hi to you too, li'l sis," he said, sauntering into the room and settling into one of the spare chairs. He propped his feet up on Corrie's desk. When she glared at him, he winked back. "Aren't you happy to see me?"

"Thrilled." She couldn't resist drowning the word in sarcasm. "Why aren't you in Newport?"

"What, a guy can't visit his sister? Not to mention his alma mater—"

"No," she cut him off. "You don't do shit like that. What do you want?"

"Fine, fine." Will put his feet down and leaned forward. "I want a job."

"What?" Corrie was incredulous. "I thought you and your fiancée were getting a place this summer."

Will grimaced and adjusted the brim of his US Sailing cap. "As it turns out, Denise's parents don't approve of the bride and groom living together before the wedding."

Corrie laughed harshly. *Oh, that's rich.* "You're fuckin' kidding me."

"Wish I were. But I didn't renew my lease and there's no way I'm moving back in with Mom and Dad. So I figured I'd spend my last summer as a bachelor hanging out here."

"Go wait tables or something," Corrie said dismissively. "I'm not giving you a job."

"Why the hell not?"

"Because I've already hired all the instructors I want," she said, meeting his indignant frown head-on. *No way are you ruining this summer for me, too.*

Will snorted. "And how many of them are Olympic sailors, huh?" He tapped the logo on his hat and arched his eyebrows in a way that was somehow patronizing. "I'm a commodity, Cor. Hell, having me on your staff will probably bring in more students."

Corrie leaned back in her chair, struggling not to grind her teeth. *Just tell him no. Tell him to get up and walk the hell away.* Except that he was right, damn him. His experience and reputation would be invaluable. And intolerable. *But I have to think of the club, first. I have to. Fuck!* He had won. Again.

"Fine," she said after a long pause. "Fine, you can have a goddamn job. But if you think for a *second* that you'll be living with me—"

Will raised one hand, forestalling her. "Save it, sis. I'm staying at the frat house."

"Your frat house," Corrie sneered. "The one you were president of five years ago, and you're just going to crash on a couch all summer?" When Will grinned, she shook her head. "Lame."

"Be nice to me and I'll let you come to some of the parties."

"Fuck off. I don't need to hang out with a bunch of cretin undergraduates to have a good time."

"Maybe you do," he said, getting to his feet. "'Cuz right now, you're in a shitty mood." He shrugged. "Or maybe you just need to get laid. Anyway, thanks for the job. I'll be around tomorrow."

As he turned toward the door, Corrie had the sudden urge to go after him—to sock him right in the kidneys and demand to know what the hell kind of right he had coming in here and asking her for help when he and Denise had betrayed her.

She grabbed the edge of the desk and hung on tightly, as though it were the gunwale of a capsizing boat. *Stay calm. Don't give him the satisfaction.* As the echo of his footsteps in the hall began to fade, she sank back into her chair. *You'll be busy,* she told herself. *Probably won't even see him very often.* It wasn't as though she'd be jockeying with him for their parents' attention or constantly trying to get better grades and faster regatta times than he did. All of that was over now. In the past. Done. So what if she saw him around from time to time? He was just passing through.

She had the moral high ground. That much was certain. And she was being the "bigger man." The fact that Will would now owe her one was nice, too, as was the fact that he would be working for her. Corrie massaged her temples briefly before gathering up the papers on her desk. Nice. Right. Nice and cold comfort—like an unexpected frost on the first day of summer.

BEARING OFF

Quinn permitted herself a rare expletive and let her lifejacket do the job of supporting her in the water as she briefly relaxed. She bobbed in the waves next to her capsized boat, one hand still gripping the exposed centerboard in case the tech suddenly began to tip all the way over. With a sigh, she looked toward shore and saw that the blue flag—indicating heavy weather—had just replaced the green.

"Could've told you that," she said, frustrated. The wind had been brisk but light when she launched earlier in the afternoon, but clouds had swept in from the east shortly thereafter. Drew had taught her ways of coping with heavy wind earlier in the week, and theoretically, she knew how to handle herself. *But all the theory in the world can't stop me from being a great big klutz!*

Just as she was about to try bearing down on the centerboard yet again, a familiar voice suddenly hailed her from astern. Quinn turned her head in time to see Corrie execute a smooth maneuver on her windsurfer board that brought her alongside the tech. Quinn couldn't help but feel both impressed by and jealous of the grace and strength with which Corrie performed the deceptively simple movement, and found herself wishing that of all the instructors, Corrie hadn't been the one to see her like this.

"Whoa there, captain." Corrie dropped her large sail and settled into a crouch on the board, her balance unaffected by the waves. She nodded at the capsized boat. "How's it going?"

"I'll be all right," said Quinn, not quite looking at her. *Just go away and let me try again. I can do this by myself!* She had to struggle to keep her voice even and light. "Drew taught us what to do."

"Okay. Just holler if you need a hand."

Quinn forced herself to meet Corrie's gaze. She even managed a weak smile. "Thanks."

She continued to watch as Corrie planted her feet and yanked her sail out of the water in one powerful movement. As she grabbed the boom and rotated her hips, the board began to move, its bow rising as the wind caught the sail. *So that's how it's supposed to be done*, she realized, having only ever seen beginner windsurfers struggling in the harbor to get themselves going in much lighter wind than this.

As Corrie moved out of her sightline, Quinn turned back to her boat, narrowed her eyes at the centerboard, and shook the wet hair off her forehead. Grabbing onto the board's end, she pulled down as hard as she could and crossed her arms over the wet surface as she struggled to right the boat with her body weight. For a long moment, it seemed that this attempt would also be in vain, and her biceps began to shake with effort.

This is ridiculous, she thought, even as she struggled to ignore the burning in her arms. *For once, it's a good thing I'm not petite, and even so, I* still *can't right this boat!* But just as she was about to let go, she felt the board begin to move down toward the water, and within a few seconds she was able to shift her grasp to the gunwales. Taking another deep breath, she reached for one of the hiking straps and managed to haul herself over the side.

"Thank god," she said as she sat in the cockpit, breathing heavily from the exertion. The mainsail flapped loudly, showering her with a fine spray of salt water that stung her eyes as she gauged her distance from land. Corrie briefly came into view a few boat lengths ahead, before she headed back downwind in a large circle. *Keeping an eye on me*, Quinn realized, and felt an unexpected surge of relief. Grabbing the mainsheet, she hauled in on it and simultaneously threw the rudder over to the other side of the boat. "But I'm not going to mess up," she told the wind. "Not this time."

It took several tries, but Quinn finally managed a successful landing just as the clock tower chimed five. Drew met her at the pier and saved her the trouble of tying up her own boat. "You okay?" he asked, frowning. "I saw you go over—"

"I'm fine," Quinn said firmly. "Just tired." This time, her arms shook from only the simple effort of boosting herself onto the dock. She sighed and began wringing out her waterlogged baseball cap. *I really need to get stronger, pronto.* "Well, that was an adventure." When Drew continued to look concerned, however, she laughed softly.

"Don't worry," she said, leaning back against his shins. "I'm still having fun. One little dunk isn't going to change that."

"Come on." He squeezed her shoulder. "I'll help you get your boat in so you can dry off."

As he returned the tech to its berth, she folded the sail and carried it, along with her soggy lifejacket, back to the equipment shed. If Jen noticed the clear evidence of her capsize, she didn't say anything, and Quinn smiled gratefully as she turned to go. But when she pushed open the double doors, Corrie was just approaching. Her biceps bulged gently with the weight of the windsurfer board, and a few strands of blond hair that had eluded her ponytail clung to her right cheek.

Oh, no. Acutely aware of the fact that she looked like a drowned rat, Quinn cleared her throat self-consciously. "Thanks again for, uh, stopping by out there."

Corrie shrugged. "You had it under control." She paused and cocked her head to one side, favoring Quinn with a long glance from head to foot. "The wet T-shirt look is good on you." When Quinn flushed and didn't reply, Corrie just winked and walked past.

She's making fun of me, Quinn thought, the sharp rush of embarrassment nearly eclipsing her chill from the strong breeze. But as she hurried back to her apartment for a change of clothes, the feeling slowly subsided. *I guess I deserved it. And she wasn't being* mean. *Not really.* In fact, Corrie's expression for those last few seconds had almost seemed appreciative. Which didn't make any sense.

Quinn pushed hard against the sticky front door and kicked off her squelching aqua shoes just inside. "You're imagining things," she told the doormat, wrinkling her pruny toes against the soft surface. She shook her head and stripped off her shirt, letting it fall at her feet with a wet *plop*. Even that simple movement made her aware of the soreness in her arms, and she grimaced slightly. The promise of a warm shower, followed by leftovers for supper and a few quiet hours of studying, was exactly what she needed.

❖

Corrie shut the blow dryer off and ran her fingers through the long mane of hair that brushed her shoulder blades. Satisfied, she stowed the appliance in her nearby locker, next to a spare set of sailing gloves. The thumping baseline of the DJ's music upstairs had replaced the dryer's buzzing hum, and Corrie felt her pulse quicken. Turning toward one of the full-length mirrors, she surveyed her reflection critically. Her black polo shirt accentuated the deep tan on her neck and arms and fit snugly across her breasts. Frayed khaki shorts sat low on her waist and came down to just past mid-thigh, giving way to long, newly shaven legs. She reached for her scuffed sandals under a nearby bench and pulled them on, stopping to adjust the brightly colored band around her left ankle in the process. An Ironman waterproof watch on her right wrist and a short, braided leather necklace were her only other accessories. She grinned at herself rakishly in the mirror. It had been a good opening week, with no major injuries or damage to the boats. And Will had gone home to Newport this weekend to visit Denise, so she didn't have to worry about him raining on her parade. That in itself was a good reason to celebrate. Corrie shut her locker and headed for the stairs that led up to the entrance of the common room. The low beat of the music grew louder with every step, and she felt it coil deep in her stomach, felt it become the familiar *wanting*. These moments of anticipation—when the night stretched out before her, long and full of promise—were almost better than anything else. *Almost*.

At the top of the staircase, the double doors were propped open, giving her an unobstructed view of the crowded room. Just in case, she looked around for Will, but when he was nowhere to be seen, she inhaled deeply and forced herself to relax, to feel the pulse of the crowd. Her heartbeat sped up again at the unmistakable swell of human energy. In situations like these, Corrie almost felt like a social vampire, as though she somehow fed off the mere presence of other people. She squared her shoulders and strolled inside.

"Hey, Corrie!"

"What's up, Mars?"

"How's it going, Cor?"

Instructors and returning students greeted her as she slowly made her way to the bar, stopping now and then to exchange a few words, shake someone's hand, or lightly touch a shoulder. She could feel the new students in the crowd watching her. They all knew who she was, of course, but most of them weren't comfortable enough to do more than nod in her general direction. Buoyed by her reception, she signaled the bartender and turned to lean against the edge of the bar when her beer arrived.

She took a long, slow swallow and let her gaze wander around the room again. The dance floor was packed, as were the leather sofas and chairs arranged in front of the fireplace. At the opposite end of the dance floor, a sliding door led out onto a wide, two-story deck. Corrie looked at her watch, grabbed the neck of her beer, and threaded her way through the crowd. *If I'm lucky, I'll still catch some of the sunset.*

As she stepped into the night air, however, she glimpsed a familiar figure standing off to one side, elbows propped on the railing. Quinn looked significantly less bedraggled in loose navy capris, a light blue button-down shirt, and sandals, but Corrie thought she might prefer her earlier appearance. The worn tee, soaked from her capsize, had outlined Quinn's full breasts, and her cotton shorts had clung to her thighs. *She's curvy*, Corrie thought as she slowly approached. *Feminine. I like that.* And yet she'd also been so very *cute*—wet and rumpled and clearly self-conscious.

"Hey," she said, coming to stand beside Quinn as the other woman turned to look at her. "Meant to tell you—nice job righting that tech this afternoon. They can be tricky."

Quinn smiled shyly. "Thanks." Corrie watched her eyes—watched them briefly flick over her body and return to her face. She noticed the slight flush, too.

"So." She took another sip from her beer. "You're in vet school, right?"

"Yes," said Quinn. "I'm just about to start my third year—if I pass my qual, that is." She met Corrie's gaze inquisitively. "What do you do? Besides all this." She indicated the boathouse and the ocean with a slight movement of one hand.

"Mechanical engineering." Corrie set her beer on the ledge and gripped it, leaning back for a better look at the clouds. "In theory, anyway." She shifted her gaze back to Quinn, who was still looking up at her. "I want to design boats when I get out of here, so practically, I do a lot of aerospace stuff and fluid mechanics."

Quinn nodded, returning her gaze to the expanse of water below. It shimmered in the light of the half-moon and earliest stars. The bells on the keelboats moored in the harbor rang intermittently in the soft breeze. "What kinds of boats?" she asked. "I mean, what's your favorite?"

Corrie smiled at the question and shifted her weight so that her right arm was brushing Quinn's left. She felt Quinn's muscles tense, but she didn't pull away. "Little boats. I'm not as big a fan of the keelboats and yachts." She tilted her head back and closed her eyes. "You're closer to the water in a small boat. And you have to do more. I think they're more challenging—" Suddenly catching herself in the middle of a ramble, Corrie laughed. "Don't get me started. I'll talk about boats all day if you let me."

"You really love them, don't you?"

Corrie was intrigued by Quinn's expression—intense and gentle, all at the same time. "You'll fall for them too, before long," she said. "But of course you're going to be a vet, so your first love must be animals."

Quinn rolled her eyes. "Oh, yes. I'm hopeless. And I completely love your dog. I'd get one just like him if I could. But then again, last week I just fell head over heels for a kitten at the shelter where I work, and next week I'm sure it'll happen again, and—" She blushed. "But don't *you* get *me* started!"

Corrie watched with amusement as Quinn's sudden animation faded back into shyness. *Sweet girl,* she thought. *She's interesting, in an innocent sort of way.* Impulsively, she stepped back and held out her hand, flashing what she knew was a charming smile. "Come inside and dance with me."

Quinn turned, startled, and pressed her back against the railing. "What?"

"Come on," she coaxed.

"I—I don't dance. Not to this music, anyway," Quinn said quickly, wide-eyed.

Corrie took a step closer and tilted her head. She reached out to tuck a stray strand of Quinn's wavy hair behind her right ear, and felt the other woman tense again. It was a struggle this time to keep the knowing smirk off her face. "What kind of music do you dance to, then? I'll tell the DJ to play it."

"I..." Quinn turned away, toward the water. "I can't. I'm sorry, I'm just not in the mood right now."

Corrie frowned at her still back, wondering what had suddenly gone wrong. *I can tell you're attracted to me. So what's up?* Determined not to lose her cool, however, she shrugged and kept her voice light. "Okay. Some other time." She let the fingertips of her left hand rest lightly in the space between Quinn's shoulder blades. No reaction. "See you."

Corrie turned and strode into the room, forcing herself not to look back. If Quinn Davies wanted to play hard to get, that was fine with her. There were plenty of other people—women *and* men—who wouldn't send mixed signals. She stopped just inside the door and was surveying the crowd again, trying to make up her mind, when she saw Drew approaching from the direction of the bar.

"What's up, Harris? Good party, huh?"

"'Course," he said casually, but his gaze was speculative. He paused for a few seconds before speaking again. "I was actually just coming outside to rescue Quinn."

"Rescue her?" Corrie frowned. "From what?"

"You know what," Drew told her. "She's not your type, Cor."

Corrie shifted her weight and crossed her arms under her breasts. "How do you know?" The question caught Drew off guard, and she watched with satisfaction as he spluttered. *I'd love to get past that shy exterior thing she's got going on and see what's* really *underneath.*

"For Christ's sake, Corrie, Quinn's just about as introverted as it's possible to be! It took me fifteen solid minutes to get her to agree to come here tonight."

"And your point is?"

Drew sighed in exasperation. "She's not about the hook-up, Mars. Not at all. Hence, not your type." When Corrie delicately arched her left eyebrow at him, he threw up his hands and nearly knocked over his neighbor's beer bottle.

"Look," he said after making his apologies. "Quinn means a lot to me. It'd be great if you were friends. But I don't...I don't want to see her get hurt."

Corrie took a step back. "That's not what I'm about, Drew," she muttered. "You *know* that."

"I didn't mean it that way, Cor—"

"Forget it," she cut him off. Refusing to meet his eyes, she glanced around the room and caught Megan Dougherty, one of the windsurfing instructors, looking in her direction from her position near the fireplace.

Barely suppressing a sigh of relief, she turned back to Drew. "I have to go. Catch you later."

Corrie walked briskly toward the bar, where she signaled for two more beers. Across the room, she knew Megs was still watching her, knew that the expression on her face stemmed from honest attraction blended with desire. *No confusion there.* Taking a deep breath to shake off Drew's interrogation, Corrie began to weave her way through the crowd around the edge of the room.

"Figured you'd be ready for another about now," she said into Megs's ear as she came up behind her, close enough to touch. She didn't touch her, though—not just yet.

The younger woman stiffened but took the bottle, her fingers brushing Corrie's in the process. Deliberately. She turned to face her. "Hey, Mars."

Corrie looked her up and down lazily, feeling a sudden rush of warmth as the first beer finally kicked in. "How's it going, Megs?"

"Pretty good. Well—very good, now. I think." She scrubbed a hand through her short, curly hair, looking a question at Corrie. Corrie took a step closer so their bodies overlapped ever so slightly. She reached out one hand to squeeze Meg's waist, gently but firmly, just above her hips.

"You think?"

"Yeah," said Megs, her voice catching. "Yeah, definitely."

❖

"You about ready to head for home?" Drew's voice came from close behind Quinn, and she turned from her view of the dark harbor to see him lounging against the doorway.

"Yes," she replied. "But if you want to stay, you should."

"I'm the one who forced you to come out tonight, remember? It's only fair if I walk back with you." He pushed himself away from the wall with a tired smile. "Plus, I'm wiped."

"Let's go, then," said Quinn, allowing him to lead her through the crowd. She looked for Corrie as she went—to say goodbye. But by the time she saw her, they were near the front door. Besides, Corrie was engaged in what looked like a deep conversation with a lean, red-haired woman. Quinn stopped short as she recognized Megs—Megan

Dougherty, whom she hadn't seen since the ill-advised bowling excursion over half a year ago. And she and Corrie looked to be pretty close, if Corrie's hand on her hip was any indication. *But it sort of felt like she was flirting with* me *earlier,* Quinn thought, *though why she'd want to do that...* Suddenly realizing that Drew was far ahead of her, Quinn hurried to catch up.

Still, as they walked the few blocks away from the Pond toward Drew's apartment, she couldn't resist asking him if Megs and Krista were still together.

Drew shook his head. "No, that didn't last for more than a month, and I don't think they were ever exclusive."

"So...is she with Corrie now? Megs, I mean?"

Drew laughed sharply. "Ah, you picked up on that little seduction scene, too?" He glanced at Quinn. "That's interesting. I didn't think you'd notice."

"Seduction scene? What do you mean by that?"

"No one is ever *with* Corrie. She has her own little circle—most of the instructors, plus some other people." He shrugged. "She sleeps with them sometimes. Whenever she gets the urge, I guess."

Quinn frowned at the pavement, trying to assimilate this knowledge into her picture of Corrie Marsten. Corrie's innate sensuality hadn't escaped her; the energy pouring from the instructor's body as they stood so close together had been nearly palpable. But somehow, this bit of news was disturbing.

"She doesn't have a significant other, then? She only goes in for random hook-ups?"

"No, no." Drew shook his head. "She had a girlfriend a while back, but something happened. I'm not sure what. Ever since then, she's made a point to hook up with friends—not random, but no strings attached."

Something about the way he pronounced "friends" made Quinn look over at him. "Does that include you?" she asked, her tone deliberately casual.

"When I'm lucky." At Quinn's raised eyebrow, he couldn't help protesting. "C'mon, Quinn, she's really attractive. Don't you think?"

"Sure, I guess so." They walked for a while in silence, then, before Quinn got up the courage to ask the next question on her mind. She was more honest with Drew than anyone else on the planet, but even they had never had a conversation quite like this. "Does...does it bother you that she also sleeps with women?"

"Uh," said Drew. "Well, no. Nope, not at all. No." Even in the dim glow from a nearby streetlight, Quinn could make out his blush. "Thing is," he said finally, "I get the feeling that gender doesn't really matter to her. That it's just another physical characteristic—like body type or something." He glanced over at Quinn. "You know?"

Quinn nodded, but really, she didn't know at all. The entire idea of casual sex—even between friends—made her uncomfortable. Sex meant losing control, and losing control meant that whoever you were with could really, truly see you. Not just physically because you were naked, but emotionally—and what if they didn't like what they saw? Even if they did, you could never take it back. Sex wasn't like blurting out a confession by accident that you could then pretend was a joke. It was permanent. That other person would always know what you were like when you were most vulnerable—what you felt like, looked like, sounded like. Unless, of course, you had faked it. But if you had to do that, then you clearly weren't getting anything out of it, so what was the point? *And what do I know about it, anyway?*

Feeling completely naïve, she kept her mouth shut for the remainder of their short walk. Her brain, however, kept working furiously. *Why does this bother me about Corrie? She isn't doing anything* wrong. *It's not what I'd do, but I shouldn't judge her, either.*

"Hey, Q?" Drew broke through her reverie as they approached the front door of a whitewashed colonial-style house, the first floor of which was his apartment. She watched him fumble with his keys.

"Yeah?"

"Corrie can be really persuasive. And I don't want to see you get hurt."

Quinn just rolled her eyes at him. "Like she'd ever go after me anyway. You're the one who pointed out how attractive she is."

Drew sighed in resignation. Quinn's insecurities were familiar territory. "I wish you wouldn't sell yourself short," he said, squeezing one shoulder. "Just be careful, okay?"

"Okay, worrywart." She looked up at him fondly, knowing that his concern was completely unfounded. "I'll be careful, I promise."

❖

"Come for me," Corrie whispered as a drop of sweat dripped from her chin to pool in the dip of Megs's collarbone. "Now."

Megs's smooth inner muscles convulsed at the command, and she pressed her mouth to Corrie's shoulder as her body surged, buoyed on the waves of climax.

Corrie stayed inside until the last flutters subsided, until Megs collapsed back on the bed, weak and gasping. Finally, gently, Corrie withdrew and surreptitiously wiped her fingers on the sheet. Megs sighed deeply as Corrie flipped over to stretch out next to her.

"God, you're good at that." Megs lazily turned her head on the pillow to meet Corrie's deep green eyes.

"You're not so bad yourself," said Corrie, remembering Megs's thumb, slick and strong against her, only a few minutes before. The insistent pressure was back already, and it was only growing stronger. *Dammit—I'm in a state tonight.*

Megs laughed breathlessly. "Such a fuckin' amazing tease. I bet you drive the guys insane."

Corrie frowned up at the ceiling. "Does it bug you that I sleep with guys sometimes?"

She looked over in time to see Megs shake her head. Her shoulders were burned a light red and sprinkled liberally with freckles. "Naw," she said, quirking a grin. "Kinda wonder why you bother, though."

Corrie shrugged against the crisp sheet. She didn't confess that it was because for some reason, seducing men made her feel powerful, somehow. Whereas women just felt *good*. Soft, warm, so unbelievably wet. Infinitely able to give and receive pleasure. And the sensation of breasts cradled in her palms, the twin puckered hardness of nipples trapped between the webs of her fingers...

When Megs gasped from beneath her, she realized that she was on top again, pressing her into the sheets, gently kneading her full breasts insistently. "I don't like being put in a box," she said, giving Megs's nipples a firm twist as she spoke. Megs whimpered.

"And I want to fuck you again. You want that, don't you?"

Megs nodded desperately, her eyes wide and hazy.

"Say yes," Corrie breathed. She bit down lightly on one earlobe. "Tell me."

"Fuck, Mars," Megs gasped. "Please, just—"

Corrie shifted her hand and slipped two fingers back inside. Megs groaned, and Corrie pressed hard against the back of her hand with one muscled thigh. She knew that Megs was good for another—for several more, actually, if she played it right. And that she'd give as good as she got.

"That's it," she murmured. "Come for me again."

KNOCK

Corrie stopped in the doorway of her cramped office as she watched Jen dump an armful of white envelopes on her already crowded desk.

"Holy...what the hell is all this?" She moved forward and grabbed the first envelope she could find, holding it up to the bright sunlight that streamed through the single window. Jen leaned against the edge of the desk and raised her eyebrows.

"Entry forms. For the regatta." When Corrie groaned, Jen shoved her shoulder lightly. "You sure did pick a good year to be head of instruction, Mars."

Corrie tossed the offending envelope back onto her desk. "I just can't believe we're already getting this shit. The race is still six weeks away!"

Jen shrugged. "Sailors are anal. *You* know." When Corrie shoved her in return, Jen just laughed. "And speaking of being type A, when's the instructor trip to Block Island going to be? I want to put that on my calendar."

Corrie sighed dramatically. "I'll take the time out of my busy schedule and fix the date right now, okay? Just for you."

"What a pal," said Jen as Corrie paged through her Dayplanner.

"No, no, no...oh." She looked up and bared her teeth at Jen. "Perfect."

"When?"

"Third weekend in July." Corrie nodded in satisfaction as she penciled in a note to herself.

"What's so perfect about that?"

"My brother won't be able to make it." Corrie snapped the book shut.

"Why not?"

Corrie's lips twisted. "That's the weekend of his fiancée's birthday." She checked her watch. "Ten of one. I have to go."

Huh, thought Jen. *I guess Corrie doesn't like his fiancée, either.* "What are you teaching this afternoon?" she asked.

"My first 470 lesson of the season." Corrie rifled through the unkempt pile of envelopes once again to retrieve her instruction folder. "Let's see who I have here." After flipping it open, she paused, then smiled with relief.

"What is it?" Jen leaned forward. "Who are your victims?"

"No one I know, really. Full lesson, though." Corrie tucked the folder under her arm and moved purposefully away from the desk. "Time for me to get out there."

Ignoring the question in Jen's parting look, Corrie hurried out of the boathouse and into the hot summer afternoon. The air was thick with moisture, and she felt even more grateful than usual for the brisk, sea-scented breeze blowing in from the east. Squinting into the haze, she looked around. There was someone down by the first pier rigging up a Laser who almost looked like—. She squinted, then blinked. Not Will. He wasn't slated to teach any lessons today, and she was glad that he wasn't just hanging around. Hell, he was probably hung over and still sacked out on whatever spare couch he'd been able to find last night.

Suddenly, Frog crossed her line of sight as he raced along the shore after an airborne piece of driftwood that was just beginning its slow descent toward the surf. Corrie turned toward the direction of the toss and grinned. *Of course.*

Quinn was dressed in a faded gray T-shirt and black mesh shorts. A Dartmouth cap kept her wavy brown hair in check and blue aqua shoes hugged her feet. As Corrie approached at a slow jog, Quinn turned in her direction. There was a brief moment of recognition in which she gave a little, self-conscious wave.

"Hey," Corrie called, just before Frog bounded up to her, his tale wagging enthusiastically. She paused to grab the stick out of his mouth and launch it along the shoreline toward the first pier.

"Nice arm," said Quinn.

"Comes from playing quarterback as a kid with my older brother's friends. I never did learn to throw like a girl."

One corner of Quinn's mouth lifted. "I'm sure you didn't. I bet your brother was proud."

Corrie grimaced. "Yeah, right. Will's never been proud of anyone but himself." She toed the sand with her left foot and stared moodily out toward the ocean. "To hear him talk, I wouldn't have a shred of athletic skill if it hadn't been for him, and—"

She looked over at Quinn and suddenly realized just exactly how much she was confessing. So Corrie did the only thing she could think of—she laughed. Too loudly. "Listen to me, revisiting childhood woes," she said, trying to be jovial. "Blah, blah, blah."

Quinn could recognize self-consciousness when she saw it, and she instinctively tried to smile in a way that would put Corrie at ease. That must have worked, because Corrie returned her expression and gestured inland.

"Shall we?"

As they turned toward the boathouse, Corrie hunched her shoulders a little. "So...I thought you might've decided this whole sailing thing wasn't for you," she said. "I mean, after you didn't come back on Monday or yesterday." *After I came on to you on Friday.*

But Quinn turned to face her, frowning slightly and shaking her head. "Oh no. I've really been enjoying it—I just had to cover for someone at the humane society. Usually I volunteer there twice a week, but one of their employees came down with a bug over the weekend, and it's kitten season right know, you know, so they really needed—" She cut off abruptly, and Corrie had to work to hide a grin as a slight flush crept across Quinn's cheeks. "Anyway, I'm looking forward to the lesson. Drew says he likes these boats quite a bit."

"They're the best." Corrie pointed to a knot of four young men gathered around one of the picnic tables. "And those must be the other students." She looked over at Quinn again and elbowed her gently just above her hip. *Soft.* "You ready?"

"Sure," said Quinn, the smile returning to her face.

"Good." Corrie waggled her eyebrows. "Because you're riding with me."

As they neared the group, her steady pace gradually shifted to a slow, rolling saunter and her attitude changed, somehow. Quinn could almost feel her withdraw, could feel the easy intimacy of a minute earlier slip away in the face of a crowd. Of men. Frat boys, even. They were all wearing the same Greek letters somewhere on their bodies. Corrie had been open and friendly just a minute before—even a little vulnerable. Quinn had seen it. But suddenly she was harder. Untouchable. *I like the earlier version better.*

"How's it going, guys?" Corrie asked, sliding her hands into the back pockets of her swim trunks. The slight motion brought her chest forward, and several of the men noticeably looked her up and down. Quinn didn't think the movement had been an accident. *What's she trying to prove to them?*

"So," Corrie said a few minutes later, after they'd introduced themselves and walked over to where the boats rested on their carts, "this is the 470—one of the boats sailed in the Olympics." She stroked the port gunwale of the nearest boat with her left hand. "Two-man vessel, sloop-rigged, built for speed and as responsive as a woman."

The guys snickered. Quinn blushed, but managed to meet Corrie's gaze without flinching. *Now you're just performing*, she thought. *Teasing.* But even so, the energy behind her jokes was real. As Corrie began to explain the benefits of having a jib as well as a mainsail, Quinn tried to figure out exactly just what threw her off about Corrie's sexuality. *I've never known anyone so intense*, she thought. *Maybe that's what it is. She's obvious in her sensuality. It's close to the surface. Aggressive, almost.*

"...so basically, when trimmed properly, the jib allows wind to pass more efficiently along the mainsail. That means more speed and better pointing." Quinn nodded quickly as Corrie's gaze swept over her again. *Way to go, space cadet*, she berated herself. *Let's hope I remember some of what was in the manual!*

"Okay, enough chitchat." Corrie had turned to look out at the waves. "Let's rig up and get wet. That's the best part, anyway."

As the guys chuckled appreciatively, Quinn kept her head down and reached for one of the sail bags. At this rate, it was going to be a long afternoon.

❖

As it turned out, once they were alone on the boat, Corrie abandoned her innuendos and focused entirely on sailing. Quinn had to admit that she was an excellent instructor—calm, patient, and full of helpful advice. She found herself benefiting almost immediately from Corrie's suggestions about how to switch sides more smoothly during a tack, and how to trim the sail to make it catch the wind as efficiently as possible. They had tacked back and forth upwind for a good half hour before returning in a series of jibes and were now circling just beyond the mooring field for man-overboard drills. Because the 470 was a two-man boat, it was important for each sailor to know how to go back and pick up the other person in case he or she were to fall out.

Biting her lip, Quinn sheeted in slightly on the line that controlled the main sail, then eased the main again as she coasted toward the bright red lifesaver just a few feet ahead. She quickly transferred the line to her tiller hand, leaned down, and snagged the flotation device out of the water.

"Nice," said Corrie, grabbing hold of the flapping jib sheets and pulling hard. "Perfect that time. Let's do it again." As Quinn tossed the lifesaver out to port, Corrie leaned forward and cupped her hands around her mouth. "I want to see two more man-overboards from each of you!" she called to the other boats. "Remember—figure eight! Fall off the wind, come up and tack, and then do a close-hauled landing *on* the lifesaver!"

"That was really okay?" Quinn asked anxiously as she steered their boat downwind.

Corrie, in the process of settling herself back on the thwart, turned and looked at her, clearly surprised. "Of course. What, you don't believe me?"

Quinn shrugged, eyes focused on the red square bobbing gently on the waves off starboard. "I just want to be sure." When Corrie slid aft along the gunwale and touched her forearm, Quinn briefly met her gaze.

"You should trust me." When Quinn didn't answer, Corrie's eyes narrowed mischievously. It was only after Quinn had salvaged the flotation device once more that she spoke up again.

"In fact," she said, gently grasping Quinn's wrist before she could toss the lifesaver back into the Pond, "you have to trust me. Because I trust you to come back and get me."

And before Quinn could open her mouth, Corrie released her wrist and pushed herself out of the boat. The splash was substantial. "Man overboard!" she shouted gleefully from the water.

"Oh…oh, crap!" Quinn struggled to keep her balance as the boat reacted to the loss of Corrie's weight by tilting up significantly so that the far end of the boom was almost touching the water. She tucked her feet under the straps inside the cockpit and hiked out, easing the sail as she extended her body out over the ocean. *All alone*, she thought, trying to ignore the ache in her abs. *I am all alone on a boat meant for two people. Shit.*

"Okay, okay. You know what to do. Just did it twice. Bear off and ease…but don't jibe. Right." Shifting the tiller away from the sail, Quinn let the mainsheet run through her fingers before risking a brief glance backward. Corrie was floating on her back and whistling, blithely unconcerned.

"I can do this." Quinn bit down anxiously on her bottom lip as she hauled in on the main sheet and pushed the tiller toward the sail so that the boat spun up toward, and then through, the eye of the wind. Quickly ducking under the boom, she banged her shin against the thwart as she jumped onto the starboard gunwale. Ignoring the sharp pain, she slipped her feet under the hiking strap and leaned back.

"Almost there. Almost." She angled the boat a little further downwind, in order to come up next to Corrie at a close-hauled course, very near to the wind. "Okay. That's it. Turn up now, and let the sail go." As she eased, the main sail began to flap heavily in the brisk wind, and Quinn felt the boat slow almost immediately. "Little more speed… and, stop."

Corrie watched her methodical approach, struggling not to laugh at the way Quinn talked herself through every maneuver out loud. *Cute. You are just really cute.* As the boat pulled up alongside her, Corrie flashed Quinn the two-thumbs up. "You're getting good at that."

Her praise dispelled most of Quinn's frown and convinced her that she really should give Corrie a hand getting back into the cockpit. "You deserve to be left behind, after that little stunt," she said. "Don't you know this is my first day sailing this boat?"

Corrie evaded her hand. "Well, in that case—" Lunging up out of the water, she grabbed the mast just above where it intersected with the boom and pulled down hard. The boat tilted viciously, and Quinn had just enough time to take a deep breath before she was plunged into the cool, salty water of Judith Pond. She surfaced a second later to the familiar sound of Corrie's laughter.

"You—you..." she spluttered, trying to find an appropriate epithet and failing miserably. Quinn finally settled for aiming a splash in Corrie's direction, before swimming around to the other side of the boat and levering herself up onto the centerboard.

"I want to see you guys capsize, too!" Corrie shouted to the frat boys as she latched onto a hiking strap and rode the boat's momentum enough to boost herself back into the cockpit. "See?" she said as she helped Quinn aboard. "We had to do that anyway, for you to get your rating." Gathering in the jib sheets with her left hand, Corrie held out her right hand and assumed what she knew to be an endearing smile. "So c'mon...truce?"

Quinn eyed her speculatively. "Only if you buy me ice cream," she said on impulse before finally grasping the cool, wet hand in her own. When Corrie raised her eyebrows knowingly, Quinn felt herself flush and hurried to explain. "I'm—I'm craving chocolate chip cookie dough." *"Buy me ice cream." Where did* that *come from?*

Corrie squeezed her hand briefly before releasing it. Her voice, when she spoke, sounded slightly lower than normal. "You've got a deal, Dr. Davies." She jerked her head westward and tightened up the jib. "Let's head for home."

❖

When the bow of their 470 lightly touched the pier, Corrie tossed some line to Drew, who had come out of the boathouse to meet them. "Good lesson?" he asked Quinn as he efficiently tied the boat off.

"Yes," she said, glancing once at Corrie, who was bent over the thwart as she raised the centerboard. "Eventful." When Corrie looked up and winked, Quinn rolled her eyes.

"What?" Drew asked from the pier, looking between them. "C'mon, what?"

"I made her do a real man-overboard," said Corrie, just before lithely swinging herself across the bow so that she straddled the mast. Drew laughed.

"You fell out of the boat?"

"Jumped out," Quinn interjected, guiding the boom down into the cockpit as Corrie lowered the sail. "Jumped right out and left me there all alone."

"Cruel. Very cruel." Drew watched as Corrie steadied the boat so that Quinn could disembark. "Want to get some practice in for the regatta?"

"In a little while," Corrie said, smoothly transferring her weight to the dock. She jerked her head toward Quinn as she tugged at the Velcro of her sailing gloves. "Give me half an hour. We need ice cream."

"Ice cream?" He frowned and looked at Quinn. *Corrie's putting off sailing for ice cream?*

"Don't worry, Drew," she said, amusement flaring briefly across her face. "I won't keep her away for long, I promise."

"I didn't—" he spluttered. "But—" The pier swayed gently as they walked away from him, toward the boathouse and the small town of Wakefield. "Okay!" he called after them. "I'll just be here..." His voice trailed off forlornly when neither of them looked back.

"Drew looked so confused," Quinn said as they fell into step on the fractured concrete sidewalk.

"It can be hard to drag me away from the water." At Quinn's curious glance, Corrie grinned flirtatiously. "What can I say, I owe you for that stunt I pulled."

Quinn didn't quite know how to reply to that, but neither was she exactly comfortable with the silence that descended between them. "So, uh, will you tell me more about the regatta?" she asked quickly.

"Oh, it's so much fun!" Corrie's step took on a slight bounce as they turned the corner and paused at a crosswalk. "The Rhode Island Invitational is open to anyone who can sail a 470, but since a lot of the Olympic sailors are from New England, it gets pretty competitive." As the light changed, they made their way across the street and turned again. "Some of the best sailors on the eastern seaboard will decide to show up. The whole thing is really just for kicks. It's not a ranked regatta or anything, but it's good practice."

"Olympians," said Quinn. "That's impressive. How do you and Drew compare?"

Corrie shrugged as she pulled open the door of the local ice cream parlor, holding it to one side and gesturing for Quinn to precede her. "We'll be somewhere in the middle of the pack, probably," she said, stepping inside. "Doesn't really matter. We'll just kick as much butt as we can and have a good time."

Quinn was surprised at her cavalier attitude but did her best not to show it. Drew had said that Corrie had very nearly been in the Olympics two years ago, and even Quinn knew that you didn't make it that far in a sport without being able to hold your own in some heavy competition.

"So," Corrie interrupted her introspection, "chocolate chip cookie dough, you said, right? Cone or dish?"

"Uh, cone." Their upper arms brushed lightly as Corrie moved past her toward the register, and Quinn couldn't help but take a step back. *Maybe that's what gets me*, she reflected, as Corrie placed their order. *She has no concept of personal space.*

"Want to walk?" Corrie asked as she handed Quinn a dramatically overburdened ice cream cone and took a large, slurping bite out of the side of her own. When Quinn nodded, Corrie held the door again and followed her out into the muggy heat.

"So," she said between bites. "Tell me about your pets."

Quinn frowned, the bridge of her nose wrinkling in a way that made Corrie want to reach one finger out and touch. "Pets?" she asked, confused. "What do you mean?"

"Well, you're in vet school," Corrie said as they began to retrace their route toward the boathouse. "I figured you had a menagerie."

"I wish!" Quinn sighed heavily. "I don't even have hermit crabs. My last landlord wouldn't allow pets of any kind." She took a careful bite off the top of her cone and shrugged. "Maybe when I move out of Drew's apartment at the end of the summer. But so many places charge extra or don't have enough space."

"Bummer," Corrie said sympathetically. They slowed to a stop to wait for traffic to pass, and Quinn had to fight the urge to put some extra distance between them. *She's just a close talker. Doesn't even realize she's doing it.*

She peered up at Corrie curiously. "How do you have the space to keep Frog? Your apartment must be huge."

Corrie looked away and cleared her throat before speaking. "House, actually," she said. "I have a house." When Quinn's eyebrows rose, Corrie found herself hurrying to explain. "My grandfather passed away a few years ago. He was a big sailing maven, and I was his favorite grandchild. Will was so damn jealous. I think he'd always thought that he would get the place. He sailed in the Olympics two years back and was definitely the golden child, but Gramps always liked me better for some reason. God knows he was the only one who..." Corrie trailed off, but when Quinn remained silent, she rolled her eyes.

"Jeez, I'm just confessing my whole life story to you today, aren't I? Anyway, whatever, point is that I got lucky. Besides, engineering internships tend to pay well."

"Nice," said Quinn, more struck by Corrie's strange demeanor than by the startling news that a graduate student could actually own a house in Wakefield. *She almost seems embarrassed, and there's definitely some kind of major tension between her and her brother.* Quinn frowned, wondering whether Drew really knew Corrie as well as he thought he did. He'd described her as beautiful but a little arrogant, charismatic but sometimes manipulative. *"Nice and always fun,"* he'd said, but also distant. And yet here she was, not distant at all—slightly flushed and slurping ice cream and having awkward moments like a regular human being.

"Well," Corrie said into the silence as they rounded the corner of the boathouse. Before them, the dark blue expanse of Judith Pond was dotted with dozens of sails in various sizes, shapes, and colors. As if by an unspoken agreement, they both paused to take in the view—just as a windsurfer went down close to shore in a spectacular flailing dive. Corrie threw back her head and howled in laughter.

"Nice biff, Brad!" she shouted. When he managed to water-start while simultaneously flicking her off, she laughed even harder. "Oh god," she said finally, nudging Quinn's arm with her elbow. "That was beautiful."

"Windsurfing looks tough," was all Quinn could think to reply.

"It's a little tricky at first." She looked Quinn up and down. "Let me know when you want to learn, and I'll be happy to teach you."

"Uh, sure," Quinn said, feeling abruptly disconcerted. "I...well, I guess you'd better go practice with Drew, huh?" She focused on taking another nibbling bite from the edge of her cone. "Thanks for the ice cream."

"Hey, thanks for being such a good sport out there." Corrie's hand rested lightly on the bare skin of Quinn's forearm for an instant. "You sure you don't want to come hang out for a while longer? I'll push Drew out of the boat so you can watch him flail around, if you want."

Quinn opened her mouth to tell Corrie that she had a metric ton of studying to do and that there was no way she could possibly afford to spend more time at the waterfront today, but what came out was, "Sure, okay."

"'Okay,' you want me to push him in?" Corrie said as they continued toward the piers.

"Do what you want. If you try to blame me, I'll plead the fifth."

"That won't stop me from—" Corrie's mouth suddenly clicked shut and she began to walk faster. "Fuck," she said through clenched teeth, glaring at the nearest pier.

Quinn wanted to ask what was going on, but didn't dare. Instead, she followed Corrie's line of sight. A small crowd had gathered at the pier along with Drew, and they were all watching the antics of someone messing around in a boat inside the mooring field. Quinn blinked in surprise; the sailor—a tall man wearing a white cap—was *standing up* on both gunwales. And singing. Completely off pitch. Quinn had seen him around the boathouse a few times, but had no idea who he was. All she knew was that if she were to ever try sailing like that, she'd be in the water faster than you could sing "Row, row, row your boat."

"What the fuck are you doing, William?" Corrie muttered as they set foot on the first wooden slat.

Her brother, Quinn realized—who, at that instant, jumped down off the gunwales into the cockpit to crouch low as he tacked through the wind, only to return to his precarious standing position despite the rocking of the boat. He let out a raucous "Yeeehaw," and waved in Corrie's direction. *How is he* doing *that?* Quinn wondered. Somehow, in the few seconds it had taken him to tack, he'd managed to adjust the jib as well as the mainsheet. *All by himself.*

"Hey, li'l sis!" Will shouted as he turned slightly downwind. "How 'bout a race? You and me, each single-handing a 470—right here, right now."

Corrie shook her head sharply. "Drew and I need to practice, Will."

"Aw, c'mon!" he yelled back. "No better practice than this!" He tacked back around and sailed close to the pier, pretending to look mournful. "Besides, I just rigged up both these boats with chutes so we could race 'em. You're not gonna let me down now, are you?"

"Corrie," Drew said urgently, "I don't know if trying to single-hand a spinnaker in this kind of wind is a very good ide—"

"C'mon, Cor, where's that fighting spirit?" Will called. "Let's go!"

"Fine," said Corrie, pointedly ignoring Drew.

Jaw set, she shook out her hair before putting it back up in a long ponytail. The end brushed against her shoulders, and Quinn suddenly wondered what her hair would feel like, sliding between her fingers—whether it was as soft and fine as it looked. She caught herself staring and immediately blushed, but fortunately, Corrie wasn't looking at her at all. *Jeez, get a grip! Yes, okay, she's attractive, but remember what Drew said.*

"The speed buoy out at the north end of the mooring field will be the windward mark," said Will. "Finish line is the same as the start—the end of this pier." He glanced up at Drew. "How 'bout you count us down, Harris?"

Drew looked from Will to Corrie, who was already putting the rudder into the second boat. "Sure, yeah. Just don't kill yourselves, okay?"

Will saluted. "Piece of cake, man."

Quinn fidgeted on the pier as Corrie raised her boat's mainsail. Corrie hadn't even looked at her once since her brother's challenge. It was like no one else existed except the two of them. *Wonder what their story is?* It made sense that they'd be competitive with each other, but it was clear that Corrie wasn't having fun. Quinn fought the urge to repeat Drew's advice about being cautious. *Why would she ever listen to me?*

Corrie untied the knot that secured her boat to the pier and gave herself a push, then scrambled back into the cockpit. "Two minutes!" Drew hollered, looking at his watch.

Quinn frowned as Corrie headed out toward the ocean, while Will circled back around the end of the dock. She moved closer to Drew. "What's going on?"

He glanced at her before returning his attention to his watch. "They're jockeying for starting position," he said. "The goal is to be as close to the line as possible, but behind it, of course, when the countdown gets to zero." He paused, then raised his head. "One minute thirty!"

Quinn watched Corrie turn back toward the pier. She was maneuvering within the boat just as fluidly as Will. "Who do you think will win?" she asked Drew quietly.

He shrugged, still staring intently at his watch. "Will was an Olympian, but he's probably out of practice by now. Thing is, he weighs more. That might really help him. One minute!"

"Help him? Isn't it better to be lighter?"

"Sometimes," Drew said, "but sometimes it's worse. The wind is gusting a lot today. Because he weighs more, Will has the better chance of being able to sail efficiently if it picks up out there. Corrie will have to let her sail out further to keep her boat level."

"Oh," said Quinn, trying to visualize the scenario in her head. Drew called out the thirty-second warning, and both Will and Corrie began to tack back and forth furiously.

"They're trying to find the best line of approach without sailing over the line before time's up." And then Drew began the ten-second countdown, and Quinn caught her breath as Will and Corrie each turned their boat on a course that could only end in a collision with each other.

"What are they doing?" She grabbed Drew's arm. He shook his head and continued the count. When he reached "Go," both boats were mere feet behind the starting line, and in less than ten seconds, their bows were going to crash.

"Starboard!" Corrie shouted at the top of her lungs. Quinn squeezed Drew's arm so tightly that he winced. "Starboard! You'd better fuckin' duck me, asshole!"

At the last possible instant, Will turned sharply downwind to avoid Corrie's boat, his bow passing within inches of her stern. Quinn sighed explosively.

"Ow," said Drew, gently trying to dislodge her grip.

"What's going on down here?" Jen asked from behind them. "What's with all the yelling?"

"Was that legal?" Quinn exclaimed, outraged at Will's close call.

"Ladies, ladies, jeez," Drew said. "One question at a time!" He turned toward Jen. "Will challenged Corrie to a duel. They're single-handing 470s with chutes." When her eyes widened and her mouth opened, he wagged one finger at her. "I tried to stop her, okay? I tried. And yes," he said, looking over at Quinn and massaging the finger marks on his skin, "that move is legal. It's called a 'duck.' Corrie had right-of-way because she was on starboard tack, but Will would have only been in the wrong if he'd actually hit her."

Quinn looked past them both to where the boats were wending their way upwind, matching one another tack for tack. Corrie had extended her body as far out from the boat as possible. She was probably hanging on to the hiking strap with her toes.

"I don't know what their deal is," Jen said, "but whenever he's around, Corrie's not right in the head."

"It's just a brother/sister thing," Drew said dismissively. "They're competitive people, y'know?"

"Yeah, but..." Jen trailed off, shaking her head. "I feel like there's more to it than that."

Quinn didn't chime in, but she agreed. Granted, she'd only spoken with Corrie a few times, but Will had always come up frequently, and never in a good way.

"They're about to round the buoy and raise their spinnakers." Drew crossed his arms over his chest. "This should get interesting."

Quinn hesitated as she debated whether to reveal her ignorance, then decided to bite the bullet. She tapped Drew on the shoulder. "Would you mind explaining what a spinnaker is, real quick?"

"Oh, sure. So, the spinnaker is this sail that looks like a parachute— which is why it's also called the chute—that gets rigged around every other sail and line and stay on a boat. When you go downwind, you raise the chute and it catches the wind that's coming from behind you, and it pulls you along." He gestured toward the ocean. "Watch. They're about to raise."

Quinn flinched as both boats jibed around the buoy. Jibing was still more than a little scary. The sail went from being all the way out on one side of the boat to being all the way out on the other in a matter of seconds, and it was easy to lose control and capsize. But, although Corrie's craft rocked from side to side, she never lost control. In fact, she was several feet ahead of her brother, and Quinn surreptitiously crossed her fingers that she'd stay that way.

"See?" said Jen, pointing. "She's pulling on the spinnaker halyard. Here it comes!"

As they watched, a bright red and white sail ballooned out in front of each boat, its edges dipping and curling like a kite. "Now they have to steer with their knees," Drew told Quinn, leaning forward in his excitement. "Because trimming that sail properly takes two hands."

Quinn could hear the concern coloring his voice. "What's dangerous about it?"

"For one thing," said Jen, "look how damn *fast* they're going! I don't know if they have enough wind to plane, but they're going to get close." She shook her head in admiration. "God, I wish I could sail like that. If Corrie keeps this up, there's no way he's going to catch—"

"Fuck, she's broaching!" Drew shouted, as Corrie's boat suddenly swung hard upwind and tilted precipitously. Quinn could see her struggling to regain control of the tiller even as she threw her weight to the high side, and the 470 hung there for several seconds, plowing through the waves on one gunwale before finally tipping completely and spilling Corrie into the water.

"Shit!" Jen was immediately running alongside Drew toward the end of the pier. "They're both in trouble."

Sure enough, Will's boat had reacted to the puff of wind in the same way, but he was slowly managing to bring it back down to a stable position. Quinn didn't realize that she'd followed Drew and Jen until she too was leaning out over the edge of the dock, trying to see if Corrie had surfaced. "Is she all right? Where is she?"

For one agonizing moment, there was nothing to be seen, but then Corrie's red lifejacket flashed brightly in the sunlight and the breeze carried over the sound of her coughing. "You okay, Cor?" Will called, his bow pointing directly toward the wind. His spinnaker fluttered like a dying red butterfly, flopping half-heartedly as he pulled it down into the boat.

Whatever Corrie said in reply was unintelligible, but she quickly splashed her way over to the centerboard and began to yank it down into the waves. Will expertly spun his boat back toward shore and completed the race a few minutes later, pulling up to the pier with a gentle bump.

"What a crazy gust," he said as Drew tied off his boat. "I haven't broached that badly in years!"

Quinn ignored Will completely, keeping her gaze fastened on Corrie as she sailed slowly toward them, her spinnaker hopelessly tangled up in her stays. Quinn took it upon herself to grab for the line that trailed off the front of Corrie's boat. "Hey," she said in the soothing tone she reserved for injured animals. "Are you really all right?"

Corrie turned to her with a scowl, but the fierceness faded as she recognized Quinn's concern. "Yeah, I'm fine." For one awful second, Corrie felt like bursting into tears. She bent over to raise the centerboard so she wouldn't have to meet those kind eyes.

"Anything I can do to help?"

"S'okay," she grunted as she pulled down hard on the sticky main halyard. "I want to do all this myself—make sure it still works right." She paused before managing a crooked grin. "But, thanks."

"Okay." Quinn gave a small wave before retreating. *That's one thing we have in common*, she thought as she slowly walked the length of the pier. She understood very well the desire to be left alone with frustration.

Will, apparently, did not. "Tough luck, sport," she heard him say. "Want a hand with that mess?"

"No." The monosyllable was clipped. Sharp enough to cut, but he seemed impervious.

"All right then." His tone was genial, but then again, he could afford to sound that way. He had won. "Nice racing out there. You mighta clinched it if you hadn't gone over."

Corrie didn't answer, and Quinn felt a sudden and totally uncharacteristic urge to trip Will as he passed her. *That's it*, she thought, *I've been out in the sun way too long*. It was time to take a break from these crazy sailors with their intense mood swings and daredevil antics, and get back to her safe, rational books.

SIDE SLIPPING

Eight days later, Quinn steadied herself in the small cockpit of the Laser before stepping out onto the uneven wooden slats of the pier. She let out a deep breath. During her first lesson on the tiny racing boat, she'd managed to dunk herself in the pond just trying to climb out. Lasers were tippy in the extreme, but, as Drew had put it, their sensitivity was the very trait that made them so exciting to sail.

"You all set, then?" asked a young man who had helped tie off her painter. He was shuffling back and forth impatiently as he waited to take over the boat.

"Yes," Quinn said. "Have fun."

She waited around long enough to give him a push out to sea, before heading back toward the boathouse to turn in her lifejacket. A slight gust of wind ruffled the strands of hair that had escaped from her hat. *What a perfect day and what a perfect sail.* It was warm but not hot, and the breeze was light and steady, save for the occasional puff. She'd done well out there. The boat hadn't capsized once, and her arm and stomach muscles were pleasantly tired from the exertion.

As she made her way inland, a bout of raucous laughter suddenly erupted from what appeared to be an impromptu party in the picnic table area. A large cooler was open on the ground between two tables, both of which were crowded with people. As Quinn got closer, she could see Drew gesticulating wildly from his position on one of the benches, while the others watched him.

"...and then, as we pull alongside the mark," Drew was saying, "there's this spectacular crunching noise as the keel hits bottom, and the boat just stops!"

"It was fucking hilarious," said a lanky blond-haired man seated at the other table. Quinn thought his name might be Brad, but wasn't sure. "All of a sudden—*bam!*"

Drew glared at him. "So while these bastards are laughing their heads off, we're scrambling, right? Just trying to get the damn keel off the sand. We're all on one side, so heeled-up the boom is almost in the water, but nothing's working—"

"And meanwhile," Brad interrupted again, "we're taking the lead—"

"Completely ignoring the fact that we'd beached ourselves," Drew said loudly. "Who knows how long we would've stayed that way, if it hadn't been for Corrie?"

When everyone turned to look at the person lounging on top of Drew's table, Quinn realized that she hadn't recognized Corrie in the glare of the afternoon sun. A few more steps forward put the bulk of the boathouse between herself and the light, and Quinn watched as Corrie, wearing frayed cargo shorts and a navy tank top, raised her beer bottle in a sort of salute before tipping her head back and taking a long swallow. Her ponytail swished lightly with the motion, and Quinn was suddenly aware of just how disheveled she herself must look. She removed her hat and combed hasty fingers through her unruly hair, hoping it looked windswept rather than like a rat's nest.

"What'd she do?" asked someone who clearly hadn't been a part of whatever activity they were discussing.

Drew reached out and gave Corrie's ponytail an affectionate yank. "She climbed out onto the boom! Can you believe that shit? Just like a goddamn monkey. And sure enough, the boat heels a few inches more, and all of a sudden we're in motion."

"It was something to see," said one of the sailors on Brad's boat, grudgingly.

Quinn watched as Corrie's lips quirked in a smug little grin. *She's like a different person when Will's not around. Easygoing, confident, secure to the point of being annoying.* She shook her head.

Perhaps it was that slight motion that caught Corrie's eye and made her turn, but when she saw Quinn, she sat up straighter and beckoned her over. "Hey, Quinn. Come join us."

Quinn didn't know whether to feel pleasure or dread at the invitation since she didn't know half the crowd, but she dutifully approached the picnic tables. "Quinn Davies, everyone," said Corrie. "An old friend of Drew's from college and one of our students." She paused and cocked her head slightly as she took in Quinn's windblown appearance and the battered lifejacket that dangled from her left hand. "Just out sailing?"

"In a Laser." Quinn smiled. "It was fantastic."

"I'll bet," Brad said.

"Perfect day for one of those," said Jen.

"Come sit, Quinn," said Drew. "Want a beer?"

Quinn sat in the place he made for her, but wrinkled her nose when he tried to hand her a bottle. "No, that's okay."

"Not so fast, D." Corrie reached out as he tried to put the drink back into the cooler. "I'll take that."

"Lush," he said affectionately as he handed it up to her.

Corrie winked at Quinn and mouthed, "Thanks." Quinn couldn't help but smile back, and found herself idly speculating about the source of Corrie's nearly palpable charisma. *It must be in her sweat or something*, she thought, barely managing to suppress a giggle.

"So, c'mon, who won the race?" asked Megs.

"Who do you think?" Drew said. "We put up our chute and blew right by 'em."

Jen thumped Drew on the shoulder. "Watch that ego, boy! You lost the second one, as I recall."

"Well," Corrie began, "I—"

But she was cut off by the sudden, high-pitched yelp of a dog, which tapered off into a barely audible series of whining yips. She frowned and craned her neck, searching for the source of the pitiful sounds until she finally caught sight of Frog, limping gingerly away from the strip of rocks bordering one side of the beach. She jumped to the ground.

"C'mere, Frogger," she called out, her voice slightly higher than normal. "Come on, bud!" Instead of obeying, the dog stopped where he was, whined even more loudly, and sat down. Corrie began to move toward him at a brisk jog. Quinn instinctively slipped off the bench and followed her, noting that Frog was favoring his front left paw.

"C'mon, Frog, you've got to let me look," Corrie was saying as Quinn approached. Her voice was tinged with desperation, as the dog shied away from her for the second time. His tail was tucked securely between his legs, and his ears were lying flat against his head—all signs that he was in pain. And Corrie, though she was trying, wasn't helping.

"Corrie," Quinn said softly, crouching down to rest one hand gently on her shoulder. Her freckled skin was hot to the touch. "He's frightened right now. You need to calm him down, first."

Corrie spun around, her face a study in anxiety. "Can *you* do something for him? Please, Quinn? I'll pay you if you want, just—"

"Oh, hush," Quinn said firmly. Crouching down before Frog, she let him sniff her hand before briefly petting his nose. "Did you manage to see whether he's hurt anywhere other than his paw?"

"His haunches, on the right side," Corrie said, her voice low and urgent. "There's a…a cut. I'm not sure how bad it is."

Quinn nodded, moving her hands to massage the scruff of Frog's neck. Slowly, she craned her head around to survey his right side. Sure enough, a red gash several inches long slashed angrily across the sleek gray coat.

"It's not much more than a scratch," Quinn said soothingly. "Looks like it's caked over already." Keeping one hand firmly but gently on Frog's neck, she ran her other hand down the injured leg and raised his foot a few inches higher into the air.

He whined softly and shook his head. "Shhhhh. It's okay, buddy." She leaned down for a quick glance.

"What is it?"

Quinn sat back on her heels. "He's got something stuck in his paw. I'm not sure what it is, but it doesn't look too serious. I can take it out and sterilize the cut, no problem." For the first time since she'd seen Frog limping along the beach, she felt a little insecure. "Unless you'd rather take him to the real vet, that is."

"I trust you," Corrie said immediately. "So, what now?"

Quinn stood briskly and dusted the sand off her knees. "Do you have iodine at home?" she asked. "And some gauze? Or something similar?"

Corrie nodded, and Quinn continued. "Okay then. Just stay right here with him. Pet his head and speak to him softly, and I'll bring Drew's truck around. We can take him back to your house to get cleaned up."

Corrie had the presence of mind to call out a "Thanks" as Quinn jogged away, but immediately turned back to her wounded dog. "It's all right now, Frogger," she said, reaching out hesitantly to scratch behind his ears. "Quinn'll take care of you."

"What's going on?" Drew asked as Quinn pulled up in front of the table and extended her hand.

"Need your keys. Frog's got a hurt foot, and I'm going to take care of it at Corrie's place."

"Want help?" he asked as he handed over the key chain.

"No, it's okay," she replied distractedly, already turning away.

Quinn pulled the truck up to the edge of the sidewalk in front of the boathouse and returned to where Corrie was stroking Frog's head. The dog looked much more relaxed, though he was still keeping that left paw clear of the sand. Corrie, on the other hand, was frowning and clearly quite tense.

"All set," Quinn said, resisting the sudden urge to reach down and touch her shoulder again. "Can you carry him to the truck, do you think?"

"Sure thing." Wrapping one arm around Frog's chest, she slipped the other under his belly and lifted him into the air. Quinn blinked in surprise at the fluid motion—the dog had to weigh at least seventy pounds.

"It'd be best to put him in the cab," she said, breaking into a jog to keep up. She ran ahead to hold the door while Corrie deposited Frog on the passenger's side. She squeezed herself in next to him as Quinn carefully backed out onto the road.

"Where to?"

Corrie guided Quinn to her house, then carried Frog through the front door and placed him on the kitchen floor. When he whined a little and tried to stand up, Quinn moved in to hold him down gently but firmly. "Stick around, buddy," she said softly. "I'll have you fixed up in a jiffy." She looked up at Corrie. "I need some warm water, a disinfectant, a towel, and that gauze."

"Okay," she said, spinning around so fast that she whacked her elbow against the kitchen counter. "Fu— ow!"

Frog's head jerked up at the interjection, but he calmed down again almost immediately under Quinn's soothing touches.

"Sorry," Corrie muttered. "Okay. Right. Back soon."

Quinn kept her eyes on the dog to hide her smile. This Corrie, frazzled and clumsy and vulnerable, was a far cry from the self-possessed woman who'd been lounging indolently on top of that picnic table. There was no doubt in Quinn's mind that Frog would be back to his old self within a day or two, but it was clear that Corrie couldn't be rational where he was concerned. *It's sweet of her.*

Despite her sudden klutziness, Corrie managed to fill a small pot with tap water and begin heating it on the stove with no further mishaps. While waiting for the water to warm, she quickly fetched the iodine and gauze from the first aid kit below her kitchen sink, then ran upstairs for a fresh towel.

"Thanks," said Quinn as Corrie finally set the pot down next to her. "Can you hold him?"

As Corrie watched, Quinn dipped a corner of the towel into the water and gently worked the caked blood out of Frog's fur. She applied iodine to the shallow cut, all the while murmuring soft words of comfort and reassurance. Corrie watched Frog's ears twitch as he lay quiescent and knew that even if Quinn's crooning made no sense to her, it was exactly what Frog needed to hear.

"Hold him firmly, now," Quinn's voice broke through Corrie's introspection. As she tightened her grip on the dog, she watched Quinn's fingers trail gently down Frog's leg. One hand immobilized the joint above the foot, while she took hold of the offending object and slowly extracted it from the injured paw. Frog whimpered once but did not move. Quinn tossed the object aside and cleaned this wound as she had the other, before deftly swathing Frog's paw in several layers of gauze. Mesmerized, Corrie's eyes couldn't help but follow Quinn's quick, sure movements. When she finally leaned back and pushed the hair away from her face, Corrie found herself blinking, as though coming out of a daydream.

"You can let him up," Quinn said. "He'll be fine, though if you want to be really careful, you might keep him at home tomorrow so he doesn't get sand into the cuts in his paw."

"Sure, okay." Corrie released the dog, who scrambled to his feet and headed immediately for his water bowl. "What was in there, anyway?"

"Horseshoe crab exoskeleton, it looked like." Quinn retrieved the broken section of spiky shell that she had extracted and wrinkled her nose in distaste. Corrie tried to hide her grin at how cute Quinn was being. For the first time since they had met, she was completely unselfconscious, and Corrie didn't want to do a thing to break the spell.

"Poor guy," Quinn said. "When he stepped on this, he must have lost his balance and scraped himself against a rock."

Corrie lightly touched Quinn's shoulder. "Thank you," she said seriously. "You're really, really good with him."

Quinn blushed and began to busy herself with tidying up the supplies. "I've seen a lot worse than that over at the humane society," she said. "It was no trouble."

"Still." Corrie grabbed Quinn's free hand and tugged lightly. "We owe you, Frog and I. Stay for dinner, will you?"

Quinn's eyes traveled down to the sight of her fingers entwined with Corrie's. Her hand was very warm. *Is she flirting with me?* But when she looked into Corrie's face, all she saw was genuine gratitude. "Are you a good cook?" she managed.

"I can whip up a mean spaghetti and garlic bread supper," Corrie said. "What do you say?" Realizing that she still held Quinn's hand, she reluctantly broke the contact, but kept her eyes on Quinn's. Why it suddenly mattered so much that she would agree to stay for a meal, Corrie couldn't have fathomed, but it seemed very important that her invitation be accepted.

"All right," Quinn said finally, nodding. "I'll stay."

❖

As promised, the meal was simple and delicious. Corrie hadn't let Quinn do a thing and, instead, had banished both her and Frog to the small deck, where a table and several chairs were set up with an excellent view of the ocean. She had even made a quick run to the nearby liquor store when Quinn had confessed that while she disliked beer with a passion, she did have a soft spot for wine coolers.

The talk over dinner had been casual and easygoing—mostly about the Sailing Center, the upcoming regatta, and school. Now, as Corrie excused herself briefly and slipped inside the house, Quinn leaned back in her chair to watch the last pinks and gold disappear from the sky. She felt relaxed and content in a way that seemed new, somehow, or at least different. She had been worried that it would be difficult to talk to Corrie—that they wouldn't have enough in common to sustain a conversation. But Corrie had been—or at least had seemed to be— genuinely interested in Quinn's job. They'd traded war stories about their introductory physics courses in college. They'd commiserated about how it was still difficult in certain respects to be women in the sciences. And they'd steadfastly avoided discussing anything really personal, for which Quinn was grateful.

Usually, after talking with another person for a good hour and a half, she was exhausted and ready to shut herself alone in her room with a good book to recoup her strength. Strangely enough, she didn't feel that way at all now. When the sounds of a light jazz CD drifted through the screen door, she stopped trying to explain the sensation and sighed happily. Corrie soon returned with a book of matches and began to light the citronella pots that ringed the table.

"What would you say to a game of cards?" she asked, fishing a deck out of the front pocket of her cargo shorts as she slid into her seat. "You pick it."

Quinn laughed. "The only game I can remember the rules for is Egyptian Ratscrew. One of my roommates in college was addicted, and we played it nonstop for hours."

Corrie shrugged and began to shuffle the deck. "Egyptian Ratscrew it is, then." She looked up to find Quinn intently watching her hands as she riffled the cards and was surprised to feel a surge of pleasure. She blinked and continued to manipulate the cards, wondering just exactly what was happening. The vibes were unmistakable, but sometimes it honestly felt like Quinn had no idea of what was going on. Was she confused? Uncertain? Playing a truly masterful game of hard to get?

Corrie took a deep breath, followed by a long sip of her beer, and decided to throw caution to the light northern breeze. "There are just two house rules," she added. When Quinn raised her eyebrows in question, she quirked a deliberately mischievous grin. "First—if two identical cards are played in a row, whoever slaps first gets the pile." At Quinn's nod, Corrie continued, "and second—each time a pile is won, the winner gets to ask the loser a question. Any question at all."

Quinn frowned and drew back slightly. "And the loser has to answer?"

"No," said Corrie, "but it'd be nice if you did."

"All right, then."

Almost immediately, Corrie threw down a Jack, and when Quinn countered with only the two of clubs, she scooped up the meager pile with an exultant flourish. Leaning back in her chair, she steepled her fingers beneath her chin and met Quinn's wary gaze. "Best kiss," she said, abruptly. "Who, where, when."

Quinn rolled her eyes and shook her head. "God, you're ruthless! And that's hard, though it's not as though I have a huge selection to pick from or anything—" She cut herself off, and even in the dim candlelight, Corrie could make out the sudden pink flush that flared across the bridge of her nose. But then Quinn raised her head, looked Corrie full in the eyes, and said defiantly, "Sue Price, freshman year, in the basement of our dorm while watching *ER*."

Corrie grinned. "Awww. That's sweet. How long did you date her?"

Quinn lightly bit her bottom lip before answering. "Three weeks. She didn't really like how much time I spent studying." She glanced down at her cards. "Pretty lame, isn't it?"

Corrie heard the strain in Quinn's voice and knew her answer would be important, especially if she wanted Quinn to keep talking about this kind of thing. She shook her head. "No, not lame. You just had different priorities, sounds like." She shrugged. "Happens all the time. Personally, I think that's why flings are easier than relationships."

Quinn looked away, frowning a little. *Shit*, Corrie thought. *I went and made her uncomfortable anyway!*

"Your turn," Quinn finally said into the silence, indicating the tabletop. She sat up straighter. "I'm out to get you back now."

True to her word, within several exchanges, Quinn had scooped up a more substantial pile and was regarding Corrie with her head tilted slightly to the side. Her eyes narrowed, and Corrie knew she was in trouble. It was a good feeling. "Same question," Quinn told her firmly. "Right back at you."

Corrie's reply was immediate, unthinking. "Denise Lewis, two years ago, in our boat after winning the—" Her voice trailed off as she realized just exactly what she was saying. She blinked at Quinn as her stomach twisted painfully, and she swallowed hard in an effort to stave off the sudden nausea. She felt her right hand tremble once against her sweating beer bottle and quickly busied herself with adjusting her ponytail. *Get a grip, dammit!* "That relationship didn't last long, either," she said, willing her voice to sound casual. "Turned out Denise liked fucking guys more than women." She licked her lips. "Her loss."

Quinn frowned slightly at Corrie's sudden shift in attitude. Her gaze was hard—almost a challenge—and once again, Quinn was struck by her aggressive sensuality. *It's a weapon*, she thought suddenly. *She uses it like a weapon.* "Your move," was all she said.

Fortunately, as the game continued, the tension that had so abruptly surfaced began to fade. By unspoken agreement, they kept the questions light and casual. Quinn discovered that Corrie's favorite color was sapphire blue. Corrie was surprised to learn that Quinn was twenty-seven—two years her senior. Corrie's favorite boat turned out to be the Laser. Quinn's childhood dog was a Great Dane. They joked and talked and even began to share small revelations outside of the game, and Corrie couldn't help but notice that Quinn's hand tended to linger slightly over or under her own each time they slapped for a double.

Nearly an hour later, when Corrie took almost all that remained of Quinn's cards with a Queen, she smiled eagerly in anticipation of the win. Quinn sat back in her chair with a heavy sigh. "Your question again," Quinn said.

Corrie frowned in thought, then shrugged. "Okay. A bit more serious this time, I guess. If you could change one thing about yourself, what would it be?"

"My weight." And then, as though the admission had startled her, Quinn clammed up and looked at Corrie with wide eyes. Corrie's frown deepened.

"Really?" she asked. "You look...well, you look fine to me. Why would you change it?" She leaned forward, intent upon Quinn's face.

Quinn sighed again. "I guess I've always wanted to be thinner." She looked out toward the ocean, then back at Corrie. "To have a body like yours."

Without thinking, Corrie reached out and took Quinn's hand. Her palm was warm, and slightly damp with sweat. "I think you have a beautiful body," Corrie said quietly. "Curvy and lush and full—"

"You mean 'chubby.'" Quinn breathed in sharply when Corrie's grip on her hand tightened.

"No, I don't," Corrie said forcefully. "I meant exactly what I said. You should believe me." Her gaze held Quinn's for a long moment, before she suddenly let go and took another sip of beer. When she spoke again, her voice was casual. "Besides, you've seen me eat. Only reason I look this way is genetics, pure and simple."

Quinn laughed softly, and Corrie felt her lips curve up at the sound. "That, and you're kind of manic."

"Ah, you've noticed that." Corrie gestured at the evidence of their unfinished game. "So—ready to meet your destiny?"

"I still have one Jack left. This won't be as easy as you think." But in the next turn, Corrie finally scooped up the last of Quinn's cards. "Famous last words," Quinn said, bemused.

"One final question. Hmm." Corrie's eyes narrowed but the curve of her lips was playful. "At that first social, why wouldn't you dance with me?"

Quinn flushed slightly as she remembered Corrie's invitation and her own discomfort, but her gaze was steady. "Actually, I told you that I wouldn't dance to the kind of music the DJ was playing," she said. "And it's because I'd feel like a complete idiot. I can only dance if there are actual steps. I learned to swing dance, in college, and that was all right."

"Neat!" Corrie promptly jumped up from the table. "Can you teach me?"

"Right now?"

"Sure, yeah. Just the basics." When Quinn hesitated, looking more than a little dubious, Corrie ducked her head and assumed such a pleading expression that Quinn rolled her eyes and stood up.

"You look just like a puppy when you do that. And I can never resist a puppy." She walked over to the small, open space between the deck railing and the table, and extended her hand. "I'll lead, you follow. Okay?"

Corrie blinked as a swift surge of arousal assaulted her yet again. *Maybe for a little while,* came the unbidden thought. *But I'm usually the one on top.* Struggling to wrestle herself under control, she took Quinn's proffered hand and stood close to her, but not touching. Dammit, she smelled good—like sun and water and just a hint of salt.

"Okay," Quinn said, her tone brisk. "Put your left hand on my right shoulder." Once Corrie had obliged, Quinn wrapped her arm around Corrie's torso so that her right hand was firmly positioned in the center of Corrie's back. Corrie felt her pulse jump as their stomachs touched lightly, and she suddenly had a hard time swallowing. *Jeez, I'm in rare form this evening. Remember what Drew said about her. But she is dancing with me, and I swear to god she's been flirting back all night.*

"I'll guide you," Quinn said, demonstrating how she could direct Corrie's movements by lightly pulling or pushing against her. "Fine so far?"

"Uh. Yep." Corrie found herself leaning in until her cheek was almost touching Quinn's right temple.

"The basic moves are very simple. One, two, rock-step. I step forward, you step backward." Quinn moved fluidly, directing Corrie with light pressure, and they soon found an easy rhythm together. "Very nice," said Quinn, pulling back slightly to look up at Corrie. A sudden fluttering deep in her stomach made her look away just as quickly. "Let's try a spin, shall we?"

Once they returned to their original position, Corrie laughed. "That was great! Let's do it again."

"All right," Quinn said, pleased at her partner's enthusiasm and trying to ignore the fact that each time Corrie's body moved against her own, a very pleasant tingle raced up her spine. "Other way, this time."

This spin was even smoother than the first, and Quinn shared Corrie's exultant grin as they came back together again. "This is fun," Corrie murmured. The cascade of warm breath against her earlobe made it suddenly difficult for Quinn to focus, and she briefly lost the rhythm.

"Sorry about that," she whispered back.

"It's okay," Corrie said softly in reply. "It can be hard to lead."

Quinn could have sworn that Corrie's lips had actually brushed the shell of her ear just then, and she swallowed hard. "I'm just not that good at it, really," she forced herself to reply.

Corrie's head began to pound as she felt sweat break out on Quinn's left hand where it gently held her right. As she touched her mouth to Quinn's ear again, Quinn's entire body trembled, unmistakably. *She wants me, I know she does, her body is* screaming *it.* "Why not let me try for a while?" she said, just before twirling them both around so that she could press Quinn gently but firmly against the deck railing.

Her lips parted in surprise, but then Corrie's hands were shifting to cup her waist just above her hips, and Corrie's head was slowly descending toward hers, and in another second, Corrie's lips were lightly brushing against her own. So soft, so gentle, Quinn's head spun, and she pressed closer, and someone—it might have been her—made a soft noise that sounded suspiciously like a whimper.

Corrie's grip tightened as Quinn clung to her shoulders. When she allowed her tongue to glide tentatively along Quinn's upper lip, Quinn clutched at the thin material of her tank top, bunching it up across her shoulder blades.

Thrilled by her responsiveness, Corrie lightly nipped Quinn's bottom lip before tasting her in earnest. Quinn's hips rocked forward at the slow slide of Corrie's tongue against hers, and this time, it was Corrie's turn to groan. Slowly, she allowed her hands to drift up along Quinn's ribcage as she continued the deep kiss. Quinn shuddered when Corrie's fingers caressed the soft undersides of her breasts, and Corrie felt her pulse skyrocket. *No one has ever reacted to me like this*, came the dim thought as she cupped Quinn's breasts, brushed her thumbs across the raised nipples, and scraped her teeth gently across her bottom lip, all at once.

Quinn tore her mouth away to suck in a deep, shuddering breath as a wash of heat radiated down from her breasts to focus between her legs—a throbbing so intense that it actually hurt. Her head reeled. *Oh, God*, Quinn managed to think. *I want—*

In a sudden instant of clarity, she pushed weakly at Corrie's shoulders. "Stop," she panted. "Please—"

Corrie drew back instantly, gasping at the loss of contact. Her eyes in the candlelight were dark and wide. Quinn turned away, grabbing at the railing for purchase.

With her back still toward Corrie, she forced herself to speak. "I don't...I can't..." She shook her head, struggling to collect her breath and her thoughts. *Remember what Drew said. This doesn't mean a thing. It's just what she does with her friends. It's only lust.*

There was a long pause before Corrie answered, her voice deceptively light. "Sorry. My bad. Didn't mean to push."

Quinn frowned and turned to face her, but Corrie was looking out toward the pond. "You didn't. You weren't. It's just that I—"

Still-dark eyes flickered briefly over her face. "So you *did* want me to kiss you? To touch you?"

Her grin was almost predatory, and Quinn didn't like it. *What just happened? Why did you change just now?* Struggling to explain herself, she ran one hand through her slightly tangled hair. "Yes...well, I mean, *no*, but it's more that I don't want...I mean, I've never, with..." She sighed in frustration and forced herself to meet Corrie's now curious gaze. "Well, with anyone, actually."

"How 'bout I try to convince you to pick me?" Corrie took a step closer.

Quinn blushed, but she held out one hand as though to ward Corrie off. "I don't know what I'm trying to say, here."

Corrie stopped moving forward, but her eyes roamed up and down Quinn's body in a way that made Quinn's face feel even hotter. "It's okay," she said. "You can be hard to get. I like that once in a while."

The resulting silence was awkward, as Quinn realized that Corrie wasn't actually getting the point at all. "I don't think I could, except with someone I loved," she said suddenly, her voice quiet but sure. "I like you a lot, but I just…I don't know you *that* well."

"Ah," said Corrie, shaking her head. "It's on principle. Well, you're missing out."

"Maybe *you're* missing out."

Corrie took a step back, as though Quinn had pushed her. The cocky smile faded. *Like closing the shutter over a window.* "Oh. I…it's my turn to be sorry," Quinn said miserably, though she had no idea why.

"What?" Corrie asked, clearly distracted. She moved a few feet away to claim her own section of railing and lean heavily against it. "No, it's not. It's just bad memories."

Quinn watched her stare out into the dark, clearly in pain. She thought back to their conversation over cards. "Of that woman," she said intuitively.

Corrie didn't answer for a while. Finally, she turned toward Quinn and sighed. "You're right, you know. It is better with someone you love."

You look so tired all of a sudden, Quinn thought. She felt a swift stab of guilt. "But?"

Corrie laughed sardonically and nudged at the railing with her toes. "But oh, all the angst when they don't return the favor." *And that's not even the half of it.*

She turned back to her silent contemplation of the night as Quinn pondered this newest piece of the puzzle. *Maybe that's why she only likes casual encounters.* She watched Corrie's hunched figure surreptitiously, wanting so much to say something that would make her feel better, but knowing that at this point, she could only offer platitudes.

Finally, she pushed herself away from the railing and moved close enough to cautiously put her hand on Corrie's shoulder. Just as it had been earlier in the day, her skin was hot to the touch. She struggled with the memory of how Corrie's lips had burned against her own before finally managing to tamp down the unfamiliar wanting and look her in the eyes. Before Corrie could stop her or she could stop herself, Quinn pulled her into a gentle hug. She felt Corrie stiffen in surprise, but then her body relaxed. Quinn couldn't help but think just how good and soft and warm she felt.

"I'm going home now," she said, fighting the urge to rub her cheek against the side of Corrie's neck. "Thank you for dinner."

In another moment, she had pulled away. Corrie watched as Quinn stopped to pet Frog before walking quickly down the steps of the deck and disappearing around the side of the house. She sighed heavily, rested her elbows against the railing, and cradled her head in her hands. *I could use more hugs like that.* Then again, all Quinn had done— besides rejecting her—was to show her just how far she hadn't come. Desire still suffused her body, but its pull was easily overshadowed by the sharp, familiar pain between her breasts. *Damn you, Denise. Damn you for worming your way in there.* The sore spot ached with every breath, and she finally freed one hand to press against it. Struggling to regain some measure of equilibrium, she closed her eyes and let the cool night breeze dry the two stubborn tears that refused to stay where they belonged.

HEELING

Corrie sighed quietly as she stepped back under the hot spray of the shower to rinse the conditioner from her hair. She braced one hand against the tiles and let the water sluice over her body, wishing for it to wash away the tension that plagued her just as it cleansed her skin of sand and ocean salt and sweat. Instead, she felt acutely the beat of the spray against her nipples, the trickle of the water as tiny rivulets converged at the juncture of her thighs. Her body was hot and full and throbbing and had been all day.

I could try turning the knob to cold, she thought briefly. But it wouldn't make a difference. Not really. The dull ache between her thighs would gradually become pain, and her skin would only grow more and more sensitive until she finally gave in to the demands of her body. *I hate this, sometimes. It frightens me.*

She heard the water shut off in the next stall over, followed by the sounds of Jen toweling dry. Raising her face toward the spigot, she let the spray pound against her cheeks, as though it could knock some sense into her overheated brain.

"So," said Jen over the noise of the water. "Are you going to tell me what's been bugging you today, or not?"

Corrie sighed again and straightened up in the shower. "What are you talking about?"

"Well, let's see. You snapped at every single person who came into your office, for one thing. And you didn't give any ratings, for another. You stayed holed up inside while everyone went out for lunch, Jeez, did you even eat anything today?"

Corrie reluctantly shut off the water, wrapping a towel around herself as she stepped out of the stall. "Wrong side of the bed."

Jen, who stood just a few feet away, was in the act of pulling on a blue, light cotton shirt. "Mmm, I don't buy it," she said, grabbing for her hairbrush. "Try again."

Corrie dried off briskly, then reached for the pair of tight-fitting khaki shorts that she had left on one of the benches. She pulled them on and, deciding to forego a bra as well as underwear, immediately grabbed her scooped-neck black top. A size too small, it clung to her breasts and stomach like a second skin.

"I'm just having a bad day," she said as she bent down to adjust the bracelet around her right ankle. *Everything would be fine if Quinn hadn't made me think of* her.

Jen looked her up and down and cocked her head. "Which is why you're going on the prowl tonight, then?"

Corrie laughed sharply. "On the prowl, huh? What makes you think that?"

"Even the gay guys and straight girls will look twice at you in that shirt."

Corrie raised her head and leered. "That include you?"

Jen rolled her eyes. "You wish." She softened the words with a light punch to Corrie's right shoulder.

"People are more flexible than you think," said Corrie, slipping on a pair of sandals. *Except for Quinn, apparently.* Her rejection still rankled. Corrie wasn't exactly used to being turned down. "Should I leave it wet, or dry it?"

"It doesn't matter." Jen's voice sounded almost resigned. "You'll have whoever you want, regardless."

"Time will tell." Corrie started for the door, and together they made their way up the stairs to the crowded hall.

"There's the gang," Jen shouted over the thumping music, pointing toward the far end of the bar.

Corrie nodded and pushed her way across the room, keeping her eyes straight ahead. Somehow the crowd was simultaneously exhausting and invigorating tonight. *I don't want to talk to anyone*, she realized suddenly, *but I don't want to be alone, either*.

As they came up alongside Drew and a few other instructors, Corrie nodded to her friends and leaned back against the warm, lacquered edge of the bar. The sunset, visible through the large windows, was spectacular, and she briefly thought back to that first social, when she had found Quinn outside similarly contemplating the nightfall.

Running With The Wind

But thinking of Quinn suddenly had her thinking about Denise again, about how it had felt to love someone instead of just fucking her, to wake up next to someone and want to hold her. Struggling to pull herself together, she turned away from her friends and caught sight of Will chatting with one of his frat buddies across the room. Mercifully, the familiar, white-hot anger surged back to the fore, purging her of the sadness, the loneliness, the grief. *You took that from me. Took* her. *She was weak, and you played her.* And then she remembered how affectionate they'd been at their engagement party and Denise's later protest that she did in fact love him.

Hell, she thought, still disgusted with herself even after all this time. *They both played me.*

Turning back, she caught the bartender's eye and gave a little wave. Beside her, Jen tucked Drew's shirt tag beneath his collar.

"You're a mess, Harris."

"Huh?" Drew asked, pulling away and turning to face her. "What was that for?"

"Your tag was out. Geek."

Drew straightened his shoulders and pretended to glare. "Who made you the Goddess of Fashion? *Jenny.*"

"How many times?" Jen's voice was shrill. "How ma—"

"Children!" Corrie said sharply, as the bartender finally made his way toward them. "Enough. Who's doing tequila with me?"

"Shots?" Drew asked, turning to face her. Corrie looked at him—really looked—for the first time that night. Strong, tan arms stood out darkly against his white T-shirt, and Corrie was momentarily entranced by the slight flicker of his abs just above the waistband of his faded jeans. When she realized that she was rather blatantly giving him the once over, she quickly met his eyes.

"Shots," she said. "Of course." She ran one hand through her still-damp hair, shaking the long strands back from her face. *Are you the one, tonight?* She knew Drew wanted her. Better yet, she knew she could make him *need* her. Unlike certain other people.

"I'm in," he said, but Corrie couldn't tell which question he was answering. She looked away, toward the others.

"Who else?"

As they waited for the round of shots to arrive, Corrie leaned back against the bar again and closed her eyes. She could feel the rhythm of the music seeping through the soles of her sandals, the skin of her feet, into her blood. The air of the room was hot as she breathed it in—hot like the aching beat as it settled between her thighs. *I haven't even touched a drink and I'm already drunk.* She gave herself up to it, surrendering to the throb of desire, letting the energy enter her, fill her, consume her until it *was* her, and she was it. Sensuality incarnate, as inexorable as the restless ocean tide.

The sensation of skin against her forearm jolted her out of the reverie. "The drinks are here," said Drew. He frowned down at her. "You okay?"

"Yes," she said while everyone around her grabbed a brimming shot glass and a slice of lime. As someone passed Drew the saltshaker, Corrie nudged him lightly. "Let me."

When he frowned again, she rolled her eyes. "Give me your wrist, silly."

"Uh," Drew managed to say. "All right."

From Drew's other side, Jen raised her eyebrows as Corrie wrapped her fingers around his left arm, turned it over to expose the soft underside, and ran her tongue over the translucent skin. When she pulled away, Drew just stood there, frozen, before his Adam's apple bobbed once in a hard swallow.

"Salt," she said, nudging him again. "Go on. And then it's my turn." She held up her own wrist with a wink.

Checkmate, Jen thought, steadfastly ignoring the abrupt surge of disappointment that bottomed out in the pit of her stomach. *That was fast.*

"What are we drinking to?" she forced herself to ask cheerfully as Drew finally finished his oral exploration of Corrie's wrist.

"The wind." Corrie's smile was triumphant, yet fierce. "Bottoms up." She delicately swiped the salt, downed the shot smoothly, turned it upside down on the bar, and closed her lips around the slice of lime. Jen watched Drew's eyes go hazy as Corrie sighed in pleasure and sucked hard on the fruit. She bit back a sigh of her own.

"The wind, then," she echoed, as the rest of the group mirrored Corrie's actions. "C'mon," she said afterward, cavalierly throwing her arms around two other instructors. "Let's dance."

Corrie didn't see the others make their way toward the dance floor; she was reveling in the slow burn of the alcohol as it rushed down her throat and into her empty stomach. *Beautiful.* Drew waited patiently beside her. *My move, and he knows it.* The power was even more intoxicating than the tequila. *God, yes, this is what I needed.*

"I'd like to hang out here for a little while," she said softly, hooking her right index finger under the waistband of his jeans and tugging. "And then, I want you to come home with me."

"My place is closer."

She cocked her head and looked at him—saw desire in the tense planes of his face, in the dark pupils that nearly drowned out the brown of his eyes. "Fine, then."

She stepped closer, settling her left hand on his waist. He curled one arm around her so that his palm rested in the small of her back. His skin burned against hers through the thin material of her shirt.

"Corrie," he said, suddenly. His face was strange, almost sad. "I just—" But then he grinned and shook his head. "Ah hell, nothing. You feel good."

Her eyes sparkled in the dim light. "Not nearly as good as you're going to feel," she said, passing him one of the beers. Her callused fingertips brushed deliberately over his knuckles. He swallowed hard again.

❖

Quinn closed the bulky textbook and set it on her nightstand with a sigh. *If I can't get to sleep now...* She yawned, stretched, fluffed her pillow, and finally turned out the light. It was past eleven. She'd been meaning to go to bed over an hour ago, but rest had eluded her. Fortunately, there was always more studying to be done.

She turned onto her side beneath the crisp white sheets and resolutely closed her eyes. *Go to sleep*, she told her exhausted brain. But, as had happened last night and all day today, as soon as there were no distractions, her body began to remember just how nice it had felt to be pressed between the soft yet firm weight of Corrie and the rigid solidity of the railing. *Caught. Trapped. No, not trapped. That means you didn't want to be there.*

She rolled onto her back and opened her eyes to stare into the dark, trying to dissect her feelings rationally. She had wanted to be there, all right—had wanted Corrie to continue kissing her, touching her. And yes, she'd even wanted more. A lot more.

That wasn't to say that she'd never considered having sex before, but previously, the thought had always been abstract. Distant. Last night had been up close and personal and not at all rational. *I wanted to give myself to her, and she wanted to take me.*

Quinn exhaled loudly. *No matter how much you wanted her, or she wanted you, you were only going to be another notch on her bedpost.* A soft breeze ruffled the curtains over her open window, bringing with it the faint sound of laughter from the street. Was Corrie still at the social? Probably not. *Who did she go home with tonight?*

Quinn shook her head, feeling her hair twist against the fabric of the pillow. *She took me by surprise. And it was nice that she wanted me.* Had any of the few women she'd dated ever approached her with the same single-minded purpose and focus with which Corrie had kissed her? If they had, she couldn't remember.

It was fun playing cards. Will we still be able to do that? She tried closing her eyes again, but now, instead of feeling the heat of Corrie's lips against the skin of her neck, she was hearing the husky timbre of Corrie's voice.

Quinn sat up suddenly and frowned into the shadows. Her eyes were open, and she was *still* hearing Corrie's voice. At the sound of the front door opening, she completely froze. *Oh my god. She came home with* Drew.

Shoulders hunched, she waited tensely, hearing only the low buzz of their speech and perhaps a sound that was the opening and closing of the refrigerator door. After a minute or two, Quinn began to relax. *Maybe they're just hanging out, having a drink or something.* She lay back in bed and closed her eyes again. *Yeah. That must be it.*

But a few seconds later, she was startled into full alertness by a loud thump that sounded as though something had crashed into the wall just outside her door.

"You didn't really want to finish that, did you?" Corrie's voice could have been clearer only if she'd been speaking directly into Quinn's ear. Her stomach plunged. *Not just a drink after all.*

"N-no," Drew said hoarsely. "God, Corrie—"

Corrie hummed, low and deep. Quinn could still hear her. "Good to know."

There was a long pause during which she started feeling hopeful that they had removed themselves to Drew's room, but then she heard a choked groan, followed by the sound of giggling. *Giggling? She giggles?*

"Stop, Mars. *Stop*. I'm gonna come in my pants if you keep—"

"None of that, now," Corrie said firmly. "You're not going to come until you're way deep inside me. Understand?"

Quinn's eyebrows shot up into her hairline. Her cheeks felt like they were on fire, and she wasn't sure that she could swallow if she tried. Even as her body responded to Corrie's explicit demand, her brain was flooded with embarrassment.

"Fuck, you're going to kill me."

Corrie's reply was terse. "Shirt. Off. Now."

Quinn squeezed her eyes shut. Dimly, she realized that she was breathing hard, her chest rising and falling rapidly beneath the light sheet. What would it feel like? Corrie tugging at the hem of her shirt, pushing it up her torso, tickling lightly along her rib cage. Quinn felt herself shiver as she remembered the way Corrie's fingers had brushed over her breasts. The exquisite friction of cotton against the tips, Corrie's palms sliding against her shoulders as the shirt slid over her head.

"You have a great body, Skipper," Corrie interrupted Quinn's reverie. "But you're not in charge tonight." Quinn heard the soft snick of a zipper being lowered, followed by Drew's tortured groan.

Heat spiraled along Quinn's spine at Corrie's command. To be ordered around like that, to be controlled. Her breath rasped softly in her throat. Corrie had taken the lead from her last night, and she was taking it again now, with Drew. Quinn remembered what it had felt like to surrender, however briefly. What if Corrie's hand had dipped beneath the waistband of her shorts? What if she had tickled Quinn's abdomen, skirting the soft brown hairs? What if she had urged Quinn's legs apart, had touched—.

Quinn blinked and shook her head, appalled to realize that her hand had snuck into her pajama bottoms—that her *own* fingers were dangerously close to rubbing against the soft place that had ached continuously since last night. She removed her hand so quickly that the elastic waistband snapped hard against her stomach. *What are you doing?* she thought, clutching the sheets so that her fingers wouldn't wander again. There was nothing wrong with masturbation, of course, except that the idea of touching herself while listening to Corrie and Drew didn't feel right at all.

This is insane, she thought wildly. *Why can she make me feel this way?*

"Need you...naked."

Drew's voice was fainter now. *They must have moved into the bedroom finally.* But the idea of Corrie naked did nothing to alleviate the throbbing pressure between Quinn's legs. Corrie didn't exactly wear all that much to work, and it wasn't hard to mentally strip her of the sports bra and swim trunks that were her usual attire. *She'd be lean and strong all over, but soft, too. I felt how soft she was, especially her breasts against mine.*

"How's that feel?" Corrie's voice—triumphant and sexy. When Drew groaned again in response, Quinn couldn't help but imagine Corrie's fingers on her softest skin, insistent and teasing, touching her in all the right places. Sure and certain fingers.

"Close, Cor, fuck." Quinn could hear Drew's deep, shuddering breaths, and she slowed her own to mere whispers of inhalation. "You gotta let me, please, inside—"

Quinn sucked in a harsh gasp. What would it feel like, to be inside of Corrie? She could only imagine the sensation of Corrie sinking down on her fingers, welcoming Quinn's touch inside her body.

"Oh, yeah. Fuck, yeah, Drew, so good—"

Quinn had read about a place inside—a place that felt very, very good. She hadn't ever managed to find it for herself, but was Drew...was he...would she hit that spot, deep inside of Corrie? Would her fingertips brush against it? Would Corrie shiver around her? Would she throw her head back, exposing her neck as she—?

A strangled cry broke the night air. Not Drew.

"C-coming...oh, do you f-feel me?" Corrie's voice was jagged.

"Yeah, tight, so good, fuck—"

Quinn closed her eyes at the sound of Drew's strangled shout and allowed herself to imagine what Corrie's inner muscles would feel like as they contracted repeatedly around her knuckles. Over and over and over, pulsing in time with her racing heart, clenching and releasing until the very last ripple of sensation had been milked from her body. *Oh god, I want that, want to feel it, feel her, can't help it I do—*

As her heartbeat finally slowed, Quinn realized that the apartment had finally gone quiet. She listened hard for several long minutes, but heard nothing except the light swish of the curtains in the soft breeze. *It's over*, she told herself firmly.

You just imagined what it would be like to sleep with Corrie, her rational brain answered back. Its tone was distinctly accusatory.

So? She's beautiful and charismatic. She kissed me last night. Why shouldn't I fantasize? Her face was still hot against the cool fabric of the pillow.

Reason was never funny, but it laughed just the same. *You've never felt this way before. Not even close. Go ahead and delude yourself if you want to, but this is uncharted territory.*

Quinn rolled over fiercely and pulled the pillow over her head. *Just...just go to sleep, dammit! Leave me alone!*

But even as she finally drifted off, she knew that she'd never be able to forget the raw, primal sounds of Corrie finally letting go.

❖

Quinn woke overheated. The sun had clearly been streaming through her east window for several hours. She threw off the covers, rolled onto her side and blinked. *What...did I miss my alarm? No— Saturday.* And then, all in a rush, the dreamlike events of the previous night came flooding back in a panoply of sounds.

The blush returned to her cheeks as she buried her head into the soft texture of her feather pillow. *Don't think about it. Just let it go. Don't think...* She focused instead on the warm sun as it caressed her back, on the dim sounds of people walking by and talking. *Sounds like a beautiful day*, she thought, as her body gradually relaxed into the mattress.

When her breathing and pulse had finally returned to normal, she checked the clock. 9:30. She's *probably gone. Coffee.*

Quinn resolutely swung her legs over the edge of the bed. She took a deep breath, stretched, and finally stood on her own two feet. Trying not to think at all about the fact that Corrie and Drew had just about had sex right outside her room, she slowly opened the door.

There was no pile of clothes, not even a mark on the wall. No evidence at all, except for her own clamoring memories. She paused, listening, but the apartment was quiet. Sighing in relief, she padded through the living room and into the kitchen only to stumble to a halt at the sight of Corrie, clad solely in Drew's blue Oxford shirt, its sleeves rolled up to the elbows. The bottom of the shirt barely even covered Corrie's butt, and the open top two buttons gave Quinn a glimpse of her breasts.

At the sound of footsteps, Corrie looked up with a half-smile that faded quickly as she saw Quinn across the narrow island dividing the kitchen's cooking space from the table. *Holy shit. How did I totally forget she was living with Drew this summer?* Corrie felt herself grow warm, partly in embarrassment, but mostly because the sight of Quinn first thing in the morning, her pajamas rumpled and her hair mussed, made Corrie want to pull her down on the couch and wake her up properly. Only to put her back to sleep, of course.

She shook her head and blinked. "Hi," she said hesitantly. She gestured to the cabinet above the sink. "I was just, um, going to make some coffee." Quinn nodded and shuffled a bit closer. "D'you want some?" *She must have been asleep by the time we came home. Had to be.*

"Sure," said Quinn. Her voice was gritty with sleep, and she looked...Corrie focused on Quinn's pajamas and nearly burst out laughing. *Adorable!* Both the light pants and the short-sleeved shirt were covered with colorful illustrations of animals. Ones you'd find in the zoo, mostly—bears, giraffes, tigers, a flamingo—and whoever had decided that the alligator's open mouth should be poised directly over the tip of Quinn's nipple was simply brilliant.

"I like your PJs," was all Corrie managed to say. Quinn looked down at herself and her blush intensified.

"Oh," she said. "Um...thanks. Younger sister gave them to me."

Corrie turned back to the sink and reached for the coffee canister, and Quinn nearly choked as Drew's shirt rode up high enough to give her an unobstructed view of Corrie's rear end. Her ass was firm and muscular, with lean curves swelling up toward her hips and a dimple above each cheek. Quinn wanted to fill her palms with those curves, to lightly rest her aching fingertips in those dimples—wanted to feel Corrie's muscles move beneath her skin as she stretched over her, beneath her. She gulped and rubbed her eyes.

Calm down calm down calm down... In the wake of the latest wave of arousal, Quinn felt anger. This was getting ridiculous. *I am* not *going to let my hormones, or* whatever *this is, take control. I'm perfectly capable of carrying on a conversation. Of being her friend. Get a grip!* Suddenly determined, she cleared her throat, looked up, and squared her shoulders.

"So, how's Frog doing?"

Corrie hit the brew button on Drew's coffeemaker and turned around to lean against the counter. Quinn fiercely kept her gaze focused on Corrie's face.

"A lot better," she said. "He was getting pretty restless from being all cooped up when I checked on him yesterday afternoon." *And you haven't been home since then, have you?* she realized guiltily. *God. Quinn must think I'm neglecting him!*

"I bet," said Quinn. "He's got lots of energy. Was he still limping, then?"

When no recrimination was forthcoming, Corrie relaxed. "A little bit, yeah."

Quinn nodded and drummed her fingertips lightly on the table. *Should I...should...oh hell, why not?* "I'd be happy to stop by and check on him later in the afternoon, if you want," she said. "Just to make sure nothing's infected. If you want, I mean." *There. See? That wasn't so hard. Friends.*

Corrie felt her eyebrows shoot up. She had expected Quinn to feel ill at ease, given the situation. *And given the fact that the night* before *last, I was trying to jump* her *bones.* But although she had clearly been startled at first, she was acting as though the awkward events of the past two days had never happened. *I should feel relieved,* Corrie thought. But she didn't. *Part of her wanted me Thursday night. I know it. I could feel it. But...if she's attracted to me at all, shouldn't she be off-kilter right now?* Corrie felt like growling in frustration. What was it about this woman that made her feel like a total novice at reading people?

"That would be great, if you don't mind," she said, her voice betraying none of her inner conflict. *At least I'm still good at pretending.* She smiled even. "Thanks."

"No problem." Quinn looked over Corrie's shoulder toward the coffee pot. "Is that ready, yet?"

"Looks like." Corrie grabbed a mug and filled it, then held it out to Quinn. "Black?"

"Absolutely." When her fingers lightly brushed Corrie's, Quinn immediately tamped down the soft flutter in her stomach. "Thanks for this. I'm going to hit the books."

As she turned away, Corrie couldn't help but admire the way the pajama shirt and pants draped over the curves of Quinn's stomach and hips. She shook her head and frowned. *Quit it!* "Uh, good luck!"

Quinn turned back at the entrance to the hall, waved, and was gone. Corrie took a deep breath and rested her hands against the counter, waiting for the faint tremor to disappear before pouring her own cup of coffee.

❖

By the time she rounded the final curve in the road before her driveway, Corrie actually felt like smiling. The promise of a hot shower and a good breakfast awaited—maybe a sail later to clear her head, or maybe she'd just avoid the boathouse entirely and stay home to read a book. *And if Quinn really does show up later, maybe I can do something nice for her. Something a friend would do...maybe baking? Do I have any eggs?*

But as her front porch came into view, her happiness dissipated. Will's truck took up most of the driveway and he was reclining on her stoop, nursing a tall mug of what was probably coffee. Corrie's jaw clenched. At the sound of her footsteps, he raised his head and blinked at her.

"Well, well. And where did *you* sleep last night?" He shifted to make room for her on the steps, but she remained standing.

"Really not your business. What are you doing here?"

He grinned, slow and easy. "Thought I'd come over this morning and get you to make me breakfast."

Corrie frowned deeply. How typical of him to expect to be her best buddy, even after he'd stabbed her in the back. To expect that she'd just forgive and forget. Maybe that had worked when they were kids, but she had a spine now. "What the fuck am I, your short-order cook?"

Will shrugged. "If you wanna be."

"No, I don't *want* to be. And I've already eaten." The lie felt good. It was what he deserved. "If you're so hungry, go to the diner with your little friends."

Will didn't move. "Nah, whatever. It's almost lunchtime anyway." He squinted up at Corrie. "So c'mon, Cor, spill the beans. Is this mystery person someone special?" When her frown deepened and she shook her head, Will rubbed the back of his neck with one hand.

"What's with you these days? You used to date, y'know? Go through a girlfriend every few months, not just hook up with someone new every couple of days." He winked at her. "Can't ya hang on to them, anymore?"

Corrie felt her face grow hot. "I cannot fucking believe you just said that," she hissed, taking a menacing step closer to him. "Who do you think you are, trying to tell me how to live?"

"Whoa," Will backpedaled, holding up one hand. "Whoa, easy. I just want you to be happy, Cor, because it's easy to see that you're not right now."

"And why is that, do you think?" Corrie grabbed onto the banister. The muscles of her right arm trembled violently.

"Clearly, I shouldn't have said anything." Will got up slowly, shaking his head. "Sometimes I don't *get* you, sis."

"Believe me," said Corrie, "the feeling's mutual." She leaned forward. "You know what I think? I think you're trying to make me into another version of you, just like you've tried all our lives. I think that since you're about to tie the fucking knot, you want me to settle down, too." She took a deep, shuddering breath. "Well, guess what? I'm not your carbon copy. I'll do whatever the fuck I want."

Will threw up his hands. "Okay, okay. This is obviously a bad time, so...I'm leaving." He turned toward his truck, then glanced over his shoulder. "Just be careful, all right?"

Corrie didn't reply. She stood still for a long time, long after he had started the car and backed it carefully out of her driveway, long after he'd disappeared down the street. But she couldn't escape his words. *"Can't ya hang on to them, anymore?"*

Finally, she turned back toward the house. Her empty house. *Not empty*, she reminded herself sternly. *Frog will be ecstatic to see me after a night away.* But deep down, she knew that wasn't enough. Deep down, she knew Will was right.

LIFT

A few days later, Quinn walked briskly down the spur corridor on the north side of the boathouse, her damp aqua shoes squelching against the polished tiles. Ahead of her, a tall man exited one of the rooms and walked toward the stairs at the far end. Quinn squinted. It looked like Will, and the office he'd just left was Corrie's. She briefly wondered what they'd been talking about, and whether Jen was right about Will's effect on his sister. *Guess I'll find out for myself.*

As she neared the door, she unconsciously slowed her pace, adjusting the brim of her cap and making sure that any stray hairs were tucked behind her ears. Maybe it was silly to care how she looked, especially after having just been out on the water, but Quinn couldn't help it. *You don't want to help it,* reason clarified. Firmly ignoring her inner monologue, she took a deep breath and tentatively rested her hand on one side of the doorframe as she poked her head into the room.

Almost immediately, she jerked backward as a wad of paper, followed by a pen, flew out the door dangerously close to where her head had been. The pen clattered against the wall.

There was a long silence as both women regarded each other, blinking in surprise. Quinn took in Corrie's flushed face and clenched fists; her desk was in disarray, papers and writing implements strewn haphazardly across the surface as though in the wake of a miniature tornado.

"Shit!" Corrie jumped up from her chair. Her eyes were dark and wild. "Sorry! You okay?"

Quinn smiled slightly, shrugged and bent down to retrieve the pen and crumpled paper. "No worries. You missed me by a few inches," she said, trying to make light of whatever it was that had just happened. When Corrie nodded and slumped back into her seat, Quinn felt her eyebrows draw together in a frown. *I've never seen her like this. She's either upset, furious, or both. And I bet I know exactly whose fault it is.*

As she moved into the office, Quinn smoothed out the wrinkled paper and glanced down. It was a registration form for the regatta. She'd seen them all over the boathouse since the beginning of the summer. The black, slanted letters at the top of the form on the line next to "Skipper" spelled out the name "William Marsten, Jr." Quinn's frown deepened. *Her brother—no surprise there.* And in the "Crew" space: "Denise Lewis."

"*Denise Lewis, two years ago, in our boat...*"

"*You're right, you know. It is better with someone you love. But oh, all the angst when they don't return the favor.*"

"Oh," she said. She looked up at Corrie, who was massaging her temples. Suddenly, the puzzle pieces were starting to fall into place.

Quinn took a step closer, and then another. She set the paper down in front of Corrie but did not touch her. "This Denise is the woman you were talking about the other night, isn't it?" she asked softly. Corrie winced and nodded. She didn't look at Quinn. "And she's coming here for the regatta? To sail with your brother?"

"Yes." The word was short and clipped. Corrie tapped her fingers against the desk.

Quinn pulled up a folding chair and sat. She wanted to touch Corrie's hand but wasn't at all certain that that was a good idea. Corrie was reminding her very much of an animal in pain, and creatures in pain tended to lash out. "I'm not sure I understand how they know each other," she said quietly.

Corrie looked out the window for several seconds, the muscles in her jaw clenching and unclenching spasmodically. "Denise and Will are engaged."

Quinn sat back hard. "Oh." She blinked as Corrie continued to gaze out toward the water. Her antipathy to Will made perfect sense, now, as did the competition between them. *Will made it to the Olympics and got the girl*, Quinn realized. *Ouch.*

"Well," she considered, keeping her voice pitched low, "do you have to let them race?"

Corrie finally met her eyes. "Of course I do. Their form is on time, and their goddamn check is for the right amount, and there's no way in hell that I can stop her from coming here."

Quinn nodded, walking the pen across her knuckles as she spoke. When she realized what she was doing, she handed it back to Corrie. "Sorry, this is yours." And then she remembered her entire reason for seeking Corrie out in the first place, and dug a pair of worn sailing gloves out of her left pocket. "As are these. Thanks again for loaning them to me."

Corrie frowned at the gloves. "Why don't you just hang on to them for the rest of the season?" Her voice was monotone. "I have several pairs."

Quinn nodded and stuck the gloves back into her pocket. "Okay. Thanks." It sounded very much as though Corrie wanted to be left alone, but as she started to get up, Corrie gestured toward the pen now lying grounded on her desk.

"Can't believe I almost *hit* you with this," she said. "I'm really sorry." She sighed and began to rub her temples again. "I just...I'm having a hard time letting it go." She returned her gaze to Quinn and shook her head ruefully. "And then when he comes waltzing in here and shoves his fucking form under my nose..." She swallowed hard, her face vacant. "Have you ever honestly seen red? It was like that—just this flash of red—so goddamn *angry*!"

Quinn finally dared to take her hand, then she squeezed once, and after a moment, Corrie squeezed back. Quinn knew she should let go, but simply couldn't. Her fingers slid perfectly between Corrie's, her palm resting against warm skin. "Do you want to tell me what happened?"

Corrie laughed harshly, her grip unconsciously tightening. "It's so silly. So fucking *trite*. It shouldn't matter. I shouldn't care anymore."

Quinn ducked her head down to try to meet Corrie's bleak gaze. "Tell me," she said gently.

Corrie looked away, gazing out her window toward the beach and the ocean. A group of students, or perhaps instructors, were playing an impromptu game of ultimate Frisbee. It was a beautiful day outside, and the breeze was light and steady, but all she could feel was the rapid, painful thumping of her heart against her ribcage.

"Two years ago, I was just out of college," she began finally, her voice so quiet that Quinn had to lean forward to hear. "Will and I were both training hard. We'd had our sights on the Olympics for years, and we were both doing well. It was an exhilarating time, doubly so for me because I had a major crush on my crew. Denise." She smiled wanly. "We worked so damn well together. And she was into me, too. It didn't take that long for us to get together."

She looked over the desk at Quinn, who nodded in encouragement. "So anyway, we had about two months together, and they were *unbelievable*. Best time of my life; I was happy and we were kicking ass and—"

"You fell in love with her," Quinn finished, her voice soft. She let her thumb rub tiny circles on Corrie's skin. *For comfort.*

"Yeah, I guess I did." Corrie's normally clear green eyes were half-black as they fleetingly met Quinn's glance. They looked like week-old bruises.

"And what happened then?" Quinn prompted, before Corrie could turn her stare back toward the beach.

"It was the first relationship I'd ever had that I couldn't see the end of," she said after a slight pause. "It was intoxicating. And I...I thought she felt the same way." She shook her head fiercely. "Long story short, she ditched me for my brother. Less than a week later, she and Will were fucking each other. I refused to sail with her, so she found another skipper; I didn't make the trials and she did. Along with Will, of course." Her eyes met Quinn's again, and they were far too bright. "Exactly out of a soap opera, see? Completely trite, completely predictable. And pathetic."

Quinn exhaled slowly, keeping her hand firmly on top of Corrie's as her brain struggled to process everything she'd just heard. *Her distance, and how she only sleeps with her friends casually, and how she's always in control.* Quinn was no student of psychology, but it was obvious that Corrie still acutely felt Denise's rejection, not to mention Will's callousness. *And soon they'll both be here at once. Invading Corrie's turf. Her safe place. No wonder she's so upset.* A sudden blaze of white-hot anger rushed under her skin, prickling like static electricity in the wintertime. Startled, she took a few deep breaths and waited for it to subside. *This is not about me. It's about her.*

"I'm sorry that she hurt you," Quinn finally said. The words came slowly, as though pulled from far away. "I wish she weren't coming here, so you wouldn't be reminded of what happened, any more than you already are. And," she said, her voice suddenly growing stronger, "I don't think you're right to say that you're silly, or that this is trite. It happened, and it was real, and you felt everything, and..." She flushed, knowing that she was babbling. "And I have no idea of what I'm trying to say, but whatever it is, I mean it."

Corrie really smiled for the first time since Quinn had poked her head around the door of her office. "Thanks," she said quietly. She closed her eyes for several seconds, enjoying the feeling of Quinn's warm hand covering her own. *Nice.* "You know, I've never...well, I've never told anyone before. Hell, nobody even knew we were dating. Denise wasn't ready to come out to her family." Her lips twisted into a frown. "Guess it's just as well that she didn't."

Quinn's eyebrows arched involuntarily. "You never even told Jen?"

"Not even her." Corrie shrugged and looked away again. Suddenly, she felt more than a little panicked. *What if Quinn says something? What if they all find out what a fool I am? Why the fuck did I just blab it all in the first pla—*

Quinn squeezed Corrie's hand hard. "I won't tell a soul." She mimicked zipping and buttoning her lips with her other hand. "I promise you."

Corrie was surprised when the panicky sensation in her gut subsided as quickly as it had come. The steady, comforting pressure of Quinn's palm and the compassion in her words were conspiring to make Corrie actually believe her, which was nothing short of a miracle.

"All I hope," said Quinn, "is that you whup them good in this year's regatta!"

When Corrie laughed, Quinn grinned back at her and suddenly realized that they'd been holding hands for several minutes. Before her stomach had a chance to get all fluttery, she uncurled her fingers from around Corrie's and got to her feet. "Come outside for a while," she said. "It's a beautiful afternoon, and all these forms aren't going anywhere." With a slight quirk of her lips, she waited a beat before adding, "Unless you throw any more of them out the door, that is."

"Ve-ry funny." Corrie stood up, pushed her chair back, and followed Quinn obediently down the twisting corridors. The anger still smoldered deep in her gut like a live coal, but she felt much more clearheaded, and the aching pressure between her breasts had subsided into a low murmur. *Thanks to Quinn,* she realized. *God, why is she being so nice to me, when I've been such an ass?* Corrie glanced surreptitiously at the woman who walked a few steps in front of her. *She's seen the worst of me, up close and personal, and doesn't even seem fazed. How's that possible?*

There was still no doubt in Corrie's mind that Quinn had a thing for her, but only now could she see that she'd been responding to Quinn's attraction in the wrong way. *Drew was right for once. She wants something...meaningful. Something real. Could I ever give that to her?*

The answer, of course, was an emphatic *no*—the mere thought of trusting someone again made her stomach try to flip inside out. But an idea slowly began to take shape, unfolding and expanding like a sail under wind. Just because she was incapable of maintaining a relationship didn't mean she couldn't pretend. She'd wipe the smirk off Will's face. She'd fool them both, dammit. *I know all the steps. I can go through the motions and they'll never be the wiser.* Quinn would be perfect for the job. And she'd get what she wanted, too. For a while, anyway.

"You've been really good to me today," Corrie said as they turned toward the front door. "I know this is kind of sudden and maybe you have other plans, but can I treat you to dinner this Friday?"

Quinn blinked up at her, clearly surprised. "Oh, you don't have to do that."

"I know, but I want to." When Quinn continued to look dubious, Corrie touched her arm gently. "No strings, Quinn. I just like hanging out with you." She stroked up toward Quinn's elbow, then pulled her hand away as though she hadn't meant to. She even managed a slightly bashful grin. "What do you say?"

Quinn's answering smile was shy but happy. "All right. That sounds fun."

"Great." Struggling to hide her triumph, Corrie held the door for Quinn, and a moment later, they were both inundated by the sights and sounds of the Frisbee game a few yards away.

Corrie watched as Jen snagged the disc out of midair, intercepting a pass meant for Megs, and quickly sent it spinning in Drew's direction. But Brad also saw the throw from his position just beyond Drew, and quickly sprinted forward to try to regain the Frisbee for his own team.

Their collision was worthy of the NFL. Brad slammed into Drew from behind, a split second after Drew jumped to make the catch, and both men went down hard, kicking up a small cloud of sand as they fell.

"Ouch!" said Quinn. "Jeez, I hope they're both okay."

Brad got to his feet slowly, but when Drew stayed on the ground, several of the other players converged on the scene. "Shit, Harris," Corrie muttered. "What the hell did you do now?" She and Quinn joined the growing circle just as Jen asked Drew what was the matter.

"Ankle," he said through gritted teeth. "Twisted it or something." He sat up, breathing heavily, and his face beneath the tan was pale. "Doesn't feel so good."

"You don't look so good," she said, clearly concerned.

Corrie watched as Jen soothingly ran one hand up and down Drew's back while supporting him with the other. Her movements were tender, and Corrie's eyes narrowed in sudden suspicion. *Does Jen like him? Can't be, they're just friends—picking at each other, joking around all the time.*

"I can drive his truck to the hospital," Quinn said, interrupting Corrie's thoughts. "We can put him in the cab, and whoever wants to follow along can meet us there."

"Oh, man," Brad began, one hand on Drew's shoulder. "I'm so sorry."

"Hang on, hang on," said Drew. "The hospital? Can't I just go home and ice it?"

Quinn frowned at him. "Let's see if it'll bear weight."

Once Brad and Jen had helped him to his feet, Drew gingerly set his foot down and immediately hissed in pain. He swayed slightly, and Corrie surged forward to help steady him. *This is bad. Our boat. There's no way we're racing now.* The vision she'd had of crossing the finish line while Will and Denise were still rounding the final buoy melted away. *Dammit!* This was not turning out to be a good day.

"It's at least a bad sprain, and it could be broken," said Quinn. "Regardless, you need x-rays."

"Fine, Doc. Fine. Let's just get it over with."

"I'll follow you to the hospital in my car," Jen told Quinn.

"Can I come with?" asked Corrie. Jen nodded, her attention still focused on Drew.

"Hang on, hang on." Drew grimaced. "Does the whole world really have to come along?"

"Shut up, gimp," Jen said fondly, "and let us take care of you."

Drew sighed in resignation, but one corner of his mouth quirked upward ever so slightly. "All right, Jenny. You win." He tightened his grip on Jen and Brad in preparation for the long hop to the parking lot. "Let's get this show on the road."

❖

A little over two hours later, Drew came limping into the waiting room on crutches, his left leg enclosed in an air cast up to the knee. He worked his way over to where Quinn and Corrie were sitting and settled glumly into the chair next to Quinn, before looking around in confusion.

"Where are Jen and Brad?"

"They went to grab some sodas from the caf," said Corrie. "What's the verdict?"

Drew exhaled and rubbed his eyes. "Grade II sprain. The ligament's partially torn. I'm on crutches for at least two days, in the cast for at least three weeks, and I'll have PT to do after that." He looked over at Corrie, dejection written plainly on his face. "There's no way I can skipper for you, Mars."

Corrie reached across Quinn to squeeze his shoulder. "Yeah, you're not wrong about that."

Drew leaned back in the bucket seat and let his head rest against the wall. "You're going to have to pull somebody in for me. Or skipper yourself and grab someone for crew."

Corrie shook her head and moved back into her own chair. "The gang's all paired up by now," she said. "You know that. It's okay. In fact, it's probably for the best." Managing the regatta was more important anyway. This was probably a blessing in disguise. *Yeah. Right.*

"God, Cor," said Drew, as though he hadn't heard her. "I'm really, really sorry. I shouldn't have been playing that stupid game, and I just—"

"It's all right, you big klutz. Quit feeling guilty, will you? Accidents happen."

There was a long, glum pause during which Drew fiddled with his crutches, Quinn patted him on the knee, and Corrie stared at the ceiling. *Would've been sweet to go up against them, though*, she couldn't help but think. *I really wonder if we could've beaten them.*

"Hey," Drew said slowly. He sat up straighter and looked across Quinn to Corrie, his face serious. "Why does it have to be another instructor? There's still a whole month before the race, why not just train someone else?"

Quinn watched as they looked at each other intently for several seconds, before turning in unison to focus on *her.* Abruptly nervous, her eyes flicked rapidly from one to the other. "Wh—what is this looking at me thing that's happening now?"

"You could do this, Quinn," Drew said excitedly. "You've been sailing a lot, and you already know the 470 pretty well. How much do you weigh?"

Quinn stiffened and glared, but Drew just continued to wait expectantly for an answer. "One-forty," she said finally, her voice nearly inaudible.

Drew nodded eagerly at Corrie. "See? That's not *that* much less than me. The boat won't feel drastically different."

"Yeah, great," Quinn said under her breath.

"It could *work*, Cor. You know it could."

"It could, yeah," said Corrie, "and besides, she has way more tact than you. You're such an ass, Drew." But her exasperation was rapidly giving way to hope. *Perfect, this will be perfect. Me and my girlfriend versus Will and his. A fitting match.*

"Huh?" Drew frowned in confusion. "What? Oh." He had the decency to look sheepish. "Did I mention I'm injured?"

Quinn rolled her eyes at him and smiled reassuringly at Corrie, who leaned forward, elbows on her knees. "So, what do you say, Quinn?"

Quinn's jaw dropped in surprise. "Wait—are you *serious*? I…I don't know anything! I just barely started!"

"Learning to race isn't hard," said Drew. "Besides, all you have to do is take orders from Corrie. She'll be the one in charge."

Quinn blinked and swallowed reflexively as her body reacted. She could feel herself start to blush as all the memories came flooding back. *Hands on my skin, lips on my neck, whispers in the dark I shouldn't have heard.*

"Like Drew said, you already know the boat," Corrie said, thankfully oblivious to Quinn's jarring trip down memory lane. "And we'll have plenty of time to train."

Quinn rubbed her eyes and tried to focus. *What about the time commitment? And heavy competition isn't exactly your cup of tea.* At that thought, she looked up sharply to meet Corrie's gaze.

"But what about Wi—" Flustered, she quickly broke off the sentence. *You just managed to convince her to trust you. Don't blow it!* "Well," she said, trying to cover her slip, "I'd never want to blow the race for you. I know how important it is."

Corrie frowned and shook her head again. "Never mind that," she said firmly. "It's just a big, fun regatta, Quinn, and I'd rather have you than anyone else."

Silence greeted this declaration, and Quinn found herself blinking in surprise yet again. "Even me?" said Drew, pretending to be miffed.

"Now that you're out of the picture." Corrie turned back to Quinn and raised her eyebrows in question.

"Well...okay."

"Okay? Really? You'll do it?"

"I'll do it. But you'll probably be sorry."

Corrie shook her head. "I don't think so."

"You're the best, Q," said Drew.

At that moment, Jen and Brad appeared at the door with several cans of soda cradled in their arms. When Jen saw Drew, her face lit up and she hurried over to them. "Back already? What's the deal? How'd it go? How are you feeling?"

Drew laughed. "Ease up, Jenny. Jeez, I'd almost think you cared or something."

Jen scoffed. "You wish. I just want to know how long I'll be able to mock you."

"Probably a few months," Drew said morosely.

"All right," said Quinn. "Let's get you home. You need to be elevating and icing that ankle, you know."

"Yeah, yeah, yeah."

As Drew grumbled and propped himself upright, Corrie lightly touched Quinn's shoulder. "When do you want to get started? Tomorrow evening, maybe? Or is that too soon?"

"Tomorrow's fine with me. I'll come to your office around five." When Corrie nodded, Quinn cracked a grin. "How about keeping your pens on the desk this time, though, okay?"

"You're very demanding." Corrie said, smiling back. She let her fingertips glide over Quinn's shoulder before pulling away. "But I'll do my best."

❖

Corrie stood at the water's edge, a half-empty beer bottle in hand. The sun had just fallen below her house, but, out past its shadow, the water flickered and glowed as though it were on fire. Frog rooted around happily near the first pylons of her as yet unfinished pier, and Corrie was glad to see that he no longer limped when he moved.

Thinking of Frog's injury made her think about Quinn, of course. Corrie took a long swallow from the bottle and closed her eyes as a gentle gust of wind blew her hair back from her face. Quinn, her project. Her crew for the regatta. *And the keeper of my secrets*, she thought dryly.

Corrie took another sip and massaged the back of her neck with her other hand. Guilt tickled her conscience as she thought about how she was using Quinn. But on the other hand...*I'm giving her what she wants, at least for a little while. And hell, maybe I can even convince her to let me be her first.* That was always gratifying—not to mention fun. *I wonder how Storm's doing?*

In the wake of a sudden wash of heat, Corrie lifted the bottle to her face, vainly attempting to cool down. How could Quinn not understand that she was attractive? Sure, she was no waif, but Corrie had been daydreaming about feeling those curves underneath her fingers again, ever since the day Frog had gotten hurt. *She's sensual. And sensitive. And admit it, you love that she's an innocent. God, wouldn't it be fun to show her what her body can do?*

Suddenly agitated, Corrie downed the rest of her beer in two gulps. The illusion of fire had faded from the water giving way to swirls of deep blue and purple. In the distance, a J-boat sailed a southeastern course toward the harbor. *I can't let my attraction to her get in the way. If she doesn't want sex, fine.* Their relationship was going to be about stability. Commitment. *About showing them I'm not broken, dammit.* She'd indulge Quinn's attraction and rescue her own pride. *There are worse reasons to get involved with someone.*

And then, of course, there was the race itself. They could be a good team; of that much, Corrie was certain. They'd be light and fast, and perhaps even better at communication than she and Drew had been. And maybe—just maybe—if they worked hard enough and got lucky, she had a chance at showing up Will and Denise.

Nodding resolutely, Corrie whistled for Frog and turned toward the house. She had dinner reservations to make, a training regimen to plan, and a few hundred extra sit-ups to do.

CLOSE HAULED

Quinn hurried out of the boathouse, looking around for Corrie as she jogged toward the piers. For the tenth time in the past five minutes, she berated the rubber-neckers who had delayed her commute from the humane society to the waterfront. As she neared the shed, however, her steps slowed. Their 470 was parked out front on its cart, and Corrie was whiling away the time by doing pull-ups on a bar attached to the side of the building. Quinn watched in fascination as she repeatedly raised her chin above the bar. Sweat glistened between her shoulder blades and on her lower back, but her smooth rhythm never even faltered. *God, she's strong!* The play of muscles beneath her skin was mesmerizing. Quinn's eyes avidly followed the contraction of her lats as they rippled upward into the powerful muscles of her trapezius, before everything released in a slow, downward slide. Even her delts were clearly visible as she segued smoothly into yet another pull.

What would they feel like? Quinn's fingers itched as she imagined Corrie's muscles rippling against her palms while she loomed over her in the twilight, pressing into and against her. When a bee buzzed past her head, jolting her from the daydream, Quinn felt her entire neck go up in flames. *Calm down,* she berated herself. *You have serious practicing to do today.*

"Hey," she called out as Corrie finally dropped to the ground, breathing hard. When the word came out as a hoarse croak, she cleared her throat and tried again. "Hey, sorry I'm late. There was an accident on Main and the traffic was awful."

Corrie turned to her with a grin. "Hi ya. And no worries. I figured it was something like that." Enjoying Quinn's appreciative gaze, she swung her arms in a few vigorous circles to limber them up.

"That was impressive," said Quinn. She gestured at the bar. "I can only do half a pull-up." When Corrie looked confused, she clarified. "The down half."

Corrie laughed. "Good one." With an effort, she turned away from Quinn and toward the boat. *Practice now, flirt later.* "Want to get started?"

"Of course." Quinn rocked on her feet. "It's spinnaker day, isn't it?" Truth be told, she was nervous about learning to sail with the chute, especially given what had happened to Corrie in her race against Will.

"Ooh, you said that with just the right amount of trepidation," Corrie said. "And yep, today we're flying chute. But since we need to make sure that it opens outside the other sails, we'll set it up last."

Quinn nodded. "Okay, so we should just rig the boat normally for now?"

Corrie's eyes sparkled. "You should rig the boat normally, while I laze about and give you a pop quiz on the stuff we've talked about over the past week."

Quinn saluted playfully. "Yes, drill sergeant!"

As she screwed in the plugs, Corrie leaned against the side of the shed and crossed her arms. "So," she said, "tell me about the kind of race we'll be sailing in. What's it called, and what's it like?"

"A triangle course," said Quinn. She fed the foot of the mainsail into the groove along the boom, her brow furrowed in concentration. "There are three buoys: the windward mark, the leeward mark, and the..." her voice trailed off and she looked up sheepishly. "Little help here, sarge?"

"The jibe mark," Corrie said. "Now get down and gimme twenty!"

Refusing to take the bait, Quinn returned to rigging the mainsail. "I can only do half of a pushup, too." She fastened the tack of the sail into its pin and worked her way along the edge of the material to find the head. "So, in this race, we'll first sail toward the windward mark, by tacking back and forth, right?"

"Right." Corrie stepped up to begin unrolling the jib.

"What happened to 'You rig this boat, peon?'" Quinn asked.

Corrie shrugged. "You're too slow." When Quinn sniffed indignantly, she grinned. "Aw, I'm just putting you on. You know that. But since you really do know how to rig up, I may as well help."

"How charitable of you." Quinn rolled her eyes. "Now where was I?"

"The windward mark."

"So we round the windward mark, and then we'll be on a broad reach—somewhere between sailing perpendicular to the wind, and completely running with it. We'll head for the jibe mark and jibe around it, before finishing a lap by tacking around the leeward mark."

"Right on," Corrie said as she tied figure-eight knots in the ends of the jib sheets to prevent them from ever coming completely loose. "How many laps will one race be?"

Quinn's brow furrowed as she concentrated on looping the main halyard through a set of pulleys at the base of the mast. "Um...three laps."

"Yep. And how many races?"

Quinn hauled briefly on the halyard, and the main sail rose smoothly up the mast for a few feet. Satisfied, she tied it off with a cleat hitch. "Six total, but only five count." She turned to Corrie. "Will we sail in all six?"

Corrie shrugged. "What do you think we should do?"

Quinn mulled over the question as she double-checked the outhaul and the tightness of the boom vang. "I guess we should probably sail the first five as hard as we can, obviously. And then, if we're not happy, we should do the last one."

"Sounds like a plan." Corrie stepped back from the boat, looked it over, and nodded. "Rigged to perfection." When Quinn joined her just off the port side, she indicated the small sail wrapped in multicolored line that waited on the ground. Beside it waited a thin, three-foot long pole that boasted what looked like some sort of clipping mechanism on each end.

"This," Corrie began, bending to pick up both objects, "is the spinnaker and the spinnaker pole. Did you get a chance to read about it, at all?"

"A little," said Quinn, reaching out to take a corner of the sail and run it between her index finger and thumb. "It's made out of the same stuff as a parachute, right?"

"Which is why it's also called the chute, yeah."

"And you only put it up when you're on a reach or running with the wind?"

"Exactly." Corrie began to unwind the line from around the sail. "The chute is the most finicky sail in the biz, no matter what boat you're sailing. It's hard to trim, but if you get it working right, your craft will just soar. This baby fills up with wind and essentially pulls us along, so fast that we'll actually start planing over the waves." She smiled brilliantly. "And let me tell you just what a rush that is—the bow lifts up out of the water and it's practically like flying."

Quinn was mesmerized. The way Corrie's face lit up when she was completely absorbed in the joys of sailing was, well, it was beautiful. *Oh, stop it*, Quinn immediately chastised herself. *Focus, idiot. This is important!* "And it'll be my job to keep it under control?" she asked.

Corrie ran her fingers along the edges of the sail as she focused on Quinn. "From the time we round that windward mark, up until the time we start to round the leeward mark, the only thing you'll be thinking about is how to keep the spinnaker filled with air."

Quinn felt her stomach drop into her aqua shoes. *Can I really do this? Corrie keeps saying it's not a big deal, and on one level she means it, but...*Quinn couldn't deny that she wanted to defeat Will and Denise out there on the water, almost as much as she knew Corrie did. For some reason, the regatta had become very important within the past week. *I will not let her down.*

Straightening her shoulders, Quinn stuffed her self-doubt into a dark corner of her brain and mentally slammed the door on it. She nodded sharply to Corrie. "All right, then. Show me how to set this thing up."

For the next hour, Corrie explained and demonstrated the mechanics of flying a spinnaker. She taught Quinn to rig it properly and showed her just how bad it would be if it were to become entangled with the jib or the main. She described in careful detail the processes of raising and dousing the spinnaker, emphasizing the need for smooth, efficient movements in order to keep the boat steady and sailing as quickly as possible. And last of all, she demonstrated the art of "jibing the pole," during which process Quinn would have to quickly detach the spinnaker from its pole, switch the pole to the opposite side of the mast, and reattach the sail while Corrie jibed the boat.

"Ready to get this thing in the water?" Corrie asked finally, as Quinn wiped the sweat out of her eyes from her efforts during their practice jibe.

"Yes!" she said, eager to feel the cooling spray of the waves. "Definitely."

She grabbed the painter as Corrie pushed the boat down the ramp alongside the first pier and efficiently tied it off in an expert bowline knot. For a long moment, she stared at the length of line, and her lips curved in satisfaction. *Guess I really have learned something.* It was a good feeling. But then she remembered just how very much she still didn't know and quickly slid into the boat to raise the mainsail and lower the centerboard.

"Here's the plan," said Corrie as Quinn shoved them away from the dock and took her place on the windward gunwale. "Since the wind's out of the northeast today, we're going to practice sailing upwind for about half an hour, fast as we can, before turning around and raising the chute. We'll do a bunch of jibes to get you familiar with how everything works. Sound okay?"

"Yes," Quinn called over the rush of the wind. They were sailing close-reached, and it was noisy. She hauled in on the jib until it stopped flapping and immediately hiked out as the boat began to heel. Beside her, Corrie was making adjustments to the traveler and the main sail.

"Let's go for a close haul!" she shouted after a few seconds.

"Okay," Quinn replied, pulling on the jib sheets once again. Corrie threw her weight out to starboard as the boat tried to tip over, and Quinn leaned back as far as she could, extending her body parallel over the water. Her stomach muscles groaned, but she ignored them. The wind was brisk against her cheeks, the salt water stung her chapped lips, and the heat of Corrie's right arm burned against her left as they both strained to level out the boat.

"Sweet breeze today!" Corrie grinned widely. She let loose with a loud war whoop, tightened the main sheet even further, and hiked out hard.

They spent the next half hour tacking back and forth across the eye of the wind. Corrie couldn't help but be impressed by how smoothly Quinn was moving. After only a week of serious work, she was already getting a feel for Corrie's style of sailing. *And the way her T-shirt rides up so I can see some skin once in a while doesn't hurt, either.*

In that instant of distraction, Corrie nearly lost control of the tiller and had to leap back inside the boat as it careened wildly toward starboard. Quinn pulled her body back in from the gunwale, her quad muscles working furiously to support her body weight. "What happened?" she shouted in concern. "Was that a knock that I didn't see?"

"No," Corrie called back. "I just fucked up. Sorry." *Focus, dammit!* Once the boat was back under control, she risked another brief glance at Quinn. "You ready to bear off and raise the chute?"

Quinn took a deep breath and nodded before remembering that on a boat, every command had to be given and accepted vocally. "Ready," she said firmly, despite the fact that her palms were sweating. *You can do this. You just went through it all on shore.* But, even she was experienced enough to know that drilling on land and performing on the water were like night and day.

Corrie watched the emotions flicker over Quinn's face, faster than the wind that drove their boat. She felt an abrupt surge of protectiveness. Quinn was trying so hard, learning so earnestly, and Corrie never wanted her to feel frustrated or anxious—especially about sailing. "Here we go," she said. "Why don't you get that pole up first, and then we'll raise the chute."

"Okay." Quinn moved as far toward the bow as she was able. Her hands fumbled as she clipped the pole into the topping lift and the mast before attaching its far end to the spinnaker guy. "Got it," she said finally.

"I'm gonna pop it." Corrie shifted the main sheet to her tiller hand so that she could haul back on the spinnaker halyard. As the red and white chute rose into the air beyond the jib, it began to inflate and the boat jerked forward sharply. "Trim, trim!" Corrie shouted, cleating off the line and adjusting the boat so that it turned downwind. She threw her weight hard out to port as Quinn struggled to keep the spinnaker inflated.

"How am I doing?" Quinn called over her shoulder, never taking her eyes from the sail.

"Beautiful," Corrie said, referring as much to Quinn as to the puffy sail. "Feel how much faster we're going?"

Quinn looked back to inspect their boat's wake, and her eyes widened at the churning waves. But, at that very moment, the wind shifted slightly and the starboard edge of the chute began to curl down toward the mast. "Watch it!" said Corrie, and Quinn immediately pulled in on the sheet so that the sail returned to maximum power.

"Finicky is right!" she shouted over the rushing sounds of the wind and the water. Her eyes remained fixed on the chute, and Corrie watched approvingly as she played the line in and out, always testing.

Just like I showed her. Jeez, she's a fast learner! "Let's go for a jibe," she said after another minute. "Remember, you pass the line back to me, jibe the pole, and then start trimming again."

"You'll jibe the mainsail afterward?"

"That's right." Corrie held the tiller extension between her legs, grasped the mainsheet tightly in her right hand, and took the line that Quinn offered in her left. Their fingers brushed fleetingly before Quinn detached both ends of the pole. She managed to clip the pole back in to the opposite side of the line, but it took several precious seconds before she managed to close the other end over the ring in the mast. In the meantime, Corrie expertly flew the chute without the pole, trimming the main all the while and making small adjustments to the rudder by shifting her legs. When Quinn finally looked up from the pole, the sight of Corrie single-handing the boat made her catch her breath in awe. It was one thing to watch from far away as she controlled the boat alone, but another thing entirely to be right there with her.

How is she doing that? God, she's good, and so intense—that sheer focus, not to mention strength. Quinn suddenly realized that she was standing in the bow gaping at Corrie when she should be taking back the spinnaker sheet and getting ready for the boat to jibe. "I've got it," she said, covering her hand briefly as she took over the line.

"Ready to jibe?"

"Ready."

Quinn ducked as the boom sailed over her head, and she immediately sat down hard on the starboard gunwale. To her credit, the chute remained inflated. She tucked her feet under the hiking strap as Corrie adjusted their sail position. "That's tough! How long does it take the Olympians to jibe the pole?"

Corrie grinned in her direction. "About five seconds."

Quinn's jaw dropped, and in that split second of inattention, the chute began to curl in again. "That's incredible," she said once she had everything back under control.

"It is. But don't worry about speed for now. Just try to make the motion as smooth as you can." Corrie shifted the mainsheet into her tiller hand so that she could reach forward to gently clasp Quinn's shoulder. "You did a great job, that time. Most people have a lot more trouble than that."

Quinn leaned out as a small puff of wind hit their sails, then hiked back in once it had passed. The spinnaker line pulled against her gloved fingers, as though the sail were a racehorse chomping at the bit. "I can do better, Skipper," she said. "Let's try it again."

Corrie squeezed Quinn's shoulder once more before settling back into the boat and returning the tiller to its position between her knees. "Aye aye, matey. Prepare to jibe!"

❖

Over an hour later, Corrie and Quinn trudged wearily up from the shoreline, their arms burdened with sails and lifejackets. "Well, I'm beat," Corrie said as they turned toward the shed. She rolled her shoulders. "Do you have lots of studying to do tonight?" She had learned right away that Quinn usually spent her mornings and evenings studying for her exam in late August.

"Mmm," said Quinn. She licked her salty lips, wishing for nothing more than a bottomless glass of water and a long, cool shower. "Large animal anatomy review."

"Large animals?" Corrie asked, shouldering open the door and holding it as Quinn brushed past her. "Like...cows?"

Quinn laughed tiredly. "Yep, like cows."

"There you are!" Jen hailed them from behind the desk. "Mars, the harbormaster called for you. Something about negotiating mooring fees for the regatta..." she trailed off and arched her eyebrows.

Corrie tossed her pile of equipment onto the desk and scrubbed her palms over her face. "He wants to charge us an arm and a leg, but I'm not gonna let him." She sighed heavily. "No rest for the weary."

"You guys look wiped," Jen said as Quinn set down her own equipment with a matching sigh. "Go home. I'll take care of this stuff."

"I owe you," said Corrie gratefully, turning back toward the door.

"You better believe you do!" Jen's sassy reply followed them out into cooling air. High cirrus clouds feathered the western sky, and Corrie tilted her head back to enjoy the caress of the breeze against her sweaty face.

"Hi ya, sis." Will's all too familiar voice immediately forced Corrie back down to earth. He stood a few feet away, a short windsurfer board tucked under one arm. The sun lit up his face and cast a long shadow behind him on the sand.

"Will." She nodded coolly.

"What'cha been up to?"

"Just out for a sail with Quinn." Corrie very deliberately brushed Quinn's shoulder with her own. "Quinn, my brother, Will." As they shook hands, Corrie watched Quinn's face. Her expression was measuring, somehow. Evaluative. And she wasn't acting shy in the slightest. *Almost seems like she wants to protect me.*

"Sweet day out there, huh?" Will asked, clearly in the mood to chat.

"It was, yes," said Quinn briskly. "A good day to practice racing."

Corrie blinked in surprise at Quinn's subtle trash talking. *Way to throw down!* Of course, that had probably gone right over Will's head. Still, Corrie felt pleased at Quinn's defensiveness. She grinned and jerked her head toward the boathouse. "I've got to get back to the office," she said.

"I'm walking your way," Quinn answered.

"Have a good one, ladies," said Will as he strutted toward the shed.

"Cocky bastard, isn't he?" Corrie rubbed the back of her neck with one hand. She always got tense when he was around. Not even Quinn going to bat for her could change that.

"I did get that impression," Quinn agreed. Her eyes narrowed slightly. "But we'll beat him."

"I hope you're right, I really do."

They paused in front of the boathouse door where they would part ways, and not for the first time, Corrie had to forcibly restrain herself from leaning in to claim a kiss from Quinn. *Don't rush her, you ass. You know she wants you. It's just a matter of time.* Why the hell was patience so damn hard?

"Have a good night." Quinn's words were accompanied by a sweet smile.

"You, too," was all Corrie said. And then she turned around, pushed open the door, and forced herself not to look back.

❖

Quinn was early for the next day's lesson—so early, in fact, that she found Corrie taking an impromptu nap on her desk. Long, blonde hair cascaded over her folded arms to fan out on the unusually clean surface, and Quinn spent several seconds watching the slow rise and fall of Corrie's hunched shoulders as she inhaled and exhaled deeply. *Wish I could see her face*, she thought idly. *I bet she'd look so innocent asleep. And young.*

She took a few steps forward, until she was close enough to reach out and lightly touch the top of Corrie's head. "Wake up, Mars." The golden hair was soft between her fingers as she stroked gently. *Just like I imagined it.*

Corrie shifted beneath her hand and inhaled noisily. She raised her face toward Quinn, her eyes blinking repeatedly as though in disbelief that it could possibly be the right time for alertness.

"Wh...what happened?" Corrie's voice was low and gravelly, and Quinn barely stopped herself from thinking about what it might be like to wake up to that sound. Barely.

"You must have fallen asleep," she said. "It's nearly five o'clock."

Corrie yawned and leaned back in her chair as her entire body vibrated in a long stretch. "Oh, man," she replied. "Sorry 'bout that! Thanks for waking me up." She rubbed her eyes and looked dazedly up at Quinn. A second later, she frowned. "You look tired."

Quinn took a step back and laughed. "And you don't?"

Corrie flushed but held her ground. "Did you sleep okay last night?"

Quinn shrugged. "As a matter of fact, I didn't." She grinned sheepishly. "I know this is ridiculous, but I dreamt about jibing the pole for hours."

"Really?" Corrie shook her head. "That's pretty crazy."

"At least I've been visualizing," said Quinn. "I've heard that can be very valuable for athletes." She paused for a silent moment, during which Corrie simply continued to blink sleepily up at her. "So," she finally broke the spell. "More chute practice today, right?"

Corrie finally got to her feet, palms pressing down hard against the desk. She stretched again, and Quinn's gaze traveled down her long torso to pause at the narrow sliver of tan abdominal muscles revealed by the sensuous movement. *She's just as sexy now as when she's wearing only that damn sports bra,* Quinn realized, before her rational brain was able to shove the thought way back into the appropriate dark, dank, cobwebby corner of her mind. It was getting positively crowded in there.

"How about..." Corrie began slowly. "What if we scrap practice today?" When Quinn's eyebrows tried to climb into her hairline, Corrie smiled. "I'm exhausted. So are you. And you're clearly stressed about the chute. Otherwise you wouldn't have been dreaming about it." She paused briefly, but when Quinn just stood still and waited, Corrie decided to go for the gold.

"So let's take a break today, and instead of sailing, we can grab a pizza and then watch *Wind* at my place. It's this movie about the America's Cup, and there's lots of sailing in it, and it's a romance too, I guess—" Realizing that she was babbling, Corrie fell silent and stared across the width of her desk at Quinn, who, she suddenly realized, was nodding.

"That sounds wonderful," Quinn replied, ignoring the clamor of her psyche's warning bells. *Oh, shut up, we can watch a film together without me jumping into bed with her.* She looked down at the scuffed floor, then back up at Corrie. "I guess I could use a day off, to be honest."

Her embarrassed admission was enough to galvanize Corrie into action. "No shame in that. We've been working hard." She picked up the phone and started dialing. "I'll take care of the pizza—pepperoni?" When Quinn nodded, Corrie dialed swiftly and placed the order.

"I have my car today," Quinn said as soon as she hung up. "It's out in the lot."

"Great, and I have the movie at the house." Corrie sidestepped the desk as she began to collect the belongings she wanted to take home. "Pizza will be ready in fifteen, they say."

Quinn shouldered her backpack. "Thanks for the break, Skipper."

Just over twenty minutes later, Quinn pulled into Corrie's driveway and cut the engine. Corrie jumped out and opened the back passenger's side door for Frog, who bounded happily around the border of his property before prancing eagerly alongside Corrie as she unlocked the front door.

"He has so much energy," said Quinn, leaning down to pat the top of his sleek head. "Like mother, like child?"

Corrie scoffed and pushed the door open. "Like I have so much energy. Don't forget who you found asleep today."

"That was a fluke." Quinn carried the warm pizza through the door, down the narrow hall, and finally deposited it on one of the kitchen counters.

"What do you want to drink?" asked Corrie, opening the fridge and peering inside. "I still have a bunch of wine coolers from—"

Corrie abruptly cut off, but Quinn knew what she had been going to say. *From when you were here for dinner. From when you let me kiss you.* She opened the pizza box and reached up for two plates, even as heat blossomed beneath her skin at the memory. "A wine cooler sounds great," Quinn said. Her voice didn't tremble, but the plates clattered together slightly in her hand.

When she turned around, Corrie handed her a bottle. She looked curious, and perhaps even a little nervous, as if she was concerned by how Quinn would react to the memory.

"Thanks." Quinn grinned up at her. "I'll never understand why you like that stuff," she said wryly, gesturing at Corrie's beer. "At least *this* is nice and sweet."

To Quinn's relief, Corrie rose to the bait and the awkwardness disappeared. "Are you kidding me? *That* tastes like cough syrup." She raised her bottle and sipped, then rolled her neck back in satisfaction. "*This* is fantastic—light and smooth and—"

"Yuck," Quinn said decisively. "And absolute yuck." She held out a plate to Corrie. "Since we're never going to agree, let's just watch this movie, already."

"Now who's the drill sergeant?" Corrie muttered as she followed Quinn into the den. Quinn settled down on the couch, while Corrie fiddled with the DVD player before sprawling on the floor at her feet.

The film began with a sailing action sequence, and Quinn found herself peppering Corrie with so many questions that it soon became necessary to pause the DVD at regular intervals so that she could adequately explain what they were seeing. Despite the fact that her body was tired and sore from yesterday's exertion, she found herself exhilarated by the racing scenes. *I really* do *love this sport*, she realized.

"See how they're using trapezes there?" Corrie asked several minutes later, as the film segued into a shot of the two protagonists on a smaller boat. Their bodies were completely extended, so that only the balls of their feet rested on the gunwales. Corrie paused the disc and pointed out their harnesses and the trapeze lines. She looked over at Quinn and quirked a grin. "The 470 is rigged for trap, you know," she said. "We'll start working on that next week."

Quinn nodded enthusiastically until a horrifying thought suddenly froze her in her seat. "But...well, you don't trapeze like that *and* trim the spinnaker at the same time. Do you?"

Corrie's eyes widened. "'Course! It's the toughest thing you'll ever do in your whole life, but it's so much fun, and the boat really flies on days when that's—"

"Nuh-uh, no," said Quinn, shaking her head. "No way. I *cannot* do that."

Corrie reached out to touch Quinn's knee, rubbing circles against her skin as she spoke. "Sure you can. Plenty of people have learned. And besides, I have complete faith in you."

Quinn blinked. She knew she should tell Corrie to take her hand away, but the warmth of her touch was irresistible. "Why?"

Corrie frowned as she realized that she really did mean it. "Because you've never given me a reason not to," she said finally, looking up to meet Quinn's curious gaze. "Because I see you out there every day, trying for all you're worth to get years of sailing experience in a matter of weeks." Suddenly uncomfortable with how downright mushy she was sounding, Corrie tried to shrug nonchalantly. "I mean, sure, you'll end up in the drink a whole bunch as soon as we start practicing that combination. But I *know* you're capable."

Quinn couldn't think of anything to say to that, so finally she nodded and indicated the remote. "C'mon, I want to see if they win." Corrie took her hand off Quinn's knee in order to press Play, and Quinn tried not to think about just how much she missed the warm pressure of her palm.

As it turned out, the main characters merrily capsized into the ocean only a few seconds later, but at least they were joking around about it. *Humor is the missing link*, Quinn decided. *No matter what happens when we're out there racing, I should be able to laugh. But how am I supposed to do that, when making a wrong move might mean that they beat us?*

Fortunately, that particular line of thought was interrupted a few minutes later as the male and female leads made their way below decks on one of the larger boats. The flirting and foreplay were unmistakable, and Quinn couldn't resist shoving Corrie's right shoulder with one bare foot.

"So," she asked mischievously, hoping to regain their previous lighter mood. "Have you ever done that?"

Corrie turned toward her with a skeptical expression. "Have I ever had sex in an America's Cup boat?" She shook her head adamantly. "No."

"Do you think it would be comfortable?" A distant part of Quinn wondered where in the hell these questions were coming from. She tilted her wine cooler up to her lips, only to discover that the bottle was empty. *Ah*, she thought. *I must be just the tiniest bit buzzed.*

Corrie, who was now grinning at her widely, jerked her head toward the bottle. "Bit of a lightweight, are we?"

"I am *not*," said Quinn. She didn't *feel* buzzed, just nice and relaxed. Quite the pleasant sensation, really. "And you didn't answer my question."

Corrie rolled her eyes. "No, I don't think it would be comfortable." She waited for a beat before adding, "But then again, sometimes comfort isn't all it's cracked up to be."

Quinn chewed on that enigmatic statement for a moment. Corrie could practically hear the wheels spinning in her head. *I'll fuck you on any boat you like, Quinn. Just name it.*

"Interesting," Quinn said finally.

Corrie could tell she was trying to play it cool. It was cute. She gestured toward the television. "Too bad they don't show more of the scene. Maybe we could get some ideas." She waggled her eyebrows.

Quinn blushed but held her ground. "They're straight. I'll pass."

Corrie laughed. "Good point. Now shut up and watch the movie."

They bantered back and forth throughout the rest of the film, and Quinn even found herself cheering for the American boat at the end. When the credits finally rolled, she got up stiffly from the couch, grabbed Corrie's plate, and made her way into the kitchen to put both plates in the sink. When she returned, Corrie was watching her critically.

"You sore?"

"A little bit," Quinn replied. "Quads and shoulders, mostly."

Corrie got to her feet and gestured toward the space in front of the couch. "I'll give you a massage, if you want." At Quinn's surprised look, she rolled her eyes. "Just a shoulder massage, I promise." She waited for a beat before winking. "Unless you'd rather—"

"That sounds great," Quinn interrupted, blushing slightly. She sat down with her back to the couch, feeling Corrie settle above and behind her on the cushions. When gentle fingers began rubbing in circles at the junction of her neck and shoulders, she exhaled slowly.

"Let me know if I'm doing this too hard." As Corrie spoke, her lips brushed Quinn's right ear, and she barely managed to suppress a shudder.

"Okay," Quinn said, allowing her head to sink down until her chin pressed lightly against her sternum. Corrie's fingers were soft but also firm, and Quinn gradually relaxed. It was so easy to close her eyes and drift under Corrie's touch—to be comforted by the gentle strokes of her fingertips as she worked across the nape of Quinn's neck, slowly progressing down toward her triceps and biceps.

Corrie felt Quinn melt into her hands, against her legs, as the tension began to drain from her body. She felt good—so soft, so warm. Corrie was about to place a light kiss on a small sunburned patch of skin on Quinn's left shoulder before she caught herself. *Dammit!* If she hadn't been trying to make this relationship thing happen, no power on earth could have stopped her from laying on the seduction, right then and there.

Suddenly, she could see exactly what she was doing, as though she were a voyeur at the window. *Leading you on. Using you.* Disgusted with herself, she bit her lower lip and backed off. *Why are you trusting me, Quinn? You really shouldn't. And what kind of monster am I to be treating you like this?*

When Corrie finally stopped touching her, Quinn had no idea whether she'd been sitting still for minutes or hours, her body was so suffused with lassitude. "Mmm," she said, raising her head with difficulty. "Thank you. You're very good at that." Instead of shifting away, she let her cheek rest lightly against the outside of Corrie's leg.

But she loves it, Corrie realized. *Look how much she loves it. She's craving this, the attention I'm giving. Hell, I'm making her dreams come true.*

"Not a problem," she replied softly. "You were pretty tense." She reached out with one hand to lightly massage Quinn's scalp. Quinn's answering moan made Corrie's pulse jump, and she shifted slightly on the couch. *Fucking hell. If I push her now she'll freak, and if I don't get off soon, I'm gonna explode!*

But asking Quinn to please leave so she could have some one-on-one time with her right hand was hardly an option. She didn't want to push Quinn away, either, especially since she felt so damn good. *But if we keep up this cuddling business, I'm going to lose it.*

Quinn hummed, her breath blowing lightly over Corrie's kneecap. "It's getting late and I know you're tired. I should go."

"No, don't." The words were out before she could stop them. Quinn pulled away and looked up at Corrie apprehensively. "I mean," said Corrie, "uh, that I have a guest room that you can stay in. You're tired too, after all."

Quinn blinked, considering her options. *Stay, stay, stay,* her body clamored, wishing for nothing more than a soft bed and a dreamless sleep. *Go, go, go* urged her brain, discomfited by Corrie's closeness and her own visceral reaction to it.

"I'll make you an omelet in the morning." Corrie was liking this idea more and more. It would fool Quinn into thinking that she wasn't just a sex fiend. "And Frog will sleep at the foot of your bed, if you let him."

Quinn's face lit up. "All right," she said. "I'll stay. Thank you."

"Not a problem. Let me show you your room."

Once she was certain that Quinn had everything she needed, Corrie left the guest room and returned to the kitchen to clean up. She found herself humming as she loaded the dishwasher, and grinned sheepishly at herself in the hall mirror as she finally returned to the second floor. It felt nice, somehow, to have another person in the house, just *being*—even if the fact that they weren't fucking was simultaneously threatening to drive her through the roof. *What the hell is going on with me?*

She paused outside the guest room and heard the slight jingle of Frog's collar. *Lucky dog.* "Good night, Quinn," she called. *What are you wearing to bed? Nothing? Doubtful. Just your T-shirt, or...*

Her cheerful mood evaporated as she suddenly considered pushing the door open. It would be so easy to step inside the room, pin Quinn to the bed, and kiss her until she stopped protesting. *I could make her want me enough. I could make her give in. It'd be so easy.* With an effort, Corrie shook her head and backed away. These mood swings were getting way out of control.

"Good night, Corrie," said Quinn, her voice muffled by the door. "Thanks again."

Corrie felt a hot trickle of shame run up her neck and into her cheeks. *Thanks. She said thanks. And you were seriously contemplating going in there and making it so she wouldn't want to say no.* Turning away before her mind could change again, she went to her bedroom, closed the door, and threw herself down on the bed. *Damn you, Denise,* she cursed silently. *If I'd never met you, I wouldn't be like this.*

In the past, these bouts of self-chastisement had often lasted for hours. Mercifully, the fatigue of the past few days claimed her almost immediately.

❖

Just a few minutes after nine o'clock, Quinn let herself into the apartment as quietly as she was able, only to find Drew sitting in the kitchen and drinking a cup of coffee. His injured leg, still in a brace, stretched out perpendicular to the table. At her entrance, he quickly turned toward the door.

"Out all night, Quinnie Quinn Quinn?" He waggled his eyebrows. "Where have you been, huh?"

"Hush, you," she said, shutting the door further behind her. "I just spent the night at Corrie's, that's all."

Drew bolted up from the table so quickly that his coffee sloshed over the top of the mug. "You did *what*? Oh *no*, I should have known she'd try something like—"

"Drew!" Quinn said sharply. When he stopped his tirade, she pointed at his vacated chair. "Sit down."

He did as she told him, though his fingers twitched spasmodically against the armrests of his chair. "Now listen to me. I spent the night in Corrie's *guest room*, because I was too tired to drive home. I didn't...I really don't appreciate you leaping to conclusions like that."

Drew looked embarrassed and opened his mouth, but Quinn forestalled him with one raised hand. "And I'm perfectly capable of taking care of myself, so will you stop worrying?"

"You don't understand," he said. "She'll want you one minute, and the next minute you'll just be her friend. She's more than a little bit predatory, Quinn, and I don't want her to hurt you."

Quinn stood still for several seconds, considering Corrie's demeanor over the past several weeks. Predatory? Sometimes. But mean? Never. Quinn felt certain that Drew was only seeing the surface image willingly projected by Corrie to the rest of the world. Arrogant, sexy, and casual—fun, but slightly dangerous—yes, Corrie was all of those things. But, she was also vulnerable and gentle and hurting and compassionate. Quinn felt the ghostly echo of Corrie's fingers against the back of her neck, and in that moment she felt very strongly that she was privileged to see further beneath the surface than perhaps anyone had before. *Maybe I'm just naïve. But you know what? I don't care.*

She squeezed his shoulder lightly. "You don't know everything about her," she said. "So don't you go judging, okay?"

Drew sighed. "Okay, okay. Sorry. I just overreacted."

"Besides," said Quinn, hoping she wouldn't blush, "it's not like that at all. We're just friends." Quickly, she turned toward her bedroom. Drew knew her too well. If he saw her face, he'd realize she was lying.

Because we're not just friends, Quinn finally dared to think. *She wants more...and so do I.*

LIGHT AND VARIABLE

Corrie shoved her keys in her pocket with one hand and slid open the bottom drawer of her desk with the other. She bent closer to inspect the row of videotapes before finally selecting two from near the front. When she straightened up, Jen was lounging in the doorway.

"Did you finally manage to kick that motorboat off the pier?" She shook her head in disgust. "Those idiots looked like they were giving you a hard time."

Corrie grimaced. "Apparently, Will told his frat boy friends that they could park at the dock for as long as they wanted. Or so they said, anyway." She moved out from behind the desk, then leaned against it. "They were sloshed. I made them leave and then called the sheriff."

Jen grinned. "Excellent." She gestured toward the tapes in Corrie's hand. "What're those for?"

"Footage from old regattas. I want Quinn to see what some real races look like so we can start simulating them."

Jen looked at Corrie skeptically. "Isn't it a little soon for that? You guys have only been practicing for what, two weeks?"

"We've got to pack in a lot if we want to do well." *If we want to beat them.*

Jen cocked her head. "And that's the point, here? Doing well?"

Corrie huffed a sigh. "Don't give me that. Quinn is into this. She wants to learn, so I'm going to teach her."

Jen cocked one eyebrow. "And is sailing the only thing you're 'teaching' her?"

"Very funny, ha ha." Corrie rolled her eyes at the innuendo.

"That's not an answer."

"It's none of your business!"

"Ooh," said Jen. "This is serious."

Corrie shrugged, knowing that Jen would read into her nonchalance. "I like her."

"You *like* her?"

"Yeah. She's nice. She's fun. I enjoy spending time with her." Corrie very nearly had to bite her lower lip to stave off laughter. Jen's face was priceless. Her eyes were practically bugging out of her head. *This will be all over the boathouse by tomorrow morning,* she thought smugly. The more *real* she and Quinn looked, the better. But, then the guilt stirred in her gut, hot and sharp. *It's not like I'm lying, either. I do like her, and—*

"Are you telling me," said Jen, "that the notoriously untamable Corrie Marsten is finally thinking of settling down with someone for more than one night?"

Corrie shrugged again, hoping her conscience would get the message. "Maybe. We'll see." She deliberately glanced down at her watch. "I've got to get going. I don't want to be late."

"Corrie's got a da-ate. This is unbelievable!"

"Yeah, yeah." She gestured for Jen to proceed out the door before her. "No need to sing about it."

"Are you kidding me? I think I may write an entire musical about this!"

Corrie looked at her sternly. She had to at least make it look like she didn't want the rumor afloat after all. "Vetoed. Period."

Jen smiled sweetly, fluttered her eyelashes, and began buffing her nails against the shoulder of her T-shirt. She didn't move. "What incentive will you give me to keep quiet?"

Corrie folded her arms under her breasts. Two could play at this game. "I won't tell Drew that you're crushing on him."

Jen's eyes widened in surprise. "What?"

"You've been spending a lot of time with him lately." Even as Corrie smirked, she watched Jen closely, hoping to discover whether what she suspected was true.

"He just feels left out, you know, since everybody is sailing except him." Jen was clearly backpedaling. "And me."

Corrie winked. "Of course." She felt another stab of guilt, though, at the memory of going home with him a few weeks ago. *You've gotta tell me these things, kiddo,* she thought uneasily. She gestured toward the door. "Shall we?"

Jen cleared her throat and promptly changed the subject. "So hey," she said as they walked down the hallway, "you should bring Quinn along to Block Island."

Corrie raised her eyebrows, realizing that in the chaos of organizing the regatta, she'd forgotten all about the instructors' annual weekend trip across the Sound to Block Island. *Next weekend, already.* "You know, maybe I will."

"Brad says he's going to beat you there this year, FYI. He's been talking a lot of smack whenever you haven't been around."

Corrie shook her head. "What a crock of shit! I guarantee he'll be riding my wake into New Harbor."

"I'll be sure to tell him you said so," said Jen, laughing. She stopped just inside the front door. "You have a good night, now. Don't do anything I wouldn't do."

Corrie just rolled her eyes once more in Jen's direction before shouldering her way through the door and into the warm, moist air of the early evening.

❖

Quinn surveyed the shirts hanging in her closet, nibbling absently at her bottom lip as she tried to figure out what to wear. The short-sleeved pink Oxford was too baggy, and the white tank all by itself felt far too revealing. She took a step back and ran her fingers through her hair, pausing briefly to work through a tangle.

"This is ridiculous. We're having Chinese food and watching old sailing videos. It does *not* matter what shirt I wear."

Except that it did matter, for some reason that Quinn truly did not wish to examine very closely, and Corrie would be ringing the doorbell any minute, and if she didn't have any shirt on at all—. Quinn couldn't suppress a hysteria-tinged giggle as she considered the consequences of greeting Corrie in her bra.

Focus, focus, focus, she told herself, returning her attention to the closet. *Not that one...no, and not that one either...and* definitely *not that one!* Her hand abruptly fell on a black, three-quarters-sleeved top that her mother had bought her during a spring visit last year. Quinn had never worn it anywhere but in the dressing room. She'd proclaimed it far too tight, but her mother had insisted that the shirt would act as incentive for Quinn to drop a few pounds.

Quinn started to put it back but found herself pulling it off the hanger instead. The shirt was surprisingly comfortable, despite its snug fit. And yes, it accentuated the fullness of her torso, but...*Corrie likes my curves,* she reminded herself shyly. *And it sure looks a lot nicer than the grubby T-shirts I've been wearing to practice in for the past two weeks.*

The doorbell rang. Quinn's reflection stared back at her with wide eyes. "Choice made," she said, before moving quickly toward the door.

Corrie stood on the other side, holding two videotapes in one hand and a bag from China Express in the other. Quinn sniffed appreciatively. "That smells really good."

Corrie swallowed hard, her eyes roving up and down Quinn's torso. *Oh man. I'm gonna have trouble tonight!* She very nearly made a flirtatious repartee out of habit but quickly suppressed the impulse and followed Quinn inside. "One order of orange chicken and one General Tso's. Did I do okay?"

"That sounds great." Quinn stood on her tiptoes to grab plates from a cupboard. "I bought some beer for you," she said. "It's in the fridge. I hope it's a kind you like."

Corrie set down the food and opened the refrigerator. A six-pack of Miller Lite lay on its side on the second shelf, and she grinned at Quinn's thoughtfulness. "Aw, thanks," she said. "That's really sweet."

A few minutes later, they were settled in front of the television, their plates heaped with food. Corrie watched Quinn as she fumbled with the remote. That clinging black shirt was only reawakening her memory of just how heavy and full Quinn's breasts had felt in her hands. *Cut it out,* she told her simmering body.

"I...um, I like your shirt," she said lamely. "Is it new?"

"Sort of." Quinn twisted around to face her, and Corrie was pretty sure she was blushing. "So, these videos, they're tapes of past regattas?"

Corrie, who had already begun to shovel food into her mouth, nodded and rapidly swallowed. "The one we've got in right now is last year's Invitational, over in Newport. Same kind of course as we'll sail in a few weeks." She wiped her mouth, took a swig of beer, and gestured to where over a hundred boats were milling together near the starting line. "The first challenge of any race is actually the start. With so many boats, it's tough to get in good position for the upwind leg toward the windward buoy."

"I can see that," said Quinn, her eyes wide.

"It's important for both of us to watch for holes—gaps that open up between boats. Often, you can take advantage of a hole to gain a better angle of approach."

"Okay." Quinn nodded. "I think I understand. It's the same principle as in horse racing; I read all of the *Black Stallion* books as a kid. Except that horses don't need to tack." When Corrie laughed, Quinn grinned back.

"A good start is important," Corrie said as the gun was fired and the boats began to head upwind, "but it isn't everything. No matter where we are in the pack, as soon as we cross that line, the goal is to keep the boat as tight and as steady as possible." She glanced over at Quinn. "You're already good at the upwind leg, so I wouldn't worry too much. Just do what you've been doing."

"It's the spinnaker that still has me worried." *If I do something wrong and we broach in a race, we'll lose for sure!*

"Watch the raise," said Corrie, pointing at the leaders as they rounded the windward mark. One after another, their spinnakers popped open for the first reach to the jibe buoy. "You know exactly what they're doing," she continued, her voice low and almost hypnotic. "You've done it all week. It's the best feeling, isn't it? When the chute pops and the boat just *goes*, like it's actually alive."

Quinn was smiling again. How could she not in the presence of that much joy, that much passion? She could see it on Corrie's face, hear it in her voice. Intensity, obsession, focus. And above all, love. "Yeah," she said. "Yes, it is."

"And now the tough part," Corrie narrated. "Jibing the pole. Remember, whenever we round one of the jibe marks, don't you worry about the chute at all. I'll have it in my hand, and I swear I'll keep it full. Just get that pole switched as smoothly as you can. Okay?"

Quinn swallowed and nodded, her eyes still intent on the television where the sailors in the video were struggling to do what Corrie had just described. One boat's spinnaker nearly landed in the water as the skipper and crew lurched around the buoy. *That will not be us. We're not even going to break stride. No way.* When she realized that her palms were sweating, Quinn rubbed them against her shorts.

"Make sure you eat, too," said Corrie, jabbing her fork toward Quinn's untouched plate. "You'll bonk at practice tomorrow for sure if you don't eat."

"Bonk, huh?"

Corrie looked affronted. "Hey now, that's accepted sports lingo."

"Yes, Skipper," Quinn said demurely.

Corrie sat back against the couch, a smug grin curving her lips. "I could get used to hearing that more often."

This time, Quinn noticed the way that Corrie's gaze lingered over her breasts. She turned her face toward the television in an effort to hide the color she could feel creeping across the bridge of her nose. *God, it feels so good when she looks at me like that. Too good.* "Don't count on it."

❖

They went systematically through the tapes that Corrie had brought. Sometimes they simply watched the races. Other times, Corrie pointed out and explained certain strategies or mistakes. By the time the last race had given way to the empty blue screen, the sky outside was completely dark, and the crickets were enthusiastically putting on a symphony.

Corrie leaned back and stared up at the ceiling. *Do we really have a chance? A might-have-been and a novice against two former Olympians?*

"You know what's weird?" Quinn's voice cut through her nervous introspection, and Corrie returned her gaze from the ceiling to find Quinn sitting Indian-style with her back to the television. Her left knee was almost touching Corrie's right thigh.

"What?"

"I've been sailing with you every day for two weeks now. We've been working hard, and I've been sore sometimes, and tired, but..." She shrugged as her voice trailed off. Corrie had no idea what she was trying to say, but since it was clearly something difficult, she nodded encouragingly.

"But I still weigh the same as I did before we started training," Quinn finished all in a rush. She risked a quick glance at Corrie before looking down at her knees. "Why is that, do you think?"

Corrie took a deep breath, all thoughts of the race disappearing. *Careful, now*, she told herself. Quinn's weight was a sore subject, and it would be easy to say the wrong thing. Or to say the right thing the wrong way. "Well," she began cautiously, "for one thing, muscle weighs more than fat. You've been building a good bit of muscle. Hell, just look at your arms now, and that muscle is heavy."

Corrie paused to gauge Quinn's reaction. *So vulnerable.* The thought suddenly made her want to feel Quinn's deliciously soft body yielding beneath hers, and she grabbed hold of the couch to keep herself from reaching out.

"For another thing," she said after she had cleared her throat, "I'm a firm believer that each body has a weight—or really, a weight range—that it *wants* to be at. Some people naturally gravitate toward a skinnier physique."

She shrugged and looked down at herself, picturing her own small breasts and flat stomach under her burgundy polo shirt. "People like me, I guess. I eat like a horse, but it doesn't really make a difference. For you..." Corrie spread her hands out in front of her, palms up. "Your body is naturally lush, Quinn. You could become a waif if you went crazy and ate nothing and ran ten miles a day, but I'm willing to bet that'd be unhealthy."

She stopped talking then, and looked down at the raggedy edges of her jeans shorts. *I said too much*, she realized, when Quinn didn't immediately respond. *Dammit, I am really not cut out for this relationship business!* She was on the verge of opening her mouth to try to clarify, when she felt the gentle pressure of Quinn's fingers on her forearm. *So warm.*

"You didn't just say those things to be nice, did you?" Quinn's voice was soft.

Corrie scoffed and reached for her beer, trying not to reveal just how pleased she was that Quinn wasn't upset with her, and that the scoop neck of Quinn's top had dipped enough to reveal the slightest hint of pale cleavage. "All this time, and you still don't trust me?"

"You *have* dunked me in the water on several occasions recently."

"You dunked yourself!" Corrie's voice rose in mock outrage. "Is it my fault that you and that damn trapeze have a love-hate relationship?"

"Yes," Quinn said firmly, and poked Corrie just below her ribs. The resulting noise sounded like a frightened chicken's squawk mixed with an injured cow's bellow.

Corrie pulled away and her eyes went wide. "You are so dead," she said breathlessly, as Quinn doubled over with laughter. "So very, very dead—"

In the next second, she had launched herself at Quinn and was doing her very best to tickle her senseless. Quinn let out a high-pitched shriek and desperately tried to squirm out of arm's reach, only to find herself teetering on the edge of the futon, struggling to lean in even as her shoulders began to tilt toward the coffee table.

Corrie surged forward to catch her, one hand splayed between her shoulder blades, the other supporting her waist. Quinn watched Corrie's left bicep contract against the sleeve of her shirt as she pulled her back from the edge. She could see the slight traces of blue veins beneath tan skin as the muscle jumped into relief, and suddenly, she wanted nothing more than to let her mouth trace the contours of that muscle, to feel its strength pulsing beneath her lips.

Her blush was deep and unmistakable. Corrie did not let go. This time, the silence lasted forever.

"You know what?" Quinn said finally, uncertain of what she would say next, but knowing that she had to speak.

"What?" Corrie's voice was just as soft. She raised her eyes to meet Quinn's and froze at the desire she saw there. Dark pupils nearly swallowed the blue of her irises, and Corrie could feel the shiver that raced down Quinn's spine.

Quinn leaned forward until Corrie could feel quick breaths pulsing against her face. Warm and wet, and *oh God you shouldn't do this stop right now don't move don't she doesn't know what she's in for she doesn't deserve this don't make the same mistake twice just don—*

But when Quinn was unable to close that last, tiny gap, Corrie groaned softly and joined their lips in a long, slow kiss. Her mouth moved gently but possessively over Quinn's, nibbling first on her upper lip, then her lower. When her tongue lightly flicked out to tease the corners of Quinn's mouth, Quinn shivered again and sighed, and one of her hands slid into Corrie's hair.

Corrie gently kneaded the curve of Quinn's waist, slipping her fingers beneath the hem of her shirt to caress the warm skin of her back and stomach. She drew Quinn closer with her other hand, and Quinn's lips finally parted beneath hers. Corrie's tongue darted inside, stroking and soothing, briefly tangling with Quinn's before retreating to lick at her lips once more. Their breathing became labored, drowning out the sounds of the crickets, but neither pulled away until Corrie's wandering hand brushed against the soft fabric of Quinn's bra.

I could have her here, right here, right on the couch and she'd let me—wouldn't stop me now, but oh god, she doesn't want that, not like this, she doesn't and you have to stop, you have to stop, you have to, you fucking idiot, stop, stop, stop!

Her body cried out in protest as she gradually gentled her kisses, easing Quinn's passion down from the remarkable high they had found together.

"That was nice," Quinn said quietly against Corrie's mouth. Later. Years later. Carefully disentangling her hand from Corrie's hair, she followed the long trail of gold down to Corrie's shoulders and briefly caressed the nape of her neck.

Corrie pulled back enough to nod, distrusting her voice. Her body still thundered with desire, and despite her good intentions, she knew that if she stayed this close to Quinn for much longer, her temporary resolve would weaken. *And what's wrong with that? Carpe diem. It's been far, far too long. Does she look like she's saying no to you?*

She cleared her throat and swallowed hard. "Uh," she said hoarsely. "I might, um, need some water."

Quinn flushed and leaned down to place a gentle kiss on Corrie's left bicep, before finally letting her hand fall away. Corrie felt the loss of connection so acutely that she barely stifled a moan. *Fuck, gotta either get off, or get out of here!*

Pushing herself up off the couch, she stumbled into the kitchen on shaky legs. She grabbed a glass and rested it on the bottom of the sink as she filled it with water, so that she wouldn't have to watch it tremble in her hand. She downed the water in several long gulps, took a few deep breaths, and stuck it back under the faucet. "D'you want anything, while I'm up?" she finally dared to ask. *Wrong question*, snarled her inner monologue.

And then the door swung open and Drew walked into the house. Corrie's eyes went wide. *Holy fucking hell, if he'd caught us—*

"Mars!" he said, surprised. "Hey. What's going on?"

"Yo, Harris." Corrie somehow managed to keep her voice level even though she felt like screaming. *Way too close for comfort.* She really wasn't prepared to go up against an overprotective Drew. "Quinn and I just finished watching some tapes of old races. Y'know, in prep for the regatta."

"The regatta," Drew said glumly, pulling back one of the chairs at the table and settling into it with a long sigh. "Yeah. Dammit, I wish like hell I could be with you out there."

"Don't worry, Drew," said Quinn as she walked briskly into the kitchen, carrying their dinner plates. When she set them down in the sink, her arm brushed Corrie's. "I promise to take care of her."

"Don't let her cut too close to the buoy!" he said, wagging a finger in admonition. "I've been watching you guys practice, and you're consistently less than two boat-lengths from the mark."

"Thanks for the tip." Quinn's gaze briefly settled on Corrie before returning to Drew. "I'm going to bed. See you both tomorrow."

"Just a sec," said Corrie, suddenly remembering Jen's idea. Besides, for some reason, she wasn't quite ready to let Quinn out of her sight. She cleared her throat.

"So, the instructors go on a weekend trip each summer to Block Island. We race there in a few keelboats, but once we're there, it's all very laid back and chill. We hang out for two days of total relaxation before coming home and getting back to work." She raised her eyebrows. "The trip is next weekend, and...well, would you like to come along?"

Quinn blinked at her. "But I'm not an instructor."

"You could be!" said Drew. "C'mon, Q, it'll be a blast. Please?"

Quinn laughed. "You guys are hard to turn down." She looked back and forth between them, clearly pleased that they both wanted her company. "I'll go. It sounds fun. But now, I really need to sleep."

"Cool," Drew replied. "G'night, then."

"Sleep well, Quinn." Corrie watched as Quinn slowly walked down the hallway toward her bedroom, and then saw her turn and smile, slowly and brilliantly, before disappearing around the corner. Her inner monologue was speechless.

"What are you smirking about?" Drew asked.

"Thinking about the race," she said, before gulping down another glass of water. The insistent pressure between her thighs had abated slightly, but she was still profoundly uncomfortable. *And kind of happy. That's so weird.*

"So, Mars." Drew's voice was a deep rumble. "You nervous about it? The regatta, I mean?"

Corrie glanced at him and shrugged. "Little bit, maybe."

His eyebrows arched. "Want to...uh...relax a little?" His face was hopeful, but despite her physical discomfort, Corrie wasn't even tempted. *Also weird.*

She moved forward a few steps to rest one hand on Drew's right shoulder. "Thanks, but I really need to catch some Z's." She pulled away before he could cover her hand with his own and began to draw on the sandals she'd left at the door.

"Oh," he said. "Sure. I get that."

Corrie grinned apologetically at him and opened the door. "See you."

"Yeah. And hey, it was really nice of you to invite Quinn for next weekend."

Corrie shrugged. "It'll be fun to have her along." And then she stepped out into the night, turning her face toward the cool western breeze. *I did the right thing,* she thought proudly. *I didn't manipulate her.* Of course, she'd done the right thing for the wrong reason, but still.

And now you're going home with a hard-on the size of Texas, the annoying voice inside her brain pointed out. *Congratu-fucking-lations.*

Corrie shook her head vigorously and broke into a jog. She could be patient. Given what had happened earlier, Quinn might just come around after all. And if the intensity of her kisses was any indication, then she'd be worth the wait. For a little while, anyway.

❖

As the door closed behind her, Quinn tiptoed into her bedroom from where she had been concealed, just beyond the bend in the hallway. For some reason, she couldn't stop smiling. *She turned down Drew! And oh, that kiss...*

This is Corrie, her rational brain pointed out. *Corrie's made out with a lot of people.*

But she's *the one who slowed down*, some other, newly awakened voice replied. *That's not like her. That's not what she did last time.*

It doesn't mean anything.

It might!

"Oh, shut up, both of you," Quinn muttered as she slid between the crisp sheets of her bed. Her lips still tingled from Corrie's soft yet insistent kisses, and she touched them with one tentative finger. They felt sensitive, somehow. Swollen and burning—the focal points of memory.

It's nothing. Over and done with. Meaningless.

Oh no, no. No. It's just the beginning. The beginning of everything.

"Shut up and let me enjoy this," she said, rolling onto her side. Corrie had kissed her, and it had felt so very good. That was all that mattered. For now, anyway.

Seconds later, she fell into sleep.

HEAD TO WIND

Harris! If you don't shut up, I'm going to beat you over the head with my oar!"

Quinn giggled as Drew pointedly ignored Jen's threat and launched into his third consecutive rendition of "We Are the Champions." Several boat lengths away off port, Brad's crew were glumly rowing themselves toward New Harbor's beach and glaring over at the winners every chance they got.

When Drew paused in his rowing to use the handle of his oar as a makeshift microphone, the uneven rocking of their inflatable dingy pushed Quinn against Corrie. Not that she minded. She didn't pull away. In fact, she moved a little closer.

"Row the damn boat, Drew!" Jen shrieked from behind them.

"Nice work with the jib out there," Corrie said softly, enjoying the sensation of Quinn's breasts pressed against her. She looked *really* good today, dressed as she was in cutoff khaki shorts and a bright blue tank that showed off her toned arms and the lush curves of her waist and hips. The outfit was nothing special, *per se*, but it just made her look fresh, somehow. Appealing. Corrie hadn't been able to stop watching her all afternoon as she worked on the boat.

Impulsively, she reached for Quinn's hand and enclosed it in her own, then rested their hands back on the rubber gunwale. Quinn's brief glance and shy smile ignited a warm, happy feeling in the bottom of Corrie's stomach, until she remembered her motivation. Then she looked away, into the dark.

Behind them, Jen elbowed Drew in the side. "Ow!" He stopped rowing again and rubbed at his injured rib. "What the hell was that for, *Jenny*?"

Jen motioned with her head toward Corrie and Quinn. When Drew looked over, his jaw dropped several inches. "Holy sh—ow!"

"What is going on back there?" asked Corrie. She craned her neck to look back at them, but didn't let go of Quinn's hand.

"I'm beating him up," Jen said quickly.

Corrie wanted to tell them to get a room but wisely decided to refrain. "Well, how about you wait until we're safely on shore, huh?"

"You heard the skipper. Row, Harris."

By some miracle, they arrived at the beach with no further mishaps. "Where are we going again?" Quinn asked. She was standing near Corrie, but they weren't holding hands anymore. She wanted to reach out, but couldn't quite muster up the courage.

"Captain Nick's," said Corrie as they began to trudge along the shoreline. "It's one of the most popular bars on the island. Really fun."

For some reason, the prospect of spending time in a loud, crowded, and probably smoky bar didn't sound as unappealing as it would have a month ago. *Face it,* Quinn admitted to herself. *You just want to be with her, wherever and whenever.*

But as they approached the brightly lit building, Drew tugged at one strap of Corrie's tank top and pulled her aside. "Mind if I talk to you for a minute?"

Corrie shrugged. "'Course not." She gestured for the others to go in. "We'll meet you in a sec." She followed Drew over to the curb. "What's up?"

He turned to face her. The streetlight just a few feet away backlit her entire body. It almost looked like she was glowing. *Like an angel.* Except that she really wasn't, not at all. Drew took a deep breath.

"What are you doing with Quinn?"

Here it comes. Corrie decided to play it dumb. She wasn't at all surprised that Drew was acting like a big brother. *He'll be harder to convince than Jen was.* "What do you mean?"

Drew sighed and shifted weight to give his injured leg a break. "You know what I mean. What's with the hand-holding thing?" His voice rose slightly. "I told you to let her be, dammit, and—"

"Whoa, whoa." Corrie frowned at him. "You see us holding hands and take that to mean that we're sleeping together?"

"What else am I supposed to think?"

"Gee, Drew, I don't know," Corrie fired back sarcastically. "Maybe that we've gotten close over the past few weeks? Maybe that we're taking things easy and seeing what happens?" She shook her head in frustration. *Does he really think I'm not capable of going slowly? Of being considerate?* Was that really how she came off to other people— as some sort of heartless femme fatale?

Drew held up one hand. "Okay, okay. I'm sorry I accused you like that. It's just—" He frowned. "Look, Cor, this isn't exactly normal for you. And I just really don't want to see Quinn get hurt."

"Neither do I." *And yet,* the niggling voice reminded her, *you're going to hurt her when this is all over.*

Drew exhaled slowly. "Fair enough. If you're both happy, then... I guess I'm glad."

"Thanks." Corrie squeezed his shoulder. *She was going to get hurt anyway. She was into me from the very beginning.* The justification felt hollow, but it was better than nothing. "C'mon, let's go join the party."

They shouldered through the crowd around the door of Captain Nick's, and Drew headed for their friends, who had managed to claim one back corner of the room. Corrie veered toward the bar. *After that, I really need a drink.* She could only imagine what Drew would think of her once this whole charade was over, but then she flashed back to Will's knowing smirk as he tossed the regatta entry form on her desk, and her resolve returned. *It's too late now, anyway.*

As she waited to place her order, she caught sight of Quinn leaning against the wall, and holy *shit*, was some random guy hitting on her? Corrie leaned forward, pressing one hand to the smooth surface of the bar. She wasn't, in fact, seeing things, despite the smoky air. A stocky, dark-haired man, perhaps in his late twenties or early thirties, had sidled over to Quinn and was chatting her up. He wasn't bad looking. In fact, he was sort of handsome, even though his nose was a bit too large for his face. But Quinn was smiling at him, dammit.

Hands off, asshole, Corrie thought fiercely, ducking out of the line to plow through the crowd. Not that he was touching her at the moment, but he would. *Not on my watch.*

"Quinn!" she said, deliberately pitching her voice much higher than normal. She grabbed hold of Quinn's upper arm and began to firmly tug her away. "Oh my god, I lost my earring over there! Help me find it, please. It's my favorite!"

"Um, sure." Quinn risked a quick glance backward at the bewildered face of her would-be companion. "Excuse me!" If he said anything in reply, neither of them heard it as Corrie steered Quinn quickly toward the door.

"Your *earring*? Are your ears even pierced?"

Corrie shook her head and bared her teeth. "Nope."

Quinn laughed and leaned against Corrie before they finally squeezed through the last of the crowd and emerged into the warm, clear night. "I hate smoke," she said vehemently. "Ugh. This is much better."

A salt-scented breeze blew off the ocean, ruffling her hair as she turned to breathe in deeply. Corrie heard her sigh of relief, watched her mouth curve up in a smile as she welcomed the fresh air. *Sensual.* Heat swirled in her gut, and she let her fingers trail down Quinn's arm as she released her.

"Somebody needs to give you lessons in how to stave off the hordes," she said, trying to keep her voice light and casual. "A big stick is always handy."

Quinn shrugged. "That's never happened to me before. Thanks for rescuing me."

"My pleasure." Feeling suddenly uncomfortable, Corrie looked out toward the harbor. *But I'm not rescuing you at all, am I?* Her newfound resolve dissipated as fast as it had appeared. *Can I really do this? She trusts me...but I'm helping her grow, dammit. I am.* Once the regatta was done and it was over between them, Quinn would be able to find a real relationship in no time. *She won't even miss me.*

"Do you want to go for a walk?" Quinn asked. Her voice sounded tentative.

"Sure, okay." The crazy thing, the scary thing, was that it felt so damn good to be with Quinn that Corrie sometimes forgot she was pretending. Corrie felt the familiar panic rise into her throat. *You just need to get laid. Easy cure. Go back inside and sneak off into a dark corner with someone and—*

"Let's walk along the beach." Quinn slipped off her sandals as soon as they reached the cool sand and paused to wriggle her toes. "I love the way it feels. Between my toes, I mean." She looked over her right shoulder at Corrie. "You should take yours off, too."

"Okay," Corrie said again. Her brain was insisting that she go back to the bar, but her gut was telling her to stay put. To stay with Quinn. She had no idea where all of this was leading—probably nowhere—but it wouldn't really hurt to find out, would it?

"My parents have a house on Cape Cod," said Quinn as Corrie removed her Tevas. "We used to stay there for most of the summer, and when I was young, I loved to build sandcastles with my brother and sister."

Corrie grinned, momentarily disarmed by the anecdote. *Cute.* "Were you good at it?"

"Oh, very. We made some very elaborate ones. And when we had finished with the moat—you always do the moat last, of course."

"Of course."

"Then, I would dig around until I found two sand crabs. And I'd wash them off in a bucket, and then put them in the throne room. As the king and queen of the castle."

Corrie laughed helplessly. "Is there any animal you *don't* like?"

Quinn thought for a few seconds. The moon, fuller than it had been last night, illuminated her concentrated frown, especially the way her tongue slightly poked out between her teeth. "Ticks," she said, finally. "I don't really see the point."

"Good call." Corrie nodded and casually reached for Quinn's free hand. She hadn't objected earlier, after all. And her skin felt so good. Warm and slightly moist. "Sucking blood until you burst...something's wrong, there."

Quinn wrinkled her nose. "Thanks for that image."

They walked silently for a while, their linked hands swinging between them. "What're your brother and sister like?" Corrie asked. She suddenly wanted to know.

"They're great. Sheila is still in college. She's a junior. Her major changes every month."

"Ah, of course." Corrie let her thumb briefly caress Quinn's knuckles. Knuckles could be surprisingly sensitive. "Does that drive your parents crazy?"

"Fortunately not. They're very supportive and tolerant."

"Good for them," Corrie said, but she was starting to get distracted. The heat in her body was rapidly rising, spiraling out of control as Quinn's hip bumped against hers and their arms brushed lightly. The wanting was strong tonight—too strong. She found herself steering them toward the largest rocks in the breakwater. They would provide some shelter from passersby. And besides, she wanted to press Quinn up against one of them, to feel the entire length of Quinn's body melting into her own. *No pushing. I just...I need...* Her stomach tightened in anticipation.

"My older brother," Quinn was saying, "is in his last year of medical residency. We've always joked that we should set up a dual clinic for both people and their pets. Like, go get your sinus infection diagnosed while your dog gets its rabies vaccine."

"Good idea," Corrie said as she maneuvered them into the shadow of a tall boulder. Within a few seconds, she had edged Quinn up against the weathered surface of the rock.

"What are you doing?" Quinn whispered. She swallowed hard.

"I've been wanting to kiss you all day." Corrie's voice was gritty and urgent. She rested her palms on the boulder, on either side of Quinn's shoulders. "Do you want me to?"

Quinn swallowed again. Her gaze darted over Corrie's face. "Yes."

"Ask me then." That rush of power—sweet and warm.

Quinn's sharp intake of breath was audible, even over the crashing of the surf. "Please—"

Corrie didn't wait to hear more. She covered Quinn's lips with her own, parting them gently with her tongue. Her hands moved to Quinn's waist—clutching, kneading, thumbs pressing into her bellybutton through the thin cotton tee.

Quinn made small, breathy noises as Corrie's palms traveled gradually up as her mouth continued to move firmly but tenderly over Quinn's. Across her ribcage, Corrie's touch lingered in the slight grooves between the bones, up and up and up, fanning over her breasts. Corrie finally pulled her head back as Quinn gasped for air, but her fingers continued to move, tormenting Quinn's nipples through her T-shirt

Out of control. Too far, too fast. But even her conscience was breathless. Maybe it was the moon, pulling her blood as it pulled the ocean, or maybe it was the low throb of the tide itself. Or perhaps it was Quinn—her softness, her surrender.

"I want you," Corrie breathed, seizing the opportunity to taste Quinn's right earlobe with her eager tongue. "I want all of you, naked, beneath me."

Quinn groaned softly. A sweet sound.

"You want that too." Corrie eased one thigh between Quinn's legs and pressed up, increasing the pressure as Quinn gasped at the sensation. "I can tell. You want my hands on you—all over you. Inside you." She lowered her mouth to Quinn's jaw line, nibbled at it with gentle nips. "You're so sensual, Quinn. So responsive. You have no idea what you're capable of, and you want me to show you. I know you do."

Corrie leaned back just enough to meet Quinn's eyes—deep pools of want darker than the shadows. "Tell me," Corrie demanded. Her voice was quiet but urgent. When Quinn simply blinked at her, Corrie rolled both nipples gently between each thumb and index finger. Quinn's eyes slammed shut. A whimper. "Tell me. It's okay. Tell me."

"Corrie—"

Then, above the rapid pounding of her heart, Corrie heard laughter. She froze. A shouted question, a louder response. Several voices— drunk and clamoring. *Getting closer.*

"Fuck." She pulled away from Quinn, who immediately sank to the ground, her back resting against the boulder. Corrie could hear her labored breaths, below the noises of the raucous group approaching them. She eased herself down to the sand, close to, but not touching, Quinn. The moment had passed.

Damn other people, always interrupting! Corrie thought, closing her eyes and gritting her teeth. She shivered as the desire raged through her muscles.

"I don't get it," Quinn said quietly, as the revelers staggered past them. "Why do you want *me*, anyway?" She looked resolutely out toward the ocean, one arm curled around both drawn-up knees. "You could have anyone. I'm not even very attractive."

Corrie turned to look at her. She said nothing until Quinn reluctantly met her gaze. "I could make you believe that you are. I could prove it."

Quinn's mouth opened soundlessly. She sat very still, trapped by the intensity written in the lines and planes of Corrie's face. Hunger. Need. Directed at her, for her. So very sexy, and yet also touching. Affirming. Quinn didn't know how to reply. Maybe there was nothing to say.

Corrie misinterpreted her reaction. "I've frightened you," she said, looking away again. "I'm sorry. I didn't mean for it to go that far, just then."

Quinn wanted to reach out and lightly stroke her back, but she wasn't sure that the contact would be welcome. "Sometimes, your drive, it can be a little overwhelming. But I trust you."

"I'm not sure that you should," Corrie muttered, so quietly that Quinn almost didn't hear. She did touch Corrie, then, one hand tentatively resting on a bowed shoulder.

"And why is that?" she asked softly. There was a long pause before Corrie finally began to talk.

"It feels, sometimes, like Denise opened up this...this dark place in me." She shook her head, struggling to articulate. *If I tell you, will you understand? Will you see through me? Will you get the hell away from me so I don't hurt you?* "Stupid, I know. But I hated myself for a long time after it was over. I'd look in the mirror and wonder where I'd gone wrong, what I could have done."

Corrie reached down to scoop up the sand. It drained through her fingers before she spoke again. "After a few weeks of self-loathing, I realized just how dumb *that* was and started hating her—and Will—instead. There are these feelings I have, emotions I know aren't healthy, but they won't go away. They just won't. And I do things..."

She lapsed into silence. Quinn sat frowning into the dark, wracking her brain for something she could say that wouldn't sound inane, wanting so very badly to be able to fix it. But this wasn't a minor scrape that could be patched up with a Band-Aid. No, this was an old wound. Old and deep and festering.

"I wish I could be like Jen," Corrie said finally. "Or better yet, like you." She glanced at Quinn, then looked away again. She barely even knew what she was saying—only that the confession was pouring out of her like the sand through her hands. "Sometimes I think about what it must be like inside your head. White and soft and clean—bright, with no dark corners—and I want to curl up in there and sleep for years and years until I forget having ever done anything I'm not proud of."

Quinn inhaled sharply, as though Corrie's words had knocked the breath out of her body. "Oh," she said shakily, "I have a few dark corners." She could feel her heart thudding against her breastbone, her hands trembling against her knees. No one had ever said anything like that to her before; no one had even come close. The shock made her skin tingle, even as she experienced an overwhelming desire to simply slide her arms around Corrie's waist and rock her until she felt peace.

Quinn swallowed. It hurt. "You feel so much. It's one of the things I—" The word teetered on the precipice of her lips. "It's one of the things that draws me to you."

Corrie's gaze skittered over her face again. She might have smiled faintly. Quinn couldn't tell in the patchy light. "You're drawn to me?"

It was Quinn's turn to look away. *You know I am.* "What did you mean," she asked instead, "about the unhealthy feelings?"

"Dodging the question," said Corrie. But when Quinn continued to stare out toward the harbor, she exhaled slowly. "Power. I started to crave it, and I guess I still do. Knowing I'm wanted, needed. Having control." She paused. "Using people." *There. I've warned you. If you don't hear it, that's not my fault.*

Quinn watched her as she spoke, the fingers of one hand curling down into the sand, a few strands of glittering blond hair fluttering against her cheek in the light breeze, the gentle bulge of her triceps as she leaned against the boulder. Strength and beauty and elegance. *Not weak. You're not weak.*

"Does it make you feel better? When you seduce someone? When you're in charge?"

Corrie's shoulders hunched, ever so slightly. "For a while. There's nothing quite like the power trip that comes from sex. When someone needs you like that, needs you way down deep in their body..." She trailed off. "Hell," she said finally, her voice flat. "I'm probably disgusting you, aren't I?"

Quinn finally did reach out then, grasping Corrie's free hand and allowing their fingers to entwine. "You don't disgust me," she said firmly. "Not at all." Her hand tightened. "Not having experience doesn't make me a prude, you know."

"Oh, I know, I didn't mean to suggest that—"

When Quinn touched Corrie's wind-chapped lips, she froze immediately. "Hush," said Quinn. "It's my turn to talk." It was difficult to pull away, but Quinn was suddenly afraid that if she continued to touch Corrie, especially her lips, they would bypass conversation altogether. Her body still pulsed with the desire that Corrie had rekindled just a few minutes ago.

"I wish she hadn't hurt you like that," she said quietly. "I wish she'd never made you feel inadequate or unwanted, because you're neither of those things. And I hope you can forgive her, forgive them both, someday, so you can get a little peace."

When Corrie looked away from her, shrugging uncomfortably, Quinn hurried to continue. "But, as for the dark places, they're part of you. Everyone fights against something inside them, and it's that fight that makes us—" Abruptly, she lost the thread of her words. This wasn't coming out right at all. "Your intensity, your passion," she tried again. "The way you do everything as though it might be your last moment. People are drawn to the fire in you, Corrie. Not despite the danger, but because of it."

As she stopped talking, she became aware of Corrie's astonished face, of her wide, shadowed eyes and slightly parted lips. Totally and completely vulnerable, for a single instant in time. And deep inside Quinn—deeper than her muscles or sinews or bones—something happened.

The sensation reminded her of when she had gone to Alaska as a child, on vacation with her parents. They had stood in a boat near snow covered cliffs in June, watching as a huge chunk of blue-tinted ice had dropped with a crackling roar into the frothing water, and their craft had pitched alarmingly from side to side in the waves that followed. Now, on a midsummer's night in New England, the air was warm enough to raise beads of sweat along her hairline. But she sat frozen as the wave thundered under every inch of her skin, raising goose bumps in its wake. Her teeth would have chattered had her jaw not been clenched.

So, she thought, somehow outside herself. *It really does feel like falling.*

"Quinn," Corrie whispered. She leaned closer.

If she kisses me, we won't stop this time, Quinn realized. The realization was relief. She closed her eyes—

"Your Red Sox are fucking pansies, Harris!" Jen's raised voice floated toward them on the light breeze. "The Yanks'll have you for breakfast this year."

"Stop yelling about it, jeez." Drew was harder to make out. "You're in Rhode Island, remember? Not really all that far from Boston? You'll get us shot!"

Quinn groaned. Corrie pulled away and buried her face in her hands. She muttered something that sounded a lot like, "I'm going to kill them," and Quinn laughed weakly. *You're not the only one.*

Corrie finally got up and dusted off the seat of her shorts. She held out her hand to Quinn who took it and scrambled to her feet. "Thanks for the talk. I guess maybe I needed that."

Quinn's answering smile was beautiful. "Thank you for trusting me."

Corrie managed a lopsided grin in return before she stepped away from the sheltering rock, freeing Quinn's hand as she moved. "Did we leave our indoor voices at the bar?" she asked Drew and Jen.

"Oh," said Jen, waving one hand expansively in her general direction. "Fuck you."

"Finally, after all these years?"

Jen peered at them suspiciously, as Quinn moved into the moonlight. "What were you two doing, eh?"

"Having a good talk," Corrie said firmly. "And now, it's clearly time to get you to bed."

"No kidding," said Drew. "She's off her rocker, talking smack like that about the 'Sox."

They walked slowly toward the pier where their J-boat was docked, Jen's hiccups intermittently punctuating their progress. Drew pulled the boat in close enough to the dock for them to all jump on board. Jen clung fiercely to the forestay.

"Where's Brad's crew?" Corrie asked. The boat next to theirs was dark and quiet.

"Still drowning their sh—sorrows," Jen slurred.

"Ah." Corrie opened the hatch and gestured for Drew and Jen to precede her into the hold, where they had layered mattresses on the floor. She clambered down after them to retrieve her sleeping bag.

"C'mon, Jen, crawl in." Drew's cajoling voice was frustrated, but gentle. "Not like that, you idiot. The zipper goes the other way."

Corrie stepped back out onto the deck just as Quinn appeared near the top of the short ladder. "I'm gonna sleep outside," she answered Quinn's questioning glance. "It's nice out."

"Okay." Quinn briefly cupped her cheek before lowering herself below. "Good night."

She wormed her way into her own sleeping bag, suddenly exhausted. And yet, when she closed her eyes, all she could feel were Corrie's hands on her body. So certain, so possessive. What would it be like to let those hands undress her? To let them touch her everywhere, with no barriers between Corrie's hot palms and her skin?

Jen began to snore loudly, but Quinn could only hear Corrie's voice. *"I could make you believe."*

She wasn't, Quinn reflected, a nice hearth fire on a cold winter's night. She was a bonfire, throwing sparks up to the heavens, crackling out of control. A supernova. A rip tide, pulling her under. Inexorable.

"I could make you believe."

Corrie cared for her—of that she was certain. But she could not—or would not—return the most important thing.

"I could make you believe."

She had promised herself that she would not give her body to someone she did not love. But that was not the issue.

"I could make you believe."

Quinn buried her face into the crumpled URI sweatshirt that served as her pillow. *I want her*, she thought dully. *I want to sleep with her. I want her to touch me, and I want to make love to her.*

I was going to say yes.

CAST OFF

Quinn stood just outside the front door of the boathouse, looking out toward the narrow strip of beach between the rocks and the first pier. Frog lounged in the shade of a nearby picnic bench, his strong chest heaving as he panted. It was hot out, and humid.

By this time tomorrow, the regatta will be more than halfway over, she realized. *I wonder whether we'll be winning or losing?*

"Go long!" Drew shouted from the shore, hefting a football in his right hand.

Corrie ran into the shallow water, her feet kicking up spray and her ponytail streaming behind her like a comet's tail. Quinn's heart thumped painfully at the sight. *God, you're beautiful.* She didn't even try to suppress the thought anymore.

It had been a busy week, especially for Corrie. When they weren't training, she had been finalizing preparations for the race. Quinn hadn't seen her much outside of their practice times, and if she hadn't known just how much Corrie had on her plate, she would have thought Corrie was trying to avoid her.

I've had it with her gentle kisses hello and goodbye. All week, Corrie had been kind and tender, even hesitant. *A banked fire.* But Quinn knew there was live coal in her somewhere, just waiting to flare up as it had the weekend before on Block Island. And she was done waiting.

Drew launched the ball into the air, several feet above Corrie's head. She charged headlong into the ocean and finally dove for it, her hands closing around the pigskin just before she crashed into the water with a loud splash. Quinn laughed as Corrie reemerged, spluttering. She raised the dripping ball into the air.

"Got it!" she crowed triumphantly. She tossed it back with a sharp flick of her wrist. The spiral was immaculate.

"Ha!" Drew smirked. "Got you all wet."

But Corrie didn't reply. She stood quite still, shading her eyes against the sun as she looked up toward the boathouse, and Quinn realized that she had been seen. "Back in a sec," Quinn heard her say. And then she was jogging away from the ocean, and the sunlight was glinting off the water that clung to her tan skin.

Quinn swallowed hard in sudden nervousness. Rubbing sweaty palms together, she tried out a smile. It probably looked sickly. "Hi," she said.

"Hey." Corrie made her voice soft, the way she'd heard Quinn speak to Frog when he had been injured. She leaned forward for a quick kiss, then stepped back. "I'm glad to see you, but what're you doing here? Day off, remember?" Corrie had insisted that practicing on the day before the regatta was a bad idea.

"I..." Quinn began. Her eyes were drawn to a drop of water that was wending its way between the slight ridges of Corrie's abdominal muscles—like a mogul skier tracking between the bumps. She cleared her throat and quickly met Corrie's eyes again, certain that she was blushing. "I figured you'd be swamped, so I came down to help out." She shrugged. "Guess I was wrong about the swamped thing."

Corrie stepped forward to wrap her arms around Quinn's waist. "You're sweet. Most everyone arrived sometime this morning and are out there practicing. See all the boats on the water?"

Quinn looked out past the mooring field and felt like an idiot. Sure enough, there were dozens of boats circling around the course that she and Corrie had set up yesterday. "I didn't even notice them," she said, leaning back in the circle of Corrie's arms. "Watching you dive after that football distracted me."

"Did it, now?" Corrie's voice had suddenly gotten deeper. Quinn loved when that happened—usually after a kiss or two.

She nodded. "Nice catch."

"Thanks." Corrie leaned down to kiss her again. It lasted longer this time.

Quinn finally tore herself away and took a deep breath. "So— what's your evening look like? Is this the calm before the storm, or will you be free?"

"Things will pick up when all those boats want to come in." Corrie looked out toward the lake again. "But I should be free about an hour after sunset. Why?"

"I was wondering if maybe you wanted to watch a movie tonight." The words came out on top of each other, all in a rush. "I mean, to rent one. And hang out. But if you need to go home and get some sleep before tomorrow..." She trailed off, suddenly certain that Corrie wouldn't want that kind of distraction the night before going up against Will and Denise. *Nice job, idiot. Now she probably thinks you're not as serious about tomorrow as you should be!*

But Corrie nodded and grinned. "Sounds good."

"Really?"

"You sound like you don't believe me." She nudged Quinn with one shoulder. "Yeah, I think that'd be great—the perfect way to relax before the regatta."

Quinn was relieved. "Are you in the mood for any movie in particular?"

For a second, Corrie considered suggesting *Bound*. Oh, it was so tempting, except that it would probably make Quinn uncomfortable. *And I did enough of that on the Island to last us a while.* She'd been extra cautious all week—careful not to come on too strong, to try to maintain at least some distance. *The closer we get, the harder it'll be on her*, Corrie reminded herself for the thousandth time. But oh, it was difficult, so very difficult, especially since Quinn always responded so eagerly to Corrie's attentions. *And now you've just agreed to spend two hours with her tonight. What were you thinking?*

But she couldn't renege, not now. And she didn't really want to, either, truth be told. Corrie blinked, suddenly realizing that she hadn't yet replied. "Anything is fine with me. You pick it. Just no slasher films, please." She winked.

"Darn," Quinn said blandly. "There went all my ideas." She squeezed Corrie's hand. "I'll see you tonight, then."

Corrie squeezed back. "Thanks for stopping by." She stood still as Quinn rounded the corner of the boathouse and passed out of sight.

"Jeez," said Drew, stepping up beside her. "She didn't even say hello or goodbye to me. You suck for my ego."

Corrie just rolled her eyes at him, refusing to take the bait. "She did seem a little preoccupied. I hope she's not too worried about tomorrow."

"Fuckin' ankle," Drew muttered. "Should be me out there with you."

Corrie patted his shoulder sympathetically and kept her opinion to herself.

❖

As it turned out, Quinn showed up at Corrie's door holding the DVD of *Homeward Bound*. The irony did not escape Corrie. She kissed Quinn to keep herself from laughing.

"Have you ever seen this one?" Quinn asked as she followed Corrie into the den.

"A long time ago. It's about the animals who try to find their family, right?"

Quinn bounced onto the couch, one leg tucked up beneath her while the other dangled over the edge. "Yep. Two dogs and a cat. It's really sweet."

Corrie smiled at Quinn's enthusiasm and gestured toward the kitchen. "Something to drink?"

"I'll just have a soda if you've got some." Corrie nodded and went to the fridge, and Quinn watched her. The white A-shirt and gray mesh shorts made her look sporty, but also soft, somehow. And her hair was down. She almost never had her hair down. It was quite long, and Quinn suddenly wanted to feel it brushing against her throat as Corrie moved over her.

"Oh god," she muttered, turning away so Corrie wouldn't be able to see the deep blush she knew had spread across her face. *I'm actually going insane.* She crouched down near the television and removed the DVD with trembling fingers. *Get a grip!*

Corrie returned with two cans and popped the tabs while Quinn set up the movie. "So after tomorrow, I'll stop making you practice for hours on end everyday." She winked. "Whatever will you do with yourself?"

Quinn wrinkled her nose. "More studying, unfortunately."

"What's the exam going to be like?"

"It's a six-hour ordeal," she said, taking the soda that Corrie offered. "Three hundred multiple choice questions. Not much room for error."

"Are you worried about it?" Corrie settled in next to Quinn, so that their knees were only a few inches from touching.

"I am, I guess." Quinn shrugged and took a sip from her drink. "The sample questions I've seen can be pretty tricky. And it costs eight hundred dollars to take the test, so it's not like I can afford to fail." Quinn leaned forward to grab the remote from the coffee table. As she sat back up, she leaned closer to Corrie—close enough that their legs were pressed together along their thighs. "Actually, I'd rather not think about it right now, if you don't mind." She gestured toward the television. "You ready for this?"

"Bring on the critters." Corrie rested her arm along the back of couch.

It was like going to the movies with your crush in middle school. As the opening credits rolled, Quinn leaned back against Corrie's bicep just a little. Corrie smiled faintly, but stayed still. Five minutes later, her patience was rewarded as Quinn snuggled closer into the curve of her body, moving her head to rest against Corrie's shoulder.

"This is nice," said Quinn.

"Mmm-hmm." Unable to help herself, Corrie shifted slightly onto her right hip so that she could bring her left hand across their bodies to rest on the gentle swell of Quinn's stomach.

The light blue cotton tee was thin, and Corrie's palm was very warm. Quinn could feel the heat soaking into her skin, radiating outward from Corrie's touch like ripples in a pond. And then, Corrie began to move her hand in slow circles, bunching up her shirt slightly as she rubbed Quinn's stomach.

The motion was soothing, and yet also arousing, especially whenever the edge of Corrie's thumb brushed against the sliver of bare skin between her shirt and shorts. Quinn no longer paid any attention to the movie. She turned her head toward Corrie's, breathing in the warm scent of her, even daring to lean closer and press her lips to the skin of her neck. She felt Corrie's body tremble once.

Corrie let her cheek brush lightly against Quinn's forehead before turning to kiss her there. And all the while, her hand continued to move, to caress Quinn's stomach, her ribs, the soft curves above her hips. The movie played in the background, unheeded. Corrie tried to relax into Quinn's sweet, cuddling touches, but her body grew tighter and tighter as it became more and more difficult not to swing one leg across Quinn's hips, pinning her in place as she pulled her T-shirt up over her head.

Quinn tilted her head back slightly, just enough to meet Corrie's gaze. And then she leaned in, all the way in, to seal their lips together. It was the first kiss she had both initiated and followed through on, and it was just like her—soft, hesitant, gentle. Her lips moved against Corrie's for a long time—testing and nibbling, pressing firmly then retreating—before her tongue tentatively touched one corner of Corrie's mouth.

Corrie groaned quietly. Quinn pulled back, her eyes wide and her face flushed. "Are you okay?"

"Okay," Corrie gasped, curling her free hand into the fabric of the couch to keep herself from taking control. "Very okay." *God, I have to stop this soon..I'm going to explode!*

Quinn's smile was blinding. She leaned forward again, and this time, her kisses were firmer. When she touched her tongue to the tip of Corrie's, they both gasped. The circles of Corrie's hand on her stomach became sporadic, and she moved higher in fits and starts—higher and higher and higher until the sides of her thumbs were rhythmically rubbing the soft undersides of Quinn's breasts through her shirt and bra. Quinn's heartbeat hammered under her palm. When Corrie's fingers curled around one breast and squeezed, Quinn pulled away again. This time, her eyes were closed as she gulped for breath.

"Quinn…" Corrie said, her voice taut. "I don't think…"

Quinn's eyes opened and Corrie's words died in her throat. The blue of her irises was barely visible, like the nimbus of the sun in an eclipse. She pressed two trembling fingers to Corrie's lips and shook her head. "Touch me. Touch me the way you want to."

It sounded so good the way she said it—quietly, with the slightest quaver in her voice. This was the sweetest kind of moment in life, Corrie thought. The instant of capitulation. Surrender. Yielding. Usually she felt pure triumph at such a confession—and there was so much more reason than usual to feel it now—but instead, she was filled with awe.

She had to swallow twice before she could speak. "Are you sure?"

Quinn nodded mutely.

Corrie breathed out a long sigh. She rose smoothly and pulled Quinn up beside her. *I know this role. Finally, I know it.* "Follow me," she said gently.

At the top of the stairs, Corrie turned and kissed her. Her mouth trailed down from Quinn's lips to trace her jaw line. "Do you trust me?" she asked.

"Yes," Quinn whispered, barely trusting her voice.

"Then close your eyes." *I'll do this right for you*, she promised silently as Quinn shut them, standing blind with her pulse fluttering rapidly just beneath the skin of her neck. Corrie led her slowly down the hallway into the bedroom. Quinn hesitated for only a second before yielding control, following her like a dance partner. At the edge of the bed, Corrie pressed Quinn's calves against the mattress and gently pushed her to sit.

Quinn kept her eyes closed. Her breaths were coming quickly. Corrie watched the rapid rise and fall of the soft, blue v-neck over her breasts.

"You're very beautiful." Carefully, she slid her fingers under the hem of Quinn's shirt and slipped it off over her head. Beneath she wore a simple, white cotton bra. Corrie's hands itched to cup her full breasts—to surround them and support them, just like the fabric.

"Scoot back," she said. She guided Quinn's body until she was reclining on the bed, her head cushioned by the pillows. And still, Quinn kept her eyes closed, trusting in Corrie's touches and commands.

Corrie knelt beside Quinn on the mattress and reached out to touch her face. Slowly, she trailed her fingers down Quinn's forehead, along her nose, across her lips. She felt a strange kind of hesitancy, like nothing she'd ever felt before. Quinn had never given herself this way. She was an innocent, and her body was sacred, somehow.

Corrie swallowed hard and continued her slow journey—over the bump of Quinn's chin, down the fragile column of her throat, moving steadily toward the valley between her breasts. *You can do this*, she reminded herself. *You know how to make people feel good.*

Beneath her touch, Quinn's heart fluttered rapidly. "Open your eyes," Corrie said. She inhaled sharply at the pleading gaze that met and held her own. It didn't matter that Quinn was still half-clothed. Her soul was naked and vulnerable and open, and Corrie was suddenly overwhelmed by a deep surge of protectiveness that left her breathing hard.

She reached around to deftly unsnap Quinn's bra and cradled her close once her breasts were freed. They felt full and heavy against the thin material of her shirt. Words spilled out of her, then—quiet words, gentle words, completely unlike the torrent of sexual banter she was used to exchanging with her partners. She had no idea where they came from, but they came.

"You feel good," she murmured. "So soft and warm." Laying her back on the bed, she let her legs straddle Quinn's hips and rested her palms lightly on Quinn's stomach. Quinn gasped at the contact. "God, I love the way your skin feels under my hands. This dip here...your curves...how full and lush you are..."

Quinn listened in wonder as Corrie cherished her body with words and touch, as Corrie's mouth slid hotly along the bumps of her ribcage and her hair brushed like thin silk across Quinn's breasts. When Corrie's tongue lapped at the sensitive undersides, Quinn felt her body arch into the air, helpless. Enchanted. A willing puppet responding eagerly to Corrie's master touch.

Corrie moved back up to kiss her as she brought her thumbs to the tips of Quinn's breasts, flicking them back and forth lightly. Quinn's body jerked, and she let out a strangled groan. Elated and painfully aroused, Corrie repeated the motion, harder.

"Oh." Quinn's eyes flew open—still pleading, but suddenly filled with fire. "God, you feel—" She surprised Corrie by tugging at her shirt, fumbling until Corrie found the presence of mind to wrestle it over her own head. Raising herself from the bed, Quinn reached for Corrie's smaller breasts and buried her face in them, breathing deeply. Corrie's senses reeled at the brief sensation of Quinn's cheeks against her sensitive skin. And then Quinn lifted her face and kissed her fiercely, hungrily, as she clutched at the strong muscles of Corrie's back.

"I knew you would be like this," Corrie gasped. "You had to be." She returned her mouth to Quinn's breasts, tormenting them with lips and teeth and tongue—sucking, nipping, massaging—drawing out little incoherent cries that sounded increasingly desperate.

Immersed in Quinn's abandon, Corrie pulled off Quinn's shorts and underwear and stretched out on top of her completely for the first time. Quinn's hips lifted into her thigh as she instinctually sought to relieve the exquisite pressure building inside her. Pressing Quinn's arms into the mattress, Corrie reared up to withhold the contact.

"Not yet."

Quinn's face was flushed, her eyes dark and dazed. "But I—"

"Hush," she said soothingly, shifting to lie on her left side, next to Quinn. "I've got you." She smoothed her right hand slowly down Quinn's body until it brushed against dark curls. Quinn froze.

"No one has ever touched you like this," said Corrie. Her gaze—

so fierce, and yet so gentle—was magnetic.

Quinn's breath caught. She shook her head helplessly. She looked up with an expression of such vulnerability and innocent desire that Corrie felt something snap, deep inside.

"When I touch you here," Corrie murmured intensely, "you are mine."

I was already yours, Quinn confessed silently. *Yours for the taking, and now you're going to...*

Warm fingers slid into the delicate folds of her softest skin— exploring, testing, stroking. Pleasure washed through her in waves of fire so intense she had to close her eyes, had to give herself up to sensation. There was only Corrie's mouth kissing the side of her neck, Corrie's breasts pressing into her side, Corrie's fingers opening her, dipping inside, then moving up again to massage her with firm, circling strokes that made Quinn want, *need* to burst open, to split apart because there wasn't room for it all for all the feeling all the fire all the light and heat and she wanted to fall, to fall forever, oh, just one final push—

Corrie watched through glazed eyes as Quinn's head fell back onto the pillows, back arching as she moaned and moved her hips in counterpoint to Corrie's rhythm. Her hands found Corrie's strong shoulders, clenching and unclenching, faster and faster, until her head snapped up and her gaze locked with Corrie's, wide and wild.

"Oh—"

The world stopped for one single, perfect instant, and then she was coming, shaking helplessly like a sail in irons. She buried her face in the curve of Corrie's neck, her short, ragged cries playing counterpoint to the jerking movements of her body as Corrie continued to touch her gently, coaxing out every last shudder. Her gasping breaths burned in her throat.

Corrie finally moved her hand up to rub Quinn's stomach again in light, comforting strokes. When Quinn's eyes opened, they were brimming with tears that quickly spilled over. Corrie brushed them away with tender fingertips and frowned.

"Did I—"

But Quinn's sudden, brilliant smile interrupted her. "I'm okay," she said haltingly. She even laughed, through the tears. "I don't know why I'm crying."

Corrie bent down to kiss her forehead. Her body begged for release after the intensity of Quinn's reaction, but she forced her hips to be still. "You're so beautiful. Do you believe it now?"

Quinn nuzzled at Corrie's shoulder, inhaled the warm, comforting scent of her. "Yes," she said, burrowing even closer. It was a miracle, but she did. Her body felt boneless—full and heavy and at peace. In this one, perfect instant, everything was as it should be.

As Quinn relaxed, Corrie's focus couldn't help but turn inward, toward the maelstrom that raged unslaked beneath her skin. Deep, steady breaths only fed the flames, and she had to fight to remain still and silent. Despite her best efforts, however, the feelings did not recede. Instead, she felt increasingly dizzy—overwhelmed by a strange vertigo that forced her to clutch the sheets for purchase.

Never been like that, she realized, on the edge of panic. *That intense, that good.* With Brad, with Megs, with Drew, she knew what to do next. *Say thanks and get on with life.* But this was uncharted territory, and once again Corrie had no idea how to proceed.

She'll probably fall asleep, and then I can get up, she thought in relief. *She's half-asleep already.*

But then Quinn moved her hand from where it had settled on Corrie's arm, stroking upward to rub lightly against her breast. Corrie's body pulsed—desire crackling to the surface like a solar flare. She bit her bottom lip hard to keep from crying out. Desperately, she hoped that Quinn might think *she* had fallen asleep, but when that hesitant touch was followed by one finger's firm pressure against her nipple, Corrie couldn't suppress a moan.

"Does that feel good?" Quinn pinched with her thumb and index finger.

"Ye-es." Corrie said when she did it again, harder. Quinn continued to explore her breasts—sometimes squeezing, sometimes stroking, sometimes caressing so lightly that Corrie could barely feel her. Each tentative touch burned between her legs, until Corrie was shifting restlessly.

When Quinn's warm mouth closed over one nipple, Corrie cried out sharply and pulled Quinn on top of her. Quinn's hungry eyes met hers before Quinn closed the gap between them with a long, thorough kiss. Corrie had an instant in which to wonder what exactly had happened to Quinn's hesitant kissing style before her rational thought was swept away on the tide that purged her brain and body of every single feeling but desire.

Her hips bucked beneath Quinn, who slid to one side and pushed Corrie's loose shorts down her legs. Quinn's hands were shaking, and she sucked in a loud breath as Corrie finally lay naked before her. Quinn was drawn to the tight, dark blond curls in the center of Corrie's body. She wanted to touch her there, to feel the crinkly hair and hot, silky skin beneath, to make her feel the same impossible pleasure. But she had been so overwhelmed when Corrie was touching her that she had no idea what Corrie had actually done. Tentatively, she let her fingertips skim over Corrie's lips. *Soft.*

Quinn's uncertainty felt like teasing, like an ecstatic kind of torture. Corrie strained desperately to feel more, but Quinn stopped and cupped her tenderly. Corrie's eyes snapped open, hazed in anguish. "God, Quinn—"

"Help me. Show me what you want."

Corrie slid a trembling hand down her stomach to cover Quinn's, guiding her middle finger inside while urging Quinn's thumb to circle the swollen knot of nerves above. "Like that...oh..." Corrie's hands fell nerveless to her sides at the exquisite pressure, both inside and out. Quinn continued the slow thrusts, watching in awe as her strokes stripped Corrie of the last shreds of control.

Corrie wanted to keep her eyes open, but the pleasure forced them shut, forced her breaths to become ragged in her throat. *Soon, soon, soon.* The pressure was building, a tidal wave behind the dam. Quinn continued her gentle touches, even as Corrie arched her hips, physically striving after the climax that hovered just out of reach. Higher and higher Quinn drove her with those tender caresses, higher and higher and higher until Corrie became mindless with passion. Her eyes opened, immediately locking on to Quinn's. The rest of the room grew dark.

"Oh, please, please I have to *please—*"

Quinn heard the strong note of panic in Corrie's voice and squeezed her clitoris gently between thumb and index finger. Despite Corrie's desperation, the pleasure was not short and sharp. It flattened her body in wave after rolling wave, as endless and eternal as the ocean. And as she watched Corrie succumb to the ecstasy, watched her ignorant fingers working this magic, Quinn felt herself fall in love all over again.

"So beautiful," she said, milking the very last of the spasms from Corrie's exhausted body. "So incredibly beautiful."

When Corrie finally lay quiescent beneath her, Quinn held her just as she herself had been held. Corrie pillowed her head on Quinn's breasts, her pale hair fanning out across Quinn's stomach.

"You feel really good," Quinn dared to confess. *I love you, god how I love you, even more than I did before.*

Corrie mumbled something incoherent and hugged her tightly. A minute later, her arms loosened their hold as she fell into a deep sleep. Smiling, Quinn managed to snag the afghan at the foot of the bed with her left toe and covered them both with it.

Right, she thought sleepily. It was her last thought before exhaustion and heavy satisfaction pulled her under. *This feels so very right.*

RIGHT OF WAY

Quinn woke to the sound of her own name and the aroma of cooking eggs. Corrie's lips were warm and soft against her ear.

"Quinn...hey, sleepy, time to get up."

She rolled onto her back and blinked as Corrie's face slowly came into focus. "Hey," she replied. As she stretched, Corrie's gaze moved down her body. For a second, Quinn felt an overwhelming urge to cover herself with the sheet, but then she saw the appreciation in Corrie's eyes and was able to relax.

"If we didn't have to race," Corrie said, her voice low and gritty, "I wouldn't let you out of bed for hours, yet."

Quinn's breaths stuttered in her lungs. "Oh." Blushing, she cleared her throat. "Um, rain check?"

Corrie laughed. "Fine by me." She sat down next to Quinn on the bed. "How does an omelet sound for breakfast? You'll need your strength today."

"Mmm, is that what I smell?" Quinn rubbed her cheek against Corrie's arm. God it felt good just to be close like this—to share this kind of intimacy. "I'd love one."

"Cool. Give me ten minutes." Corrie leaned down to gently kiss Quinn's forehead. "Do you regret it?" she asked softly. "I know...I know you broke your rule."

Quinn looked up at her for several silent moments. "No. I don't regret it at all."

Corrie smiled—a little bit in relief, Quinn thought. "Good." She leaned down to press a lingering kiss on the corner of Quinn's mouth. "See you downstairs in a few."

Quinn watched her walk away, already clad in her token sports bra and swim trunks. *And I didn't break my rule,* she thought at Corrie's tan back. *I love you. But I'm afraid if I tell you, I'll break the spell.*

She lay still, feeling the crispness of the sheet against her back, the warmth of the sunlight on her chest. *Do I feel different?* She sat up slowly and shifted so that her feet were touching the wood floor. Her clothes were lying folded on the desk chair; Corrie must have picked them up when she'd awakened earlier. Experimentally, she rolled her shoulders and flexed her quads. Her muscles felt relaxed, and her head was clear. Crisp. Free of the hazing desire that had so plagued her the night before.

Am I different? She looked down at herself—at her breasts, at her familiar, too-round belly, at the patch of curly hair between her legs. Corrie had mapped her body, had touched her everywhere. *And I...* She raised her fingers to her nose and breathed in. *Oh, god.* That scent, musky and pungent, made her want nothing more than to feel and be felt all over again.

But breakfast awaited, and then the race. Quinn got to her feet and quickly pulled on her clothes. It was time to stop dilly-dallying. If they could win, maybe Corrie would finally feel better. Stronger, not as threatened by Will, and perhaps even able to forgive Denise. Who was, Quinn realized, even more of a fool than she had originally thought.

"She loved you, and you refused to honor that," Quinn said to her reflection in Corrie's mirror. *But I'm not going to make that mistake,* she pledged silently as she headed for the stairway. *Even if she never says the words.*

❖

Quinn made her way down the hall, weaving between small groups of sailors as she headed toward the skipper's meeting in the chart room. Technically, she wasn't obligated to be there, but it didn't make any sense to wait at home once she'd stopped in to retrieve her sailing gear. And more than that, she wanted to be with Corrie for any showdowns she might have with Will and Denise.

Quinn stopped just inside the door, leaning against the wall as she surveyed the buzzing crowd. She was immediately surprised by the diversity of the group. At least a third of the skippers were middle-aged. She had expected to see more men than women, but even that split was less drastic than she had anticipated. Everywhere she looked, people were talking and gesturing excitedly, and Quinn felt herself start to relax. *Casual. The atmosphere's a lot less competitive than I thought it would be.*

But then she finally caught sight of Corrie, and her pulse jumped back into hyper-drive. *Oh, she looks so good.* Quinn suddenly felt thirsty and just the slightest bit dizzy. Shaking her head, she moved toward the familiar figure.

Incredible. It was the only word she could think of. Corrie owned several "rash guards," as Quinn had heard her call them—skin-tight shirts made from a special kind of polyester that blocked both sun and salt water—but she had never seen this particular one before. It was a deep blue, with bands of gray at the collar and on both short sleeves, and as Quinn drew closer, she could make out Georgetown's crest above Corrie's left breast. The shirt left nothing to the imagination. Quinn could *see* the prominent bulges of her biceps, and her six-pack abs, and the contours of the muscles that flared out slightly just above her hips. Tight, dark gray shorts struggled to contain her strong legs, finally giving way to tan skin several inches above her knees.

Quinn suddenly flashed to the sight of Corrie's *naked* body, bow-tight beneath her in the fragile instant before orgasm. She breathed in sharply as her own body sparked at the memory, as her fingers ached to be enclosed again by the wet grip of Corrie's inner muscles.

"Quinn, hey!" Corrie's voice, uncharacteristically high-pitched, shocked Quinn out of her reverie. She had no memory of crossing the room, but there she was, standing next to Corrie, who was facing off with her brother and a petite, perky brunette whose painted-on smile nearly out-dazzled the morning sunshine. A rather large diamond glinted on her left hand. *Denise.* It had to be. And she was much, much prettier than Quinn.

"Glad you're here," Corrie said, her voice noticeably strained. She slipped one arm around Quinn's waist and drew her close. A few weeks ago, Quinn probably would have minded the show of possession, but after last night? It felt right, somehow. She rubbed her cheek briefly against Corrie's shoulder and tried to look relaxed. "You've met Will, but this is his fiancée and crew, Denise Lewis. Denise—Quinn Davies, my crew and my girlfriend."

Both Will and Quinn looked surprised at Corrie's use of that particular word. Despite having never really liked it, Quinn found that she didn't mind it applied to her now. Especially with that "my" in front of it.

"Pleased to meet you," said Denise. Her smile was surprisingly wide as she focused in on Quinn.

Weird, Quinn thought. *She almost looks relieved.* She shook hands and tried not to let on that she could feel Corrie vibrating with suppressed tension. Her back was ramrod straight, and Quinn suddenly understood why every single one of her muscles was jumping out in high-definition. *At this rate, she'll waste all her adrenaline, just by standing still.*

"So," Denise asked conversationally. "How long have you been sailing?"

The question was presumably meant to rattle her, but instead, Quinn found herself enjoying the prospect of being the underdog. "I started lessons in early June," she said, shrugging, "so, not long at all, really." When Denise nodded benevolently, Quinn pointed to her sleek white US Sailing shirt and pretended ignorance. "Were you in the Olympics as well?"

"Yes," Denise said, "though we haven't been on the circuit for a few years now." She turned then to look up sweetly at Will. "That's where we met." Will grinned back indulgently.

Quinn barely stopped herself from rolling her eyes and instead brushed her hand surreptitiously along Corrie's forearm in a meager attempt to soothe her. Corrie's skin nearly burned the tips of Quinn's fingers. *That's it*, she thought suddenly. *She's driving herself crazy here.*

"That's so great," she said, before lightly gripping Corrie's wrist. "I hate to say this, Mars, but don't you have a meeting to run?" Quinn used the nickname deliberately, hoping to catch Corrie's attention.

"Oh," Corrie said, pulling back and nodding. She shrugged in what passed for an apologetic manner. "I really should be going, I guess."

"Sure, Cor," said Will. "See you on the water."

"It was good to see you again, Corrie," Denise chimed in. "And nice to meet you, Quinn."

Quinn successfully reined in her impulse to trip Denise as she and Will wandered off to find seats. She looked up into Corrie's dilated eyes and deliberately squeezed her hand. "How are you doing?"

"Okay. I'm okay."

"Try to stay calm for now," Quinn said as she stroked the back of Corrie's hand with one thumb. "Save it for the water."

Corrie nodded. Her face was suddenly very vulnerable, and if they hadn't been in a crowded room, Quinn would have dared to lean in for a kiss. "I'm glad you're here," Corrie said quietly. "I think maybe you rescued me, just then."

"You would have been fine on your own."

"No," Corrie replied vaguely. "I'm not sure you're right about that." But she looked down at her watch, and her eyes widened slightly. "I actually *do* need to get started." This time, the note of apology in her voice was genuine. Quinn could tell.

"Okay." She was turning away to find a spare strip of wall to lean against, when Corrie caught her shoulder.

"Meet me in my office, an hour before the start," she breathed into Quinn's ear. The gentle, prickling sensation forced goose bumps to the surface of her arms.

"Okay."

When she turned around, Corrie had melted into the crowd.

❖

Corrie, ensconced in the swivel chair behind her desk, twisted from side to side as she gazed out the window. The boathouse's flag streamed steadily in her direction. She had checked the radar only a few minutes earlier. *No storms in the vicinity. Fourteen knots, no gusting.* She rolled her shoulders and flexed her biceps experimentally. *A perfect day.*

At the sound of approaching footsteps, she immediately looked up, expecting Quinn. But the doorway remained mysteriously empty, until—

"You're not going to throw anything, are you?" Quinn's voice sounded wary.

Corrie grinned. "The coast is clear. Come on in."

"Hi." Quinn closed the door behind her, walked right up to Corrie, and leaned against the desk instead of sitting on her lap, as had been her original intent. *Chicken.*

Fortunately, Corrie read her mind. "This is softer," she said, patting her thighs. For some reason, she was feeling the overwhelming urge to be in physical contact with Quinn every chance she got. *And I'm not in the mood to deny myself—not today. Not after last night.*

Quinn settled warmly into Corrie's embrace, loving how easily they meshed together. "You feel good."

"So do you." One of Corrie's hands rubbed circles on Quinn's stomach while the other lightly stroked her knee. "Are you feeling okay about the race?" Corrie asked. Her words were warm against Quinn's neck. "Anything you want to go over one last time before we head out?"

"Hmm." Quinn traced Corrie's bicep through the rash guard as she thought. "Well, as much as I hate to bring them up, you've seen Will and Denise sail, right? Is there anything we can focus on that will specifically help us beat them?"

Corrie shifted so that she could look directly into Quinn's eyes. They swirled from blue to gray and back again. *Like the ocean on a partly cloudy day.* "You know...you know it's okay if we don't, right?" she asked, frowning. "If we don't beat them, I mean."

Quinn gazed back at her steadily. "I understand why you need to say that to me right now, but I also know that it's not exactly true." She gently stroked the back of Corrie's head. "I want to help you win, because it's important to you. And I care about what's important to you, because I care about *you*. Okay?"

Corrie nodded, not daring to trust her voice. *I really, really don't deserve you*, she thought as she stared out the window toward the waiting ocean. Her gut twisted painfully. *Don't think about it. Not now. Later. After.* "I guess we should get down to the boat," she said, finally.

"Yes. The boat." Quinn leaned in for a kiss. "Unofficially, though," she murmured against Corrie's lips, "I'd rather stay right here."

Corrie laughed as they both rose to their feet. "You're good for my ego, you know that?"

Quinn shook her head, reached for Corrie's hand, and pulled her toward the door. "And you're good for mine."

She led Corrie out into the brilliant sunlight, blinking as her eyes adjusted. A dozen questions still pounded against the walls of her brain like the surf against a cliff—big questions, frightening questions, questions about the future, about relationships, about love. Hopeful questions. But for now, the wind and water beckoned.

❖

Jen and Drew were helping to orchestrate the distribution of sailing equipment from the shed as Corrie and Quinn approached. "I was beginning to wonder about you two!" Drew called, tilting his head toward their boat on its cart. "Everything's in there—sails, rudder and tiller, vests. Some spare line as well."

"Thanks," Corrie said. She squeezed his shoulder, just before Quinn stepped up to give him a quick hug.

"Good luck, Q," said Drew. "Kick some ass for me."

"You betcha." Quinn tried to look brave.

"What am I?" asked Jen, arms folded imposingly beneath her breasts. "Chopped liver?"

"Yep," said Drew, grinning from ear to ear.

"Not at all," Quinn answered graciously. "Thanks for the extra-crispy sail." She indicated the brand new tube of material in the bottom of their boat, and gave Jen the thumbs-up as she unfurled its foot along the boom.

"Don't forget to tell the staff to fire up the grills at five o'clock," Corrie said, fitting the tiller and rudder together. "If we don't have food for the masses when the races are over, we'll be hoisted on our own petards."

"How àpropos," Jen scoffed.

"Yes'm," said Drew, snapping a smart salute.

At that instant, Will walked by, hand-in-hand with Denise. She balanced a sail on her right shoulder while he hefted the tiller in his free hand. The pair was clearly headed for the piers and their waiting boat. "Hey Cor," he said jovially. "Hi, Quinn. See you out there." Denise nodded at them.

Corrie nodded back frostily and began running the tapes of the spinnaker with far more vigorous movements than were strictly necessary. "Sure, see you." Her head turned to follow them and she muttered a string of obscenities under her breath.

I guess Corrie's fighting spirit is back in full force, Quinn thought. She was more than a little relieved. Now was not the time for Corrie to feel vulnerable.

"Who's the girl?" Jen asked, once they were out of earshot.

Corrie ground her teeth. Quinn winced at the sound. "His fiancée."

Drew frowned. "What's her deal? Why are you making that awful noise?"

"I'm ready for the chute," Quinn said matter-of-factly, holding out her hand. As the sail was handed over, Quinn made sure to brush Corrie's knuckles with her fingertips in an effort to soothe her. *Don't think about them. Think about me. Think about how you kissed me, and how I felt inside you. Forget she ever touched you.* "Pay attention while I rig this now," she said. "I don't want to do it wrong. Not today."

With an effort, Corrie turned away from the retreating forms of Will and Denise. "Okay." She even mustered up a half-grin. "Right. I'm watching."

"Is she evil?" Drew persisted, still watching Denise.

"How about we make sure the judges' boat doesn't leave without us, Harris?" Jen asked sweetly. Quinn shared an appreciative smile with her before turning back to the rigging. Drew was so hopelessly illiterate at subtext.

"But—"

"Come on," Jen said, grabbing his elbow and shepherding him toward the dock.

For a few minutes afterward, Corrie and Quinn worked together in silence. "I think we're good to go," Corrie said finally, surveying the boat one last time. The spinnaker sheet clearly extended around the outside of the forestay, and the pole was tucked securely under one hiking strap. Quinn had tied figure-eight knots in every important piece of line. Both sidestays sported telltales made from unwound cassette tape that would flutter in the wind to help them navigate.

"Shall we?" Corrie asked, taking a deep breath and looking out toward the water. *Wind still looks steady. Good.*

"You're the skipper." Quinn grabbed one side of the cart's handle and began to maneuver their boat toward the nearest pier.

"Yeah, but you're calling most of the shots these days," said Corrie. She slid her right hand over the back of Quinn's before taking hold of the other side of the handle.

"Careful now," said Quinn, her voice soft. "You'll give me ideas."

Corrie sucked in a quick breath as her body reacted to Quinn's innuendo by breaking out in goose bumps despite the eighty-five-degree temperature. "Hold that thought," she said, resolutely willing the sensation into the background. "We have some races to win."

❖

Quinn flinched noticeably as a boat that had been about to broadside them ducked below their stern at the very last minute. "Way too close," she muttered, keeping one eye on the jib and one eye on the crowd of boats off starboard.

"Don't worry," said Corrie, her own gaze intent on the starting line. "We're doing just—oh!" By now, Quinn knew that an exclamation like that one was a good reason to duck.

"Tacking," Corrie called belatedly as the boom swung above Quinn's head. There was no time for the normal sequence of commands during the mêlée just before a race's start. The precious gaps that suddenly developed between boats would disappear just as quickly if they didn't act fast.

As the boat returned to a close haul on port tack, Quinn noticed the bright flash of Megan Dougherty's orange windbreaker off to their left. "Look, Megs and Brad," she said as they first pulled alongside and then began to pass the familiar pair.

"Howdy, strangers," Corrie said jovially. Her quick eyes picked up on a developing gap on the other side of Brad's boat and she raised her voice. "Hole off starboard, Brad, two o'clock!"

"Thanks, Mars," said Brad as they quickly tacked to take advantage of the room.

Corrie made a minor adjustment to the tiller and returned her focus to the mass of boats between her and the starting line. "Never hurts to lend a helping hand," she answered Quinn's curious look. "Besides, we're gonna whup them anyway. May as well be sportsmanly about it."

When Quinn laughed, Corrie winked, and at that moment, three short whistle-bursts pierced the hazy air. *Thirty seconds.*

"There!" Quinn cried suddenly, her left arm snapping out to point as the paths of two boats just in front of them diverged to create an empty space.

Corrie looked along the line of Quinn's trembling muscles and realized that it was the ideal trajectory. Just inside the port buoy, on an excellent course for the windward mark. They'd be in perfect position. She pushed the tiller hard to starboard, even as Quinn anticipated the movement and hurriedly brought the jib across. Their tack was flawless and fast, and within seconds they were darting forward toward the starting line.

Two whistles. Twenty seconds. The mainsail snapped taut as they surged ahead, and Corrie watched in supreme satisfaction as they passed Will and Denise in their twin US Sailing uniforms. She couldn't help it, she war-whooped. Loudly.

"All we have to do is stay ahead of them!" she shouted. She spared a second to meet Quinn's gaze. "*You* did this; your good eyes."

Quinn hiked out further and smiled. Ahead of them, the last short whistle sounded. Ten seconds. For the first time since they had climbed into their boat an hour earlier, she felt her nervousness abate, to be replaced by a surge of exhilaration. *We can do this*. And then they were crossing the starting line, passing near the judge's motorboat, and she could distantly hear Drew and Jen shouting words of encouragement that were almost immediately lost in the wind. Ahead, several boats were struggling to point as high as they could, as they made for the bright orange windward buoy. Behind, the majority of the pack was trying desperately to catch up to the leaders.

Quinn glanced back at Corrie and was immediately reassured by her intense focus on the boats ahead and her steady hand on the tiller. *She's so beautiful like this*. Her tan, freckled face, the strong muscles in her arms that leapt into definition as she trimmed the mainsail, the swell of her breasts beneath her tight shirt—she belonged exactly where she was. *Really, incredibly beautiful.*

The epiphany was as swift as their tack had been—a change of direction, a sudden crossing of the wind. *I don't want this to end.* Quinn felt the truth of it in the pit of her belly—in the joy and fear that rippled under her skin like static electricity. The odds were against her, of course. Could she really keep Corrie's attention? Would she grow too needy and scare her away? A night here and there would never be enough. *Not for me.*

"Prepare to tack!" Corrie called, reading the wind on the water before it reached their boat.

"Ready," Quinn replied automatically. *Stop thinking.* Now was not the time for ogling or introspection. *Later.* Now was the time to focus. To put to the test every skill she'd learned in the past two months. Resolutely, Quinn crossed the middle of the boat and swung her weight out to port, settling in for the upwind leg.

❖

"Quinn," Corrie said to Quinn's back, as they made their way from the shoreline toward the boathouse. "*Quinn,*" she called more loudly, when there was no reply.

Quinn stopped and turned back so quickly that Corrie nearly crashed into her. She pulled up short just in time and stood looking down into profoundly unhappy blue-gray eyes. "I know," Quinn choked out. "It's completely my fault, and if I don't get my act together this afternoon, we'll have *no chance* of beating them!"

Corrie reached for her hand, but Quinn pulled away. The agony on her face felt like a sucker punch to Corrie's gut. *Idiot, idiot, idiot,* she berated herself. *She's taking this way too hard. What have you done?*

"It doesn't matter," she said urgently. "I never meant to make you think—"

"We've been over this already." Quinn's eyes were far too bright. "It *does* matter. You want to show them that you're better. That you don't need either of them. And I want to *help* you, and then I go falling out of the boat..." She paused, bright eyes flickering across Corrie's face. "You know I'm right."

"One bad race is not a big deal. It's not. I mean it."

Quinn's shoulders slumped and she turned away, swiping at her eyes. "Please don't lie to me," she said, beginning to trudge toward the boathouse. "That's not fair."

Her heartfelt words slammed into Corrie's gut like an uncontrolled boom. *How will I ever come clean? I've been lying to you for weeks.* But then she realized that Quinn was moving away, and she shoved her guilt to the side. The sand churned wildly beneath her feet as she darted to catch up.

"But I'm *not* lying." *Not now, anyway.*

This time, when Quinn tried to pull away, Corrie would have none of it. She squeezed Quinn's hand gently. "Remember that we can get rid of one of our times. So let's just pretend that last race never happened."

She grinned winningly. "Shazam. Poof. Gone. We're tied with them, one to one."

For the first time since Quinn had hiked out too far on her trapeze, lost her balance, and swung out to collide with the bow of their boat, she smiled. Sort of. "We *did* beat them by a good margin in the first race."

"Yeah!" said Corrie, nodding enthusiastically. "That was an incredible sail."

"So, we should be okay, as long as we win twice and don't lose another one badly—right?"

Corrie nodded again, and finally gave in to the urge to move forward and tuck a few stray strands of Quinn's wavy brown hair back behind her right ear. Quinn leaned into her touch. "It'll all come down to how the times add up in the end," she said quietly. Quinn's face was soft and smooth and she leaned down to press her lips to where her fingers had been. "But that strategy sounds good to me."

Quinn took a deep breath. "Okay."

"Okay?" Corrie raised both eyebrows. "You're still with me, then?"

Cute, thought Quinn. "It looks like I am." Corrie's evident relief made her chest hurt, but in a good way. She took another deep breath and looked toward town. "I'm going to take a walk and grab something to eat. I want to get away from this for a while."

"Sure." Corrie let go of Quinn's hand with obvious reluctance. "I understand. See you in an hour."

Quinn walked briskly toward Main Street, but just before she turned out of Corrie's line of sight, she looked back. Corrie was watching her. She even gave a little wave. Quinn's heart flip-flopped again.

This is bad, she thought. Apparently, falling in love was the same as any other kind of falling in its rapid acceleration. *Very, very bad.* Who knew what would happen after all this excitement was over? *She'll just be left with little, boring me. How will that be enough?*

But despite the familiar doubt, she was smiling.

❖

Corrie tugged hard on the mainsail and hiked out even further as the boat heeled up in response. Testing her line of approach, she turned the bow just a bit further into the wind, and when the sail did not begin to flap, she crowed in triumph.

"We're pointing better than they are," she shouted to Quinn over the sound of the wind. "Just keep her steady and we should catch them at the mark!"

"Okay," said Quinn. Her body was extended completely over the water, her knees only slightly bent. She rigorously watched for puffs, even as the ocean spray battered her face and soaked her shirt and shorts. The wind had picked up since this morning, which meant that Quinn had literally been trapezing for hours. Her quads were on fire and her biceps ached, but this was the last race.

Just hang on, she told herself. *Hang on and don't mess up.* The windward mark drew rapidly closer with every passing second, and she mentally prepared herself for the flurry of activity that would attend their rounding of the buoy. Keeping the boat balanced on the windward leg was a piece of cake compared to raising and flying the spinnaker. And as soon as they rounded the orange sphere now bobbing just fifty feet away from them, she would have to do just that.

The race leaders had already made the turn, but ten feet ahead, Will and Denise were clearly visible against the deep blue backdrop of the late afternoon sky. Quinn caught her breath in excitement as she realized that Corrie was right. They were gaining on the pair. And as long as they could nose their way even with the stern of Will's boat, Corrie would be able to demand right of way around the buoy.

Quinn held her breath as they edged closer, and closer, and even closer.

"Room!" Corrie bellowed, as soon as the bow overlapped. "Get the fuck out of my way, Will!"

When Quinn saw Corrie let out their sail by several feet of line, she jumped back into the boat, immediately reaching for the spinnaker pole. As quickly as she could, she attached the topping lift before hooking one end of the pole to the mast and the other to the edge of the sail. For once, the entire process didn't take more than ten seconds. "Raise, raise, raise!" she shouted, as soon as all three points of the pole were attached. Corrie pulled hard on the spinnaker halyard, and the blue and white sail began to inflate off port.

As the boat tilted precipitously, Quinn secured the guy, grabbed the sheet, and launched herself backward until only the balls of her feet were in contact with the gunwale. From her precarious position on the trapeze, she continually trimmed the spinnaker, testing the fullness of the sail by alternately tightening and easing the line. As soon as the boat was level in the water, she felt its bow rise up powerfully out of the waves.

"Planing," she whispered reverently. She risked a quick glance backward to watch the water stream behind them and realized that they had somehow managed to pull ahead of Will and Denise by a little more than a boat length. *Five seconds. Jen said we need to beat them by five seconds to come in ahead overall.*

"Nice!" said Corrie, grinning broadly at their sudden lead. She tucked her feet under the hiking straps and leaned out slightly to help balance the boat. "Long as we keep the chute full, we'll hit the jibe mark ahead."

Quinn nodded, never taking her eyes from the spinnaker. She played it delicately as Corrie worked the tiller and watched for sudden gusts. *Keep it full*, she told herself, over and over. *Just keep it full.* The rest of the world receded. There was only wind and water and the impatient tug of the sail, straining hard against her aching palms. *Just hang on. Just keep it full.*

"Jibe mark in fifty," Corrie said. "We're still a boat length and a half ahead."

Quinn nodded again. *Moment of truth. Last chance to make this perfect.* Denise and Will were former Olympians, and Corrie had once told Quinn that most Olympians could jibe their spinnaker pole in under five seconds. She took a deep breath and visualized what she was about to do, even as she continued to trim the chute.

"All right, Quinn," Corrie shouted, as she let the mainsail out completely. Crouching low to maintain her balance, she threw one leg over the tiller extension so that she could steer with her legs while flying the chute with her hands. "One last time. Hand me the sheet!"

Quinn bent her knees and swung into the boat, reaching back as she did so to transfer the line into Corrie's gloved palm. As soon as she was safely inside the boat, she unhooked her harness from the starboard trapeze clip and reached forward to jibe the pole. For the first time in her life, Quinn managed to release the pole and reattach it in the same motion. In a burst of speed, she reset the spinnaker lines and hooked herself into the port trapeze clip, then grabbed the sheet from Corrie and propelled herself out of the boat.

Corrie let go of the spinnaker sheet completely and grabbed at the purchase system of the mainsail. Mesmerized, Quinn took her eyes off the newly inflated spinnaker to watch the muscles in Corrie's arms and back leap into sharp relief as she manually yanked the boom across the thwart while shoving the tiller away from the sail with her knees. The boat lurched and spun quickly around the buoy—so quickly that it only registered as a bright flash of orange in Quinn's peripheral vision before they had cleared it and were racing toward the leeward mark.

"That was beautiful!" Corrie yelled into the wind as she trimmed the sail. "*You* are beautiful!"

Quinn laughed triumphantly. The spinnaker tugged against her grip like a creature possessed, but the ache in her arms and legs was gone. "How far ahead?" she shouted, not daring to look back at their competition.

Corrie risked a quick glance. "Enough!" she crowed. "Enough. Just keep her full."

And Quinn did, all the way until the windward mark. She pulled the spinnaker down with smooth, efficient movements as Corrie spun them around the buoy and headed back upwind toward the finish line. The boats ahead were meaningless. Only the one behind them counted. As soon as the sail was tucked securely into its bag, she swung out again on the trapeze. Their boat responded by darting forward, as though it knew just how important these final seconds were.

"Still enough?" Quinn gasped. Her arms were suddenly aching again.

"Yes," said Corrie, her voice strong and sure. She stretched as far out of the boat as she could, and briefly met Quinn's eyes. "Just a minute more."

Quinn's legs shook, her thighs and stomach burning as she struggled to maintain her balance on the trapeze. And then, out of the corner of her eye, she could see it—the judges' boat, only a few seconds away. She leaned back for all she was worth, forcing the hull down *hard* to ride flat against the water until the high-pitched blare of a whistle signaled their finish. Corrie released the mainsail immediately, and Quinn somehow found the strength to lunge back into the boat before collapsing against the thwart.

Several seconds later, the whistle shrilled again. As one, they looked toward the judges' boat, where Jen was waving her arms frantically in their direction. "You did it!" they heard faintly.

"Holy shit," said Corrie. The boat was rapidly losing momentum, as it spun up into irons. She looked over at Quinn and grinned tiredly. "We beat them."

"Yeah," Quinn said weakly. Her heart, she was certain, was trying to force its way out between her ribs. "We did."

"You were amazing. Incredible. That last jibe..."

"You were pretty amazing yourself," Quinn managed.

The boat finally stopped its forward movement, hanging motionless for just an instant before the wind and the waves began to push it backward. After another minute, Corrie wiped the sweat from her forehead with one arm and sat up slowly. She turned toward Quinn, and her eyes were bright.

"Thank you," she said. Inexplicably, she blinked back tears. "God, Quinn, thank you so much."

But Quinn shook her head. "Don't thank me for something I wanted to do." She reached out to touch Corrie's arm above her sailing glove. The skin beneath her fingertips was hot and moist with sweat. And then Corrie leaned in to briefly rest her head on Quinn's shoulder, her eyes closing as she sighed deeply.

I hope this brings you peace, Quinn thought as she grazed Corrie's temple with her lips. *You deserve it.* Corrie's vulnerability was humbling. It made her ache inside. *I love that you trust me. I love you.*

"Come on, Skipper," she finally said. "Let's head in, so we can celebrate our victory."

GALE FORCE

Quinn stretched her sore legs out beneath the table as Jen handed her another drink. Tequila sunrise. Quite possibly a new favorite. "Oh, thank you," she said, immediately pressing two fingertips to the cool glass and transferring them to her face. *Cool. Nice and cool.*

"Either you're pretty buzzed, or you got a wicked sunburn," Jen said, smirking. "'Cuz you're all red, y'know."

"Sunburn. I forgot to put more lotion on, during the lunch break."

"Ah." Jen took a sip from her glass—some kind of hard liquor on ice—and raised her eyebrows. "You must be feeling pretty good, though. About beating Corrie's brother, I mean."

"Oh," said Quinn, nodding perhaps a bit more enthusiastically than she would have, had she not already consumed one tequila sunrise. "Yes, definitely. I feel *great*." *And about out-crewing Denise. Especially about that.*

"Bet Mars does, too."

"I hope so," Quinn said, suddenly serious. "She should. In fact..." She sat up straighter and craned her neck. "Where did she go?"

"There." Jen pointed, and Quinn twisted around in her seat until she could see Corrie, who was deep in conversation with Brad and Drew just a few feet away. An unfinished beer bottle hung down by her side, resting in the vee between her index and middle finger. She was still wearing the rash guard, and Quinn's eyes were drawn to the gentle curves of her breasts. They weren't full and heavy, like her own. In fact, she was willing to bet that Corrie could get away with not wearing a bra without feeling discomfort. But they matched her lean physique, and they had fit so perfectly into her palms, and god, she wanted to feel them again, to kiss them as she smoothed her hand down Corrie's taut stomach and—

Will strode into her field of vision, Denise in tow, and Quinn was immediately on high alert. Denise looked reluctant to be there; she was frowning a little and biting her bottom lip. As she stood behind him and slightly off to one side, he clasped Corrie's shoulder. Quinn grimaced preemptively. *Uh oh.*

"That last race was amazing, Cor," Will said jovially. "The way you stole our wind like that was just clutch. You guys were sharp!"

Quinn didn't realize that she was holding her breath until she exhaled in surprise. Corrie's expression as she turned to look up at Will was not fiercely triumphant, as she had expected it to be, or even angry. Her face was curiously blank, almost as though she didn't recognize him. Her mouth opened slightly, then closed.

"And Quinn was incredible, too," he said, his hand still resting on her shoulder. "Especially seeing as she only started learning this season."

Corrie said nothing in reply, but Quinn could tell when the rage began to sweep over her, could see it in her face and in the set of her body—like watching a thunderstorm move across the water. Denise was actually fidgeting, and Quinn wondered whether she could read Corrie's mood as well. The thought bothered her.

"Anyway, that was a solid ass-whupping you gave us, but we'll be out to get you back next year." He reached out to thread one arm around Denise's waist. "Right, honey?"

"Sure," said Denise. She glanced once at Corrie, then away.

The storm hit. Corrie trembled once, violently. Her eyes were as wide and dark as they had been while Quinn had touched her the night before, but her fists were clenched at her sides and the tendons in her neck leaped out in relief as she struggled to keep her fury in check. She trembled again, squared her shoulders, and turned toward the double doors. They boomed shut behind her, a clap of thunder.

Will turned toward Denise, tugging in frustration at the brim of his cap. "What the hell was that all about? What did I say? I congratulated her, for fuck's sake!"

"Just let her go," Denise said, grabbing for one hand. "Come on, let's head back to our table." She tugged lightly, but Will remained rooted to the spot.

"No." He shook his head. "No, I'm going out there, and I'm going to find out what her goddamn problem is."

"Will—" she sounded genuinely frightened for some reason.

Quinn paused in the act of raising her glass to her lips. What was Denise trying to hide? She tracked Will's progress across the room before looking down into the pink and gold swirls of her drink. "They'll either have it out once and for all," she said to Jen, "or one of them will end up in the ocean."

❖

Corrie kicked up small clouds of sand as she hurried across the beach toward the docks. "Fuck you both," she muttered. "You and your bullshit, treating me like some kind of baby..." Will's condescending congratulations had been the proverbial last straw. Who the hell did he think he was to give her a pat on the head? His message had been loud and clear. *Nice sailing, kid sister, but we all know what's really important. What I have and you don't, what I won and you lost.*

She turned aside at the first pier and threw herself onto the slats, dipping one foot down to kick furiously at the glittering water. Leaning back on her elbows, Corrie looked up at the stars—so very bright in the clear, still sky. But all she could see were the dark spaces between them.

Behind her, a loose board creaked. Her head whipped around. "Get out of here!" She spun around and surged to her feet in the same movement.

"No." Will stopped a few feet away. "I'm sick of this passive aggressive bullshit, Corrie. It's been going on for far too long, and I should've called you on it a long time ago." He crossed his arms over his broad chest. "So whatever the hell is bothering you, out with it, okay? Right here, right now. 'Cuz I've been wracking my brains, and I don't have a clue."

"What the *fuck*?" Corrie took a menacing step toward him. "Wracking your brains, huh? I always knew I was a fuckload smarter than you, but this just takes the cake!"

"Oh, get off it," Will growled. "I'm sick and tired of you going on about what a little genius you are! Ever since you got into Georgetown, you've been rubbing my face in it."

Corrie's fingernails bit into her palms. "Oh, and you've never rubbed my face in anything, have you? 'Course not. Not you. Prince Charming William."

Will threw his hands up in the air. "What the hell are you talking about now?"

Corrie took another step forward. "Denise, you asshole!" she yelled back. "Or have you already forgotten how you stole her, fucked her, and fucked me over?"

Will froze. "What?"

"You heard me." Her words were missiles, sparking over the gulf between them, finally finding their marks.

"You...and Denise." Will looked stunned. "You and Denise had a...a thing?"

"A *thing*? I was in love with her! I had it all planned out! We were going to win the gold and move to Provincetown so we could get married and—" Suddenly, the import of his questions hit home. She reached out for one of the pylons, to steady herself. "Holy shit. You didn't—"

"Of course I didn't know! I just thought you guys were friends. You never said anything about it. I had no idea."

"How could you not—"

"What the fuck? Do you expect me to read your mind or something?" Will scowled deeply. "Cut me a little slack here, for once in your life. I have *no idea* how your oh-so-brilliant brain works, okay?"

"And that's my fault?" Corrie sucked in a deep breath. "You never bothered to really get to know me. All I've ever been to you is a fucking benchmark you always had to exceed."

"Oh, thanks a lot, Cor. Thanks a *lot*." Will shook his head. "Who the fuck taught you how to throw a football? Kick a soccer ball? It sure as hell wasn't Dad. I taught you how to *sail* for god's sake!"

"All you taught me," Corrie snarled, "was how to royally fuck up someone's entire life. And you didn't even have to try that hard."

"I told you, goddammit, I didn't have a clue that you guys had been an item. Not a fucking clue!"

Silence descended between them, then, as Corrie realized the import of what he was saying. "She never told you." She shook her head in disbelief. "I mean, yeah, she didn't want to come out to her *parents*, but how the hell did she manage not to tell *you*?"

"She—she told me she thought you were jealous of her because she made it to the Trials and you didn't." He shrugged, clearly confused. And upset. "What...what happened, Cor?"

Corrie looked down at the dock. Suddenly, she didn't want to yell anymore. Her righteous anger didn't stand a chance in the face of his honest confusion. "We were together for two months." Her lips twisted. "I had it so bad...and then, one day, she just broke it off. Said she couldn't 'do this' anymore, whatever the hell that means." She sighed heavily and glanced up at Will before rubbing the back of her neck with one hand. "Next thing I know, I see her getting all cozy with you."

Will looked out toward the water, running his fingers lightly over his five o'clock shadow. "Fuck."

Corrie nodded in silent agreement. "You and I," she began hesitantly. "We've always been competitive. Too competitive, about everything. And maybe it's my fault. Maybe I let the pressure of always being in your shadow get to me."

"My shadow?" Will grimaced. "I had to fight just to stay one step ahead. You lit a fire under my ass, you know? Always on the verge of catching up and passing me by."

Corrie laughed, but it wasn't a happy sound. "God, what a pair we make."

"No shit." Will stretched both arms above his head. "I feel like I'm in one of those soap operas Mom used to watch when we were kids."

"I hear you."

They stood still for several minutes—not moving, not saying a word, but closer than they'd been in years. Will sighed. "I think Denise and I need to have a long talk." He glanced at her, then back out at the water. "You and I...uh, are we...?"

"I don't think this is going to get fixed in one day," Corrie said quietly. "But this—it's a start, I guess. Or something."

"Temporary truce?" When Corrie shrugged, he held out his hand. "Do you want me to spit in my palm, or what?"

She turned away, but Will thought he saw the shadow of a smile curve her lips. "I'll pass, thanks."

He jerked his head toward the boathouse. "Want to head back?"

"Yeah, okay."

When they stepped through the doors of the chart room, Will headed one way and Corrie another. Quinn had to grab her chair handles to keep herself from jumping up and asking what had happened between them, but fortunately, Corrie made for her table after a brief stop at the bar.

"You okay?" Quinn asked softly as Corrie sat down next to her. Corrie nodded. Her expression was vacant, as though she were looking at something far away. *God, she looks so tired.*

"He didn't know," she said. "All this time, I thought he was gloating. I even thought he might've done it on purpose just to get at me, and he didn't know."

Quinn sat back hard in her chair. *So that's what she was hiding. Why would she* do *that?* "God."

"Yeah." Corrie took several swallows off her beer. She closed her eyes. "I think I'm going to go home. Party's winding down anyway. I'll clean all this shit up tomorrow."

Quinn reached out to stroke Corrie's quads with a light, soothing motion. The muscles were tense beneath her palm. "Okay." She bit at her lip. "Do you want, um, company?" *Please say yes. I want to help you, to comfort you.*

Corrie opened her eyes and smiled but shook her head. She covered Quinn's hand with her own. "I sort of just need to be alone tonight. To think."

"Sure," said Quinn, smothering her disappointment. *How can you blame her?* "Sleep well, okay?"

Corrie kissed her lightly on the lips, then stood up. "You, too. I'll talk to you tomorrow." She paused to brush her knuckles down the side of Quinn's face. "And sweet sailing out there today."

Quinn didn't look away until the doors closed behind Corrie's back. She sighed and swirled the last few swallows of her drink in the bottom of her cup. *I wanted to hold her tonight. To just hold her until she fell asleep, then maybe wake her up in the morning...*

"Hey, Q, you all right?" Drew slid into the chair that Corrie had just vacated.

"Sure, just fine."

"You were making a weird face. All scrunched up, like—" When he demonstrated, Quinn laughed.

"I sure hope I didn't look like *that*."

"Yeah, you kinda did."

Quinn relaxed into the friendly banter, but deep down, she knew she'd be unsettled until she saw Corrie again—until she held her, touched her. *Tomorrow,* Quinn thought. *Tomorrow, I hope.*

COMING ABOUT

Corrie woke to birdsong with the early morning sun in her eyes. She lay still, blinking as she remembered. *Yesterday, the regatta. Will.* Relief spread through her body—aloe over sunburn. She hadn't wanted to admit it last night, but their talk had been new. Different. *Good, I guess.* She flexed her toes and took a deep breath before rolling over in the hopes of getting more rest. *God, I never realized how tiring it is to be angry all the time. For years now.* She snuggled back into the pillow and pulled the sheet up to her shoulders. *But now I don't have to be angry—not at him, anyway.*

Denise, however, was a different story. Corrie felt the tension begin to return, despite her efforts to relax into the springy firmness of the mattress. *He didn't even have to try to steal her away*, she realized. *She was so eager to forget me, she never even told him about us.*

Turning onto her side, she closed her eyes again and tried to focus on nothing—on the sheer sensation of being so snugly cocooned in warmth and softness. But her brain was awake, now, and it churned like the waves before a rising wind. *The past is in the past*, she thought firmly. She had allowed Denise to break her—had given her that opportunity—and she'd never do that again. She was safe.

Then what are you doing with Quinn?

Restlessly, Corrie switched positions onto her other side, drawing her knees up almost until they pressed against her belly. She could feel the trip-hopping of her pulse between her breasts and tried taking a deep breath. Her entire reason for being with Quinn was gone. Eradicated by Will's revelation last night. What did that mean?

That it's time to move on.

Suddenly wide-awake, Corrie slipped out from beneath the sheet and threw her legs over the bed. "Focus," she muttered. "Coffee." Coffee and breakfast first—then thinking. She stood up so quickly that the edges of her vision blurred in dizziness. *Easy*. The relief was gone. Her stomach rolled like a boat about to be swamped by the waves. *Take it easy*.

Frog followed her downstairs, eager for his kibble. She poured the dry food into his bowl and turned on first the coffee pot, then her laptop. As both machines whirred to life, she stared out the window at the waves rippling onto her small beach. *Must be some good wind already*. The thought was automatic.

When the coffee pot chirped its readiness at her several minutes later, she was still looking out toward the water. Where she and Quinn had triumphed, yesterday. *That doesn't change the facts. It's time to let it go—to break it off*. She snagged a mug from the cupboard above the sink, but somehow managed to spill at least half a cup's worth of coffee all over the counter when she tried to pour.

"Ow!" she yelped as the hot liquid cascaded over her thumb. "Jeez, you klutz."

The burn on her hand echoed the growing pain in her chest. *But I don't...I don't want that*, she realized. *I don't want to break it off*.

Corrie practically choked on her bite of powdered donut as panic and dread flooded her brain. *No. No way*. This charade had gone on for far too long—so long that she had begun to believe it. *Going through the motions. That's all it was. Play-acting. Make-believe*.

There was really only one solution. It had to be now. No easing off. Just a clean break. Quinn would get over it. She'd be hurt, but she would recover. *She'll chalk it up to my m.o.,* Corrie realized guiltily. At least it was proving to be good for something. Sort of.

Corrie threw the rest of her donut away. Her stomach didn't feel so good, all of a sudden. When she walked into the den to open the drapes, she remembered sitting behind Quinn on the futon and giving her that massage. She remembered those mind-blowing kisses only two nights ago, just before they'd first made love. *Never again. If you break it off with her, you'll never have that again*. Quinn trusted her, and she was about to betray that completely. *But what else can I do? I can't give her what she wants. I can't. It's not in me*.

Agitated, Corrie returned to the kitchen. *Gotta get out of here. Gotta do something*. She focused on her computer screen. The forecast called for 15-20 knot winds out of the north. Another perfect sailing day. This decision, at least, was an easy one. The wind wasn't complicated:

it demanded intelligence and strength. She gave it her love because it never asked for anything in return. And if it failed her, she could be certain that she wasn't at fault.

You'll find someone, Quinn. Someone who deserves you, someone who can love you like you deserve. She paused in the bathroom to pull back her hair, to put on her Hoyas hat. *I'm not that person, Quinn. I'm like the tech simulator—busted up, broken, fit only for pretend-sailing.*

Down the stairs, out the front door, Frog bounding gleefully at her heels—she ran.

❖

Late in the afternoon, Quinn found Corrie taking down old posters from the boathouse's bulletin board. The strong muscles of her shoulders rippled in tandem with her calves as she stood on tiptoe and reached. *I love your body.* The thought was unbidden.

"Hi," she said softly, from a few feet away. *God, I've missed you.* She hadn't been able to sleep the night before—not for more than an hour or two before waking, alone in the dark.

Corrie spun around and dropped her sheaf of papers. She bent to gather them all up before finally looking Quinn in the eyes. "Um, hey."

"I, um, just wanted to...say hi, I guess. And to see how you are. After last night, I mean."

Corrie forced the corners of her lips to curve up. For the first time, she was thankful for Quinn's hesitancy, for her shyness. If Quinn touched her, Corrie wasn't sure she'd be able to go through with her resolution. *But you have to. Short-term happiness is not worth anymore long-term pain.*

"I'm relieved, actually," she said. About this, at least, she could be truthful. "It feels really good to know that Will didn't...that he wasn't—"

"Out to get you?"

When Corrie nodded, Quinn smiled back. Her expression was definitely the genuine article. But as quickly as it had bloomed on her face, it was gone. Quinn cleared her throat.

"I also wanted to ask you whether maybe you wanted to get some dinner tonight." The words came out in a rush. "A pizza? Or something nicer?"

"I can't," was Corrie's immediate reply. Her eyes darted up and down the hallway as she wished desperately for someone else to come along. A distraction. "Sorry." She shrugged. "It's just, I have to finish up all the paperwork from the regatta, and then read these instructor applications before Tuesday night's meeting so we can short-list."

"Oh, okay." Quinn nodded and stuck her hands in her pockets. "Maybe some other time." The awkwardness was palpable. Corrie could taste it. It tasted bitter.

"Sure," she said. "Yeah." *It's better this way,* she thought at Quinn's back, as she watched her walk away. *You want someone who doesn't exist.*

❖

Quinn deliberately waited two days before trying again—two distracted days, two aching nights. Corrie had awakened her body and her heart, and now both were starving. *You knew this might happen,* she scolded herself as she approached Corrie's office half an hour before the weekly instructor meeting. *You knew and you walked in with open eyes.* Her knock on the door was tentative.

"Come i—" The words stalled in Corrie's throat as she looked up to see Quinn framed in the doorway.

"Hi."

"Uh, hey."

"I brought you cookies."

Oh, fuck, Corrie thought. *An edible toaster.* "Oh, thanks!" she said cheerfully, leaning back in her chair as Quinn approached.

"I know you have that meeting tonight," said Quinn. Her face was flushed. "I thought you might get hungry."

"Definitely." Corrie tried to nod in a convincing manner. "Yeah, thanks."

"So," said Quinn, leaning one hip against the desk. "How's it going? With the applications, I mean." Her gaze roved across Corrie's face eagerly, like a searchlight.

"Slowly," Corrie said, shrugging. "It's going to be a busy week while we decide."

"Ah." Quinn looked down at her feet, then back up at Corrie. Her eyes were bright. "Too busy to go out for a movie, then?"

"Probably, yeah." Corrie had to look away when Quinn's face fell. She twirled a pencil between the index and middle finger of her right hand and felt her stomach mirror the motion. "Sorry."

"No, no." Quinn deposited the cookies on Corrie's desk, took a step backward, and smiled sadly. "I understand." *You pursued me, and you caught me. You had me, and now it's over.* From some deep corner of her gut, pride asserted itself. If Corrie wasn't interested anymore—fine. Quinn wasn't going to beg. She would retreat to a safe place to rest and lick her wounds, just like the animals did.

Quinn didn't return to the boathouse for the rest of the week. Corrie didn't ask Drew about her, nor did she make any effort to talk with her. *She'll only be hurt more. A clean break—that's the best thing. Just let it go.*

But if this really was the best course of action, then why did she feel so damn miserable?

❖

It was late Friday afternoon before Drew took drastic measures. Quinn sat on the couch, apparently engrossed in a textbook on mammal microbiology while he and Jen watched old reruns of *90210*. But when she hadn't turned the page for an hour, Drew finally closed the book for her. Quinn looked up at him and blinked, startled.

"Okay," he began gently. "How about you tell me what's wrong, huh?"

"What are you talking about?" Her tone was defensive.

"You've been on that page for an hour, now."

She glared at him. "It's a hard page."

"No, it's not," he said good-naturedly. "I've read it three times, and I understood it right away."

"Good for you," she snapped, returning her attention to the book. But Drew's gentle yet heavy hand on her shoulder was disarming.

"Come on, Q," he said softly. "I'm worried about you." He glanced over at Jen. "We both are."

"It's the test," she said. "Just the test, stressing me out."

He shook his head. "Nice try. You've had to worry about the test all summer, but you've only been all spaced out for the last few days. Give Corrie a call or something, huh? Go out—have a good time. Or hell, stay in and have a good—" He cut off abruptly and leaned forward. Beneath his hand, Quinn was suddenly trembling. And she had gone very pale.

"What's going on?" Drew asked, perhaps more sharply than he intended. Quinn looked away. "Did something happen with Corrie?"

Helplessly, Quinn nodded. She swallowed hard, unable to speak. "Did she break up with you?" Drew's voice was only getting louder. Quinn winced and shrugged.

"Drew." Jen touched his shoulder in an effort to calm him down, but he shook her off.

"Fucking hell! I'm going to—"

"It's not a big deal," Quinn said. Her words sounded more like a plea than a statement of fact. "We never really talked about what was going on, so..." She had to stop to swallow again and blink fiercely. The cover of the textbook on the table swam in and out of focus. "So it's not a break-up, really. Everything just kind of fizzled out." She nodded again and cleared her throat.

Jen got up and gave her a hug, which Quinn gratefully returned. "I think I'm going to take a walk," Quinn said, once she thought her voice would be steady again. She stood, then looked down at them both. "*Please* don't say anything about this to Corrie. Please don't. Promise me."

"I promise," said Jen immediately, understanding Quinn's reluctance. Drew took a little more convincing, but between the two of them, they managed to make him swear that he wouldn't interfere.

"Come to the social later on," he said, looking down at his watch. "It'll be fun—a good distraction. Please?"

"Maybe." Quinn's voice was firm and brooked no arguments. "See you." After a brief detour into her bedroom, she headed resolutely for the door.

"Godammit!" Drew exclaimed as soon as it had shut behind her. "They were so fucking good together! How the hell did Corrie screw it up?"

"I thought they just might make it, too," Jen said sadly. "Hell, now I owe Brad ten bucks."

Drew rolled his eyes. "You made a *bet*?" When Jen stuck her tongue out at him, he settled back against the cushions. "Do you think maybe we should go have a talk with her? Corrie, I mean? No matter what Quinn says?"

Jen shook her head. "No. Especially since we promised not to. But damn, wouldn't it be fun to go yell at her like there's no tomorrow?"

❖

Quinn trudged along the road leading to Corrie's house, holding a small plastic bag in her right hand. The sun was setting. Corrie wouldn't be home. She'd be at the social, flirting with someone, seducing them, letting them touch her—

Stop it, she told herself desperately. *You knew this would happen. You always knew.*

It didn't matter that she had hoped. Corrie did not do relationships, and she did not fall in love with people, and the fact that Quinn wanted both meant that she was being naïve and unrealistic and just plain dumb.

She stopped at Corrie's driveway. Unable to help herself, she looked up at the bedroom window. *She touched me, there. Made lo— no, no, had sex with me. There, in that room.* A whisper of heat stirred in Quinn's belly, and she looked away. *It's over. No, you never had anything to begin with. Touches in the dark. Let it go.* She blinked back tears and wrestled open the mailbox.

In went Corrie's backup pair of sailing gloves.

They remind me of you. Of sailing with you, of your strong hands. Every time I looked at them this week, I hurt. So she had washed them, and she had hung them out to dry, and all that time she had wished so very badly that it was as easy to purge her self of emotion—to drown and sanitize and burn it all out—as it was to put clothing through the laundry

"Goodbye," she said to the quiet house, before turning back toward town.

But before she had taken more than a few steps, a dark blue convertible pulled up next to the curb. Quinn frowned deeply when the driver stepped out of the car, looked up, and froze. *Denise.* Some small, detached part of Quinn's brain clamored for a six-shooter. *Showdown.*

"Oh," said Denise. "Hi."

"Hi." Quinn had to force herself not to shuffle. Denise was very beautiful and very poised, and Quinn suddenly felt like she was right back in middle school, cowering in the presence of one of the popular girls.

"You're Corrie's girlfriend, right?

Quinn shrugged, even as her anger at Corrie's behavior churned sluggishly beneath her skin at the question. "I really don't know."

It was Denise's turn to frown. "What does that mean?"

"I think Corrie doesn't really do the girlfriend thing." Denise's hair was perfect and her waist was trim, and by the looks of her car and the small diamond necklace that glinted in the v-line of her shirt, she made plenty of money. *How can I ever compare to you?* The waves of anger rose higher, fanned by resentment.

Strangely, though, Denise looked surprised. "I thought maybe she got over that with you."

"No," Quinn said unable and unwilling to suppress the bitterness in her voice. "I guess you were the last one."

Denise took a step back and wrapped her arms around her waist in a protective gesture. "Oh my god, how many people has she told?"

Her puzzling reaction derailed Quinn. "Just me, I think." But Denise's long sigh of relief only fed the flames. "After what you did," Quinn said, her voice growing louder and stronger as she spoke, "why would she want to tell anybody?"

Denise's shoulders straightened, her eyes glinting as they caught the dying light. "It was never as easy for me as it was for her!"

Quinn shook her head once, sharply. "*What* wasn't?" A significant part of her wanted to step forward, grab Denise by the shoulders, and shake her until she started making some sense.

"Her mother tells her to bring girlfriends to family picnics, her brother thinks it's cool that she seduces women, her friends think she can do no wrong. It's never been like that for me—*never*."

"Wait," said Quinn. Comprehension clashed fiercely against the tide of her anger. "Is *that* why you left?"

"I am not a lesbian!" Denise said shrilly. "I want a *real* relationship. A husband that I can be proud of and children that come from us and only us." She gesticulated wildly as she spoke, her hands slicing through the cooling air. "Corrie and I...it would never have—"

"You are such a coward." Quinn's voice was quiet, but it cut off Denise's diatribe just the same. She took a step forward, leaning into Denise's personal space. The fear, the intimidation, was gone. "You were afraid of what everyone else thought, so you just gave up?" Quinn wanted to slap her, to sting her with her words. To get below the skin and indelibly brand her betrayal. "She loved you. It doesn't get any more real than that."

Denise's jaw worked silently for several seconds, before she finally spun on her heel—only to take a step backward as she saw Corrie lounging against the passenger's side door of her car. Quinn sucked in a quick, surprised breath as she too recognized the familiar figure.

"Did you hear that?" Denise asked.

"I heard enough." Corrie's voice was inflectionless.

"Good, then I don't have to repeat it." Denise yanked open her door. "I'm sorry. I'm going home."

Corrie held up one hand. "I just need to ask you one thing." When Denise paused, Corrie continued to speak softly, her voice completely devoid of rancor. "I want you to convince me that you're marrying my brother for him alone." Quinn rubbed her arms, wondering whether the evenness of Corrie's voice was genuine, or the prelude to an outburst. "That you'd still marry him even if you'd never met me. That you're not going to decide someday that he isn't 'real' enough for you."

Denise's grip on the door tightened visibly. "I told you, I love him." She paused, finally daring to meet Corrie's gaze across the car. She swallowed hard. "I...I loved you, too. I couldn't stay with you, but I swear I'll stay with him."

Corrie held her gaze for a long moment, then nodded. When she stepped away from the convertible, Denise got in and gunned the engine. Within a few seconds, she was gone.

Corrie exhaled slowly as she watched the car disappear around a curve. *She didn't have the courage to tell the truth.* She ran one palm across her eyes, then looked over at Quinn. *I'm not going to be like her.*

"I owe you an explanation," she said quietly. "It's not pretty, and it will hurt you, but you deserve my honesty. If...if you still want it."

Part of Quinn wanted to reach out, to take Corrie's hand and pull her in for a long embrace. To tell her that her confession didn't matter. That it didn't change the facts. That her love was unconditional. But at the same time, she needed to know. And perhaps more importantly, she sensed that Corrie needed to tell her.

"Let's go inside."

Frog skittered across the floor as Quinn stepped into the house, his paws clicking loudly against the wood. But he didn't wag his tail. Instead, he whined low in his throat and pushed his nose into the palm of Quinn's hand.

There was a long pause, during which Corrie swallowed audibly. "We should go sit down." The suggestion was more of a ploy for time than anything else, but when Quinn perched on the edge of the couch, so very nervous yet also clearly determined, Corrie knew that she had to deliver what she'd promised. *I have to tell her—to tell her everything.* The guilty anticipation was a sucker punch, and it left her breathing shallowly.

"Here's the thing," she said, looking down at the floor. "I...I used you. When Will accused me of not being able to keep a relationship going, I decided I'd prove him wrong, and went after you." She smiled bitterly. "It worked even better than I could have hoped, except for the fact that my entire reason for wanting to show him up never existed in the first place."

She gripped the armrests of her chair and leaned forward, watching the hurt ripple across Quinn's expressive face. "So now you know. Now you know exactly just how messed up I am—enough to lie to you and manipulate you. All for nothing."

Quinn's hands trembled as she clutched at her knees, the newly developed muscles in her arms leaping into sharp relief. "What gives you the right?" she finally said. Corrie could hear the snarl of tears that blocked her voice. "I never did anything to you. I wasn't a part of this until you made me—"

She cut herself off and surged up out of her seat. Corrie sat back in surprise. "What gives you the right?" she asked again, her voice louder and stronger. She moved forward until she was standing only a foot from Corrie's chair, her eyes so bright they burned.

"Dammit, Corrie, you have a *responsibility.* You're beautiful, you're fun, you're so charismatic it's scary." Two tears freed themselves and cascaded down her red cheeks, only to cling to the corners of her mouth. "You have power over other people—over how they feel about themselves—and you're *selfish* with it."

Her tongue flicked out to catch each tear, absorbing them back into her body. "Go ahead and ruin your own life, if you want to. Go ahead and make yourself miserable. But leave other people out of it. Please."

Quinn's agonized words pressed in on Corrie, forcing her shoulders to bow. "I know what I did to you. I know it was wrong. I just...I'd take it back if I could, okay?" She gulped noisily and ducked her head. "I want you to know that I would."

Quinn began to pace. Corrie could feel the energy flowing opposite its usual course—from her, and into Quinn. *Taking back what I stole from her. Reclaiming herself.* It would have been a beautiful sight, had she not felt so guilty.

"Just tell me this much." Quinn paused near the window. "Just tell me one thing, and then I'll leave and you can move on to your next *victim*." Corrie winced and looked down at the hem of her shorts. One of the threads was coming loose. She'd have to cut it; if she pulled, it would unravel completely.

"Did you really pretend all of it?" Quinn's voice, insistent but somehow softer, forced her to look up. "Was it all just a...a game? Or was there ever..." Her voice trailed off again.

Corrie looked down at her strong, tan hands. *When I touch you like this, you are mine.* There had been something so special about that night. Something unique. Something powerful. But what she felt for Quinn went far beyond the purely physical. Memories of the past two months collided with the hollow sensation in the pit of her gut, sparking and merging. Quinn had made her feel strong, capable, secure. Loved.

It was the moment of deepest truth, the ultimate confession. Corrie took a long, shuddering breath and finally let go. Her heart unfurled, a becalmed sail waiting desperately for just a puff of wind.

"No," she said. "It wasn't just a game." And then her breath hitched and her shoulders began to shake as first one, then several tears dripped hotly onto her knees, scarred and bruised from so many years of sailing. She refused to look anywhere but down, certain that within a few seconds, the front door would slam shut, and that would be the end. *The end of the only real relationship you've ever managed.* And that was the irony, wasn't it? What she had begun cynically had somehow become genuine. Authentic. *True.*

But the door did not slam. Instead, two moist palms covered her knees, and warm breath cascaded against the skin of her forehead and for some unknown reason, Quinn was kissing her—her lips moving gently as she traced Corrie's hairline.

"I'm glad," she said. Callused fingers massaged her head, gently raising it until Quinn could press her lips chastely against Corrie's. "So very glad."

"Don't," Corrie whispered, her eyes closed. "Don't forgive me. Not for this."

But Quinn kissed her again, and then again—over and over, her lips sliding softly against Corrie's until Corrie couldn't help but respond. Quinn pulled back then and waited for Corrie's hazy eyes to focus on her face.

"Don't tell me what to do," she said, her voice quiet but firm.

A shaky smile curved Corrie's lips, but quickly faded. "You knew that I might hurt you," she said. "And I did." Her voice trembled. "Why did you let me? Why did you risk it?"

Quinn knelt down on the floor at Corrie's feet. "People do that—hurt each other," she said finally, meeting Corrie's tortured gaze. "We can't help it, unless we go off and live in cave or something. And even then, we'd be leaving someone behind." She sat back on her heels and restlessly smoothed the fabric of her shorts. "It's happened to you. It happens to everyone. The most important thing is not to do it on purpose."

Corrie swallowed loudly. "I...god, I'm sorry. I know that doesn't mean anything, but—" She sniffled and tried to breathe in deeply. "I tried to convince myself that I was just going through the motions. But I wasn't. I guess maybe I was afraid." She blinked her swollen eyes. "Hell, I'm still afraid."

"Why?" Ever so slowly, Quinn slid one her hand between them. When she laced her fingers with Corrie's and rested it on her knee, Corrie's breath hitched.

"Afraid that once you've thought about all this you'll realize I'm not nearly good enough for you—not by a long shot. Like Denise did."

Quinn raised their joined hands so that she could press gentle kisses to the tan skin below Corrie's knuckles. "You heard what she said. She didn't leave you because you weren't good enough. She left because *she* wasn't. She couldn't find the courage to live her own life."

Corrie had closed her eyes at the first gentle touch of Quinn's lips to her skin. When she opened them, she saw Quinn in a different light. *You really are older than me,* she realized.

She exhaled slowly. Something loosened in her chest, like a chunk of ice trying to break free from its berg and melt away into the ocean. It left her feeling a little empty, and scared. "But...how can *you* still want me?" she asked, almost childlike. "After what I did? After I lied? How?" *Why would you ever give me another chance, Quinn? Help me understand.*

Quinn looked away, considering. "I think we have to say yes to the good things that find us," she said, finally. "Even if bad things have already happened, or might happen later. Even if saying yes hurts— better that than to never have anything at all." She met Corrie's eyes, then looked away again. "And that's ridiculously simplistic." She shook her head and released Corrie's hand. "Should I...do you want me to go? You're exhausted, I can tell."

But as she began to stand up, Corrie recaptured that hand. She squeezed gently. "No. Please don't." She cleared her throat and tried again. "I don't want you to."

"No?" Quinn's eyes were dark and hopeful and sad. Corrie hated herself for causing that sadness, even as she understood that she was the only one who could make it disappear.

She licked dry lips. "I want to say yes to you." *I need you, Quinn. I do. And you need me to finally admit it.*

Quinn's smile was slow and radiant and new. It was perfect. She rose smoothly to her feet and pulled Corrie up beside her. "Then follow me."

At the top of the stairs, Quinn turned and kissed her. Her mouth trailed down from Corrie's lips to trace her jaw line. "Do you trust me?" she asked against her skin.

"Yes."

"Then close your eyes."

Quinn led her into the bedroom, then stepped into the circle of her arms. She walked Corrie backward until her hamstrings pressed against the edge of the bed. "Sit down," she said gently. She cupped Corrie's face, smoothing her freckled cheeks with both thumbs. So beautiful, so beloved. *I can't resist you. I don't even want to try.*

"Now open your eyes," she said, "and tell me what you need."

Corrie's expression was as hazy as the late afternoon air had been.

She blinked up at Quinn, tired and wanting and so very vulnerable. "I know, I *know* I don't deserve you. But I need..." She stopped and breathed deeply. "Could you hold me? For a little while?"

Quinn's earnest face—such a *good* face—was serious as she settled onto the bed. "I'll do anything for you, you know," she said, blinking back sudden tears. "I love you. I didn't mean to, and part of me still doesn't want to, but I love you."

A slow shiver ran through Corrie's body at the words. Quinn felt it. She knew a kind of power, then—a sweet, gentle power that buoyed her up and helped her understand what to do next. Flashing a lopsided smile, she turned to grasp Corrie's shoulders, pushing her back onto the covers with gentle pressure.

"Turn," she said, maneuvering Corrie onto her side and curling around her. She tucked her hand beneath Corrie's breasts and sighed contentedly against the nape of her neck.

Corrie pressed back into her and pulled her arms into a tighter embrace, shivering a little and then falling quiet. "You feel so good." Quinn tangled her legs with Corrie's, entwining their feet and ankles together.

They lay quietly for a long time, long enough for their breathing to synchronize, for their bodies to melt into each other and their warmth to mingle. Long enough for Quinn to feel the wanting awaken in her blood—sharp and sweet and urgent. Her fingers tightened almost imperceptibly around Corrie's breast, and her lips brushed the back of her neck.

"Corrie," she murmured reverently. "I want you. To claim you."

Corrie moaned and her hips rolled involuntarily at Quinn's hesitant touch. "Quinn, yes..."

Quinn teased the tip of Corrie's breast through her shirt. Corrie tensed in her arms and let out a soft cry. Slowly, Quinn shifted her grasp to the hem and began to work it loose—to slide the shirt slowly, tantalizingly, up and over Corrie's head.

After a few seconds, Quinn tugged gently at Corrie's waist, urging her to lie on her back as she slipped her loose shorts down over her hips. As Corrie's body was bared, Quinn caught her breath in wonder. The small areas just around Corrie's nipples were the most beautiful shade of dark pink—like the high, wispy clouds during a hazy sunset. She watched the skin pucker under her gaze, watched the nipples harden and grow darker. When she met Corrie's eyes, they were wide and pleading, but also nervous in a way she had never known them to be.

Quinn cupped her cheek briefly before drawing converging spirals around Corrie's breast. She traced the dusky circle around her nipple with soft fingers, and Corrie whimpered helplessly.

"I love your body." The words were shy and quiet, but when Corrie groaned, Quinn's confidence grew. "I love how soft you are, here." And then her palm moved into the dip between Corrie's breasts before tracking down, down across the tawny plain of her stomach. "And how firm you are, here." She let her touch skitter lightly across Corrie's ribcage and felt her body tighten immediately. Corrie gasped. "And I love that you're ticklish." Corrie laughed shakily.

Quinn reigned in her mischievous fingertips and concentrated on the slight dips between Corrie's abdomen and thighs. Muscles rippled beneath her touch. She looked up to meet Corrie's wide-eyed gaze.

"I love that you're lying still, letting me feel you." Quinn narrowed her touch to the tips of two fingers, sliding down so slowly until they brushed the golden brown curls between Corrie's legs. "I love that you trust me."

"Yes," Corrie surrendered, her back arching, her legs opening. "God, Quinn...need you, so much."

Quinn smiled brilliantly as she slipped her hand into Corrie's warm folds, squeezing gently as she explored. She gasped as wetness coated her fingertips. And then she leaned forward to kiss Corrie, to tangle their tongues together as she massaged her, rubbing in light circles around, then over the tiny hard place nestled in the midst of such exquisite softness.

Corrie's body trembled, and she made tiny pleading sounds against Quinn's mouth. Her hips lifted and Quinn switched to long, firm strokes—up and back, up and back, first with one finger, then with two. Corrie tore her lips away from Quinn's, her breaths coming short and shallow. Quinn felt the muscles in Corrie's stomach contract and knew she was close.

"Look at me," she said quietly.

Corrie's green eyes—nearly black, now—snapped open. Trying desperately to focus through Quinn's tender, relentless touch, she stared into her eyes.

"I love you," Quinn said.

Corrie tipped over the edge into the longest, gentlest climax she'd ever experienced, anchored through it all by Quinn's eyes.

Hours—it had to be hours later—she registered that Quinn was looking down at her—calm, peaceful, content. Corrie felt the last shreds of fear melt away in the warmth of that smile. "I love you," she whispered back. Nothing had ever been more right, more certain.

When Quinn's eyes filled with sudden tears, terror stuck in the back of Corrie's throat. She pulled Quinn close, cradling her face in the crook of her shoulder, feeling the warm drops cascade into the dip of her collarbone. "Oh," she said anxiously. *What is it? What's wrong? What if she's changed her mind?*

"I'm s-sorry," said Quinn, her mouth warm against Corrie's skin. "I just...I never thought I'd hear you s-say that."

Corrie relaxed and kissed Quinn's forehead. *I swear you'll always know*, she vowed silently. *From now on.* "I love you," she said, stroking her back with gentle, soothing hands. "I'm sorry it took me so long to figure it out. I'm sorry, so sorry that I hurt you. I love you, Quinn."

The sensation of Corrie wrapped around her finally banished Quinn's tears. "I'm glad," she whispered. "So glad." She pulled back slightly, needing to see Corrie's face. "I don't say those words lightly, you know. I want...well, I mean..."

When Quinn faltered, Corrie took up the slack. "I know the wind is finicky," she said, holding Quinn's gaze with her own. "But I really like the direction it's blowing in right now. I say we run with it." She leaned in for a kiss, the light strokes of her hands along Quinn's sides a sensual promise. "What do you think?"

Quinn arched into Corrie's loving touch as desire sparked beneath her skin. "Full speed ahead, Skipper," she whispered. They were the last coherent words she spoke for a long time.

CLEAR AHEAD

Will's perpetually tousled head poked out from behind the doorway leading into the living room. "Glad you could make it, sis!" he called. "See ya!"

Corrie grinned over her shoulder and waved at him, then turned back to follow Denise down the hall toward the front door. Quinn was still at large. She had protested that she needed to say goodbye to someone, but Corrie suspected that the excuse had been a front to ensure that she and Denise had some brief alone time. Quinn could be devious like that, she was learning.

"Thank you for coming," Denise said as she turned to open the door. Her voice was heartfelt. Relieved, even.

Corrie lounged against the doorframe, essence of cool. "We appreciated the invitation. Congrats again."

"It was good to get to talk to Quinn some more," Denise persisted. "I like her."

Corrie's eyebrows arched. Denise had been overcompensating all evening, and Corrie couldn't help but feel a small rush of satisfaction. Denise hadn't brought up the uncomfortable conversation they'd shared a few weeks ago, but then again, maybe going out of her way to make them feel welcome was her version of "I really am sorry." *Not as if it matters, anyway. Not really. Not anymore.*

"Good," she said. "I like her, too."

"Like who?" Quinn asked as she turned the corner and walked briskly toward them.

"You." Corrie leaned forward to kiss her. She meant it to be a light peck, but Quinn leaned forward to prolong it.

When she finally broke away, Quinn turned back to Denise and smiled calmly. "It was fun to meet your friends and family, Denise. Thank you."

They shook hands, and Corrie nodded at Denise. "Have a good night." She eased her arm around Quinn's waist as the door closed behind them.

"So?" Quinn asked, as she unlocked the car. "How are you feeling?"

"Much better after that kiss." When Quinn flushed slightly, Corrie nudged her with one elbow. "So you were *trying* to make her jealous?"

"Maybe just a little." Quinn squinted diligently out the windshield as she pulled away from Denise's family home.

Corrie rested one hand on Quinn's thigh and squeezed lightly. "You're sweet. Thank you." She closed her eyes and rolled her shoulders, mentally testing out her mood. "I feel okay, actually. Which is a miracle, considering that only a few weeks ago, I would have actively sought out opportunities to strangle her."

Quinn briefly covered Corrie's hand with her own. "I'm glad. I love you and I don't want you going to jail."

"Ha ha ha." Corrie looked out the window toward the cheerfully lit streets of Newport. "Y'know, I pity her, I guess. Does that make any sense?"

"Of course it does." Quinn glanced at Corrie. "And I pity her, too. Though to be honest, I had the strangest urge all night to do a victory dance to the tune of, 'I won, you lost, neener neener neener.'"

Corrie laughed, long and hard. "I take it back," she said finally, once she'd managed to catch her breath. "You *don't* act like the older one."

A comfortable silence stretched between them as Quinn eased the car onto the freeway that crossed over the Narragansett Bay. Corrie closed her eyes and enjoyed the feel of the salt-tinged summer air against her face and the light pressure of Quinn's palm over her knuckles.

"I think I sort of forgive her," she said finally as the second bridge ended and they returned to the mainland. "And I think the only reason I'm capable of that is you." She turned her head to take in Quinn's profile.

"How do you mean?" Quinn asked softly. She squeezed Corrie's hand with her own.

"You forgave me. I feel like I should pay it forward."

Quinn nodded, her gentle smile illuminated by the red lights of the dashboard. "I'm glad. But as far as I'm concerned, making peace with her is the harder job by a long shot."

"Making peace." Corrie smirked. "Is that a new euphemism?"

Quinn pretended to look alarmed. "In that case, please *don't* 'make peace' with anybody but me!"

Corrie reached out to touch her cheek. "You don't ever need to worry." She paused. "You do know that, right?"

"I know." Quinn looked away from the road just long enough to kiss the tips of Corrie's fingers.

"I need to stop and check on a few kittens at the humane society," she said a few minutes later as they passed the Wakefield town sign. "Shall I drop you off first, or do you want to come with?"

"I'll tag along. I'd like to see it, actually. I've still never been inside."

They pulled up to a low brick building and Quinn unlocked the entrance. She led Corrie down several hallways before finally pausing in front of a set of double doors.

"This," she said as she pushed them open, "is the recovery room for kittens that have just been spayed or neutered." She pulled Corrie inside. Corrie looked around, noting the rows of small cages, many of which were temporarily housing a slumbering feline.

"It's kind of bleak," said Quinn, gravitating over to the cages in the far corner, "but they get moved out to the roomier enclosures within a few days." Corrie followed and grinned when Quinn turned around with a tiny black ball of fur in her arms. The kitten yawned, giving her a view of its pink tongue and gums.

"This is Rogue," Quinn said, nuzzling the kitten's head with her cheek. "I named her for the character in the *X-Men*. See the white stripe she's got, here?" Corrie moved closer and slid her arm around Quinn to peer down at the top of the kitten's head. Sure enough, a streak of white fur trailed from her left ear down to just past her neck.

"Hey, Rogue," Corrie crooned, reaching out to trace the marking. She looked down at Quinn. "Is she your favorite?"

Quinn's expression grew wistful. "Oh, yes. I've never wanted to take home a kitten so badly." She shifted Rogue until the cat was cradled against her neck. Immediately, Rogue began to purr and stretched both paws out until she was hugging Quinn.

"See? She's such a sweetheart." Her face fell even as Rogue

continued to purr and began to munch on her hair. "But she'll be put up for adoption tomorrow, and I know someone will snatch her up right away."

Corrie's sudden idea made her mouth go dry, but she felt the rightness of it, even through her anxiety. She cleared her throat. "Uh," she said. When Quinn looked at her expectantly, she pulled away. "Well...why don't you move in? With me. Into the house. There's more than enough room, and that way you'll be able to adopt Rogue, you know, and I'm sure Frog will love the company."

Quinn's clear shock drove whatever else Corrie had been about to say out of her mind. She stuck her hands in her pockets and hunched her shoulders. "What do you think? At least until you find your own place that'll let you have a cat." She frowned. "Not that I want you to find your own place, because I don't, but if you *did* want to then that'd be cool and—"

Quinn took one step forward and kissed her, wrapping her free arm around Corrie's waist. The kiss didn't end until Rogue, now sandwiched between their bodies, mewed indignantly and squirmed. Corrie laughed breathlessly.

"Are you sure that's okay?" Quinn asked, her voice soft.

Corrie smiled and reached out to stroke Rogue's silky head as she kissed Quinn again. This time, the kitten didn't protest. "Frog doesn't like it when you leave," she said when she finally pulled back. "And besides, I love you."

About the Author

Nell Stark grew up predominantly on the east coast of the USA. She attended a small college in New Hampshire, where she was lucky enough to fall in love with both New England and Lisa, her partner. She is now pursuing her doctorate in medieval English literature in Madison, Wisconsin. Nell spends most of her free moments writing lesbian-themed fiction. When she's not researching, teaching, or writing, she's either spending time with Lisa and their two cats, reading, sleeping (though she wishes she didn't have to), cooking, exercising, or playing *World of Warcraft©*. Nell is also a contributor to several erotica anthologies, including *Erotic Interludes 3* and *4* (BSB), *Wild Nights* (Bella), and *After Midnight* (Cleis).

She can be reached at *nell.stark@gmail.com* or by visiting *www.nellstark.com.*

Books Available From Bold Strokes Books

Blind Curves by Diane and Jacob Anderson-Minshall. Private eye Yoshi Yakamota comes to the aid of her ex-lover Velvet Erickson in the first Blind Eye mystery. (978-1-933110-72-1)

Dynasty of Rogues by Jane Fletcher. It's hate at first sight for Ranger Riki Sadiq and her new patrol corporal, Tanya Coppelli—except for their undeniable attraction. (978-1-933110-71-4)

Running With the Wind by Nell Stark. Sailing instructor Corrie Marsten has signed off on love until she meets Quinn Davies—one woman she can't ignore. (978-1-933110-70-7)

More than Paradise by Jennifer Fulton. Two women battle danger, risk all, and find in one another an unexpected ally and an unforgettable love. (978-1-933110-69-1)

Flight Risk by Kim Baldwin. For Blayne Keller, being in the wrong place at the wrong time just might turn out to be the best thing that ever happened to her. (978-1-933110-68-4)

Rebel's Quest: Supreme Constellations Book Two by Gun Brooke. On a world torn by war, two women discover a love that defies all boundaries. (978-1-933110-67-7)

Punk and Zen by JD Glass. Angst, sex, love, rock. Trace, Candace, Francesca...Samantha. Losing control—and finding the truth within. BSB Victory Editions. (1-933110-66-X)

Stellium in Scorpio by Andrews & Austin. The passionate reuniting of two powerful women on the glitzy Las Vegas Strip where everything is an illusion and love is a gamble. (1-933110-65-1)

When Dreams Tremble by Radclyffe. Two women whose lives turned out far differently than they'd once imagined discover that sometimes the shape of the future can only be found in the past. (1-933110-64-3)

The Devil Unleashed by Ali Vali. As the heat of violence rises, so does the passion. A Casey Family crime saga. (1-933110-61-9)

Burning Dreams by Susan Smith. The chronicle of the challenges faced by a young drag king and an older woman who share a love "outside the bounds." (1-933110-62-7)

Fresh Tracks by Georgia Beers. Seven women, seven days. A lot can happen when old friends, lovers, and a new girl in town get together in the mountains. (1-933110-63-5)

The Empress and the Acolyte by Jane Fletcher. Jemeryl and Tevi fight to protect the very fabric of their world: time. Lyremouth Chronicles Book Three (1-933110-60-0)

First Instinct by JLee Meyer. When high-stakes security fraud leads to murder, one woman flees for her life while another risks her heart to protect her. (1-933110-59-7)

Erotic Interludes 4: Extreme Passions. Thirty of today's hottest erotica writers set the pages aflame with love, lust, and steamy liaisons. (1-933110-58-9)

Storms of Change by Radclyffe. In the continuing saga of the Provincetown Tales, duty and love are at odds as Reese and Tory face their greatest challenge. (1-933110-57-0)

Unexpected Ties by Gina L. Dartt. With death before dessert, Kate Shannon and Nikki Harris are swept up in another tale of danger and romance. (1-933110-56-2)

Sleep of Reason by Rose Beecham. While Detective Jude Devine searches for a lost boy, her rocky relationship with Dr. Mercy Westmoreland gets a lot harder. (1-933110-53-8)

Passion's Bright Fury by Radclyffe. Passion strikes without warning when a trauma surgeon and a filmmaker become reluctant allies. (1-933110-54-6)

Broken Wings by L-J Baker. When Rye Woods meets beautiful dryad Flora Withe, her libido, as hidden as her wings, reawakens along with her heart. (1-933110-55-4)

Combust the Sun by Andrews & Austin. A Richfield and Rivers mystery set in L.A. Murder among the stars. (1-933110-52-X)

Of Drag Kings and the Wheel of Fate by Susan Smith. A blind date in a drag club leads to an unlikely romance. (1-933110-51-1)

Tristaine Rises by Cate Culpepper. Brenna, Jesstin, and the Amazons of Tristaine face their greatest challenge for survival. (1-933110-50-3)

Too Close to Touch by Georgia Beers. Kylie O'Brien believes in true love and is willing to wait for it, even though Gretchen, her new boss, is off-limits. (1-933110-47-3)

100th Generation by Justine Saracen. Ancient curses, modern-day villains, and an intriguing woman lead archeologist Valerie Foret on the adventure of her life. (1-933110-48-1)

Battle for Tristaine by Cate Culpepper. While Brenna struggles to find her place in the clan, Tristaine is threatened with destruction. Second in the Tristaine series. (1-933110-49-X)

The Traitor and the Chalice by Jane Fletcher. Tevi and Jemeryl risk all in the race to uncover a traitor. The Lyremouth Chronicles Book Two. (1-933110-43-0)

Promising Hearts by Radclyffe. Dr. Vance Phelps arrives in New Hope, Montana, with no hope of happiness—until she meets Mae. (1-933110-44-9)

Carly's Sound by Ali Vali. Poppy Valente and Julia Johnson form a bond of friendship that becomes something far more. A poignant romance about love and renewal. (1-933110-45-7)

Unexpected Sparks by Gina L. Dartt. Kate Shannon's attraction to much younger Nikki Harris is complication enough without a fatal fire that Kate can't ignore. (1-933110-46-5)

Whitewater Rendezvous by Kim Baldwin. Two women on a wilderness kayak adventure discover that true love may be nothing at all like they imagined. (1-933110-38-4)

Erotic Interludes 3: Lessons in Love ed. by Radclyffe and Stacia Seaman. Sign on for a class in love…the best lesbian erotica writers take us to "school." (1-9331100-39-2)

Punk Like Me by JD Glass. Twenty-one-year-old Nina has a way with the girls, and she doesn't always play by the rules. (1-933110-40-6)

Coffee Sonata by Gun Brooke. Four women whose lives unexpectedly intersect in a small town by the sea share one thing in common—they all have secrets. (1-933110-41-4)

The Clinic: Tristaine Book One by Cate Culpepper. Brenna, a prison medic, finds herself drawn to Jesstin, a warrior reputed to be descended from ancient Amazons. (1-933110-42-2)

Forever Found by JLee Meyer. Can time, tragedy, and shattered trust destroy a love that seemed destined? Chance reunites childhood friends separated by tragedy. (1-933110-37-6)

Sword of the Guardian by Merry Shannon. Princess Shasta's bold new bodyguard has a secret that could change both of their lives: *He* is actually a *she*. (1-933110-36-8)

Wild Abandon by Ronica Black. Dr. Chandler Brogan and Officer Sarah Monroe are drawn together by their common obsessions—sex, speed, and danger. (1-933110-35-X)

Turn Back Time by Radclyffe. Pearce Rifkin and Wynter Thompson have nothing in common but a shared passion for surgery—and unexpected attraction. (1-933110-34-1)

Chance by Grace Lennox. A sexy, funny, touching story of two women who, in finding themselves, also find one another. (1-933110-31-7)

The Exile and the Sorcerer by Jane Fletcher. First in the Lyremouth Chronicles. Tevi and a shy young sorcerer face monsters, magic, and the challenge of loving. (1-933110-32-5)

A Matter of Trust by Radclyffe. When what should be just business turns into much more, two women struggle to trust the unexpected. (1-933110-33-3)

Sweet Creek by Lee Lynch. A celebration of the enduring nature of love, friendship, and community in the heart-warming lesbian community of Waterfall Falls. (1-933110-29-5)

The Devil Inside by Ali Vali. The head of a New Orleans crime organization falls for a woman who turns her world upside down. (1-933110-30-9)

Grave Silence by Rose Beecham. Detective Jude Devine's investigation of ritual murders is complicated by her torrid affair with pathologist Dr. Mercy Westmoreland. (1-933110-25-2)

Honor Reclaimed by Radclyffe. Secret Service Agent Cameron Roberts and Blair Powell close ranks to find the would-be assassins who nearly claimed Blair's life. (1-933110-18-X)

Honor Bound by Radclyffe. Secret Service Agent Cameron Roberts and Blair Powell face political intrigue, a clandestine threat to Blair's safety, and the seemingly irreconcilable differences that force them ever farther apart. (1-933110-20-1)

Innocent Hearts by Radclyffe. In a wild and unforgiving land, two women learn about love, passion, and the wonders of the heart. (1-933110-21-X)

The Temple at Landfall by Jane Fletcher. An imprinter, one of Celaeno's most revered servants of the Goddess, is also a prisoner to the faith—until a Ranger frees her by claiming her heart. The Celaeno series. (1-933110-27-9)

Protector of the Realm, Supreme Constellations Book One by Gun Brooke. A space adventure filled with suspense and a daring intergalactic romance. (1-933110-26-0)

Force of Nature by Kim Baldwin. From tornados to forest fires, the forces of nature conspire to bring Gable McCoy and Erin Richards close to danger, and closer to each other. (1-933110-23-6)

In Too Deep by Ronica Black. Undercover homicide cop Erin McKenzie tracks a femme fatale who just might be a real killer…with love and danger hot on her heels. (1-933110-17-1)

Stolen Moments: Erotic Interludes 2 by Stacia Seaman and Radclyffe, eds. Love on the run, in the office, in the shadows…Fast, furious, and almost too hot to handle. (1-933110-16-3)

Course of Action by Gun Brooke. Actress Carolyn Black desperately wants the starring role in an upcoming film produced by Annelie Peterson. Just how far will she go for the dream part of a lifetime? (1-933110-22-8)

Rangers at Roadsend by Jane Fletcher. Sergeant Chip Coppelli has learned to spot trouble coming, and that is exactly what she sees in her new recruit, Katryn Nagata. The Celaeno series. (1-933110-28-7)

Justice Served by Radclyffe. Lieutenant Rebecca Frye and her lover, Dr. Catherine Rawlings, embark on a deadly game of hide-and-seek with an underworld kingpin who traffics in human souls. (1-933110-15-5)

Distant Shores, Silent Thunder by Radclyffe. Dr. Tory King—along with the women who love her—is forced to examine the boundaries of love, friendship, and the ties that transcend time. (1-933110-08-2)

Hunter's Pursuit by Kim Baldwin. A raging blizzard, a mountain hideaway, and a killer-for-hire set a scene for disaster—or desire—when Katarzyna Demetrious rescues a beautiful stranger. (1-933110-09-0)

The Walls of Westernfort by Jane Fletcher. All Temple Guard Natasha Ionadis wants is to serve the Goddess—until she falls in love with one of the rebels she is sworn to destroy. The Celaeno series. (1-933110-24-4)

Change Of Pace: *Erotic Interludes* by Radclyffe. Twenty-five hot-wired encounters guaranteed to spark more than just your imagination. Erotica as you've always dreamed of it. (1-933110-07-4)

Honor Guards by Radclyffe. In a wild flight for their lives, the president's daughter and those who are sworn to protect her wage a desperate struggle for survival. (1-933110-01-5)

Fated Love by Radclyffe. Amidst the chaos and drama of a busy emergency room, two women must contend not only with the fragile nature of life, but also with the irresistible forces of fate. (1-933110-05-8)

Justice in the Shadows by Radclyffe. In a shadow world of secrets and lies, Detective Sergeant Rebecca Frye and her lover, Dr. Catherine Rawlings, join forces in the elusive search for justice. (1-933110-03-1)

shadowland by Radclyffe. In a world on the far edge of desire, two women are drawn together by power, passion, and dark pleasures. An erotic romance. (1-933110-11-2)

Love's Masquerade by Radclyffe. Plunged into the indistinguishable realms of fiction, fantasy, and hidden desires, Auden Frost is forced to question all she believes about the nature of love. (1-933110-14-7)

Love & Honor by Radclyffe. The president's daughter and her lover are faced with difficult choices as they battle a tangled web of Washington intrigue for...love and honor. (1-933110-10-4)

Beyond the Breakwater by Radclyffe. One Provincetown summer, three women learn the true meaning of love, friendship, and family. (1-933110-06-6)

Tomorrow's Promise by Radclyffe. One timeless summer, two very different women discover the power of passion to heal and the promise of hope that only love can bestow. (1-933110-12-0)

Love's Tender Warriors by Radclyffe. Two women who have accepted loneliness as a way of life learn that love is worth fighting for and a battle they cannot afford to lose. (1-933110-02-3)

Love's Melody Lost by Radclyffe. A secretive artist with a haunted past and a young woman escaping a life that has proved to be a lie find their destinies entwined. (1-933110-00-7)

Safe Harbor by Radclyffe. A mysterious newcomer, a reclusive doctor, and a troubled gay teenager learn about love, friendship, and trust during one tumultuous summer in Provincetown. (1-933110-13-9)

Above All, Honor by Radclyffe. Secret Service Agent Cameron Roberts fights her desire for the one woman she can't have—Blair Powell, the daughter of the president of the United States. (1-933110-04-X)